I0680729

Books by Liz Crowe

Single Title
FireBrew
Sweet Bitter Honey

Brewing Passion
Tapped
Lightstruck
Conditioned
Adjunct Lovers
Gravity
Infusion

SWEET BITTER HONEY

LIZ CROWE

Sweet Bitter Honey
ISBN # 978-1-83943-854-7
©Copyright Liz Crowe 2019
Cover Art by Erin Dameron-Hill ©Copyright February 2019
Interior text design by Claire Siemaszkiewicz
Pride Publishing

Published in 2020 by Pride Publishing, United Kingdom.

SWEET BITTER HONEY

Dedication

To my ever-patient friend, editor and advisor,
Rebecca.

Chapter One

A strange, thin wail broke through Ryan's fog of exhaustion. He pulled the pillow over his head and willed the bizarre dream out of his subconscious. His body ached from his hair to his toenails, a familiar feeling from the days when he used to work out daily to improve at his scholarship sport. But the weak noise got stronger, piercing his eardrums and making his heart pound with a newly familiar anxiety.

He rolled onto his stomach, breathing in a lung full of the ubiquitous scent of brewery. The ever-increasing noise, now a distinct shriek of fury, and the smell of his life working as an assistant brewer for the Charleston Brewing Company all clashed around in his half-dreaming state. When the brain-numbing shrieking stopped, as if a switch had been flipped, he sat straight up, his newfound radar pinging.

Throwing off the covers, he stumbled over boots and jeans jumbled at the bedside and nearly broke a toe on the doorjamb in his haste to get out of the room. "Shit!

Fuck! Hell! Goddamn it!" He hopped down the hall and slid to a stop outside the second bedroom door.

"Ryan James Shannon, I did not raise you to curse like a sailor." His mother stood, cradling a small bundle in her arms, frowning at him. She was fully dressed, made up and coiffed the way she always had been for as long as Ryan could remember, even at this ungodly hour. "You'll hurt the poor wee man's ears." She snuggled the impossibly tiny infant against her cheek. "Isn't that right, young James? Papa must watch his language or fear for his immortal soul." She frowned at him once more when she passed him in the hall on her way to the kitchen, crooning singsong nonsense into his son's ears.

His son.

Ryan slid down the wall, covering his eyes, ignoring the piles of half-packed boxes and general chaos that ruled his world. The room reeked of shit and sour milk. In the six weeks since he'd walked into that hospital a single man and walked out a single dad, he'd operated on less sleep and more stress than he'd ever experienced in his entire existence. But a renewed sense of purpose kept propelling him forward. A bizarre, almost counterintuitive feeling of empowerment had filled him from the moment the small boy had been handed over, along with a mind-boggling hospital bill. It had kept him buoyant and focused. For that, he would be eternally grateful.

Although he'd be the first to admit that this whole newborn-baby thing was a nightmare of the highest order. The second he'd realized that the doctor who'd called him that morning was not kidding, that he was not being punked by a fellow beer slinger from the pub where he worked, he'd experienced two simultaneous emotions—terror and elation. When he'd held his son for the first time, all awkward elbows and hands and fear, and looked into the child's deep blue eyes, a calm had settled over his nerves. Until he'd got the kid home, of course, and the crying had started and had not ceased until Ryan's mother raced to their rescue after his brother, Quinn, broke the news.

"Ryan," his mother called out over the baby sounds of bottle consumption.

He looked up from an apparent nap on the floor into her eyes. She smiled. "Go on, son, get a few more hours' sleep. I've got our little man here. We'll be just fine, won't we, my fine boy?"

To her credit, Moira Shannon had asked no questions when presented with her third grandson. She'd been missing the twins since Quinn's ex had decamped to California with them. Ryan's mother had walked in the door of his miniscule apartment, put down her suitcase and held out her arms for the baby. While he packed up in preparation for the trip back to Michigan, Ryan let her take over. He had to—he had absolutely no knowledge of what to do and had bungled making bottles—too hot—and changing diapers—too wet—to the point that the kid was red at both ends and had cried so much he'd been hoarse by the time of the Grandma rescue.

He drifted off, letting his fevered brain calm for a few more moments, replaying the doctor's words the second he'd walked into the neonatal intensive care unit. *'Mr. Shannon, meet your son,'* the man had said without a single shred of irony. *'He needs a name, and I need to know who will be responsible for this bill.'* The nurses had been a bit more sympathetic and let Ryan hold the baby—too small to come home for at least a couple of weeks, but by all expensive testing accounts, healthy.

'*Jamie*,' Ryan had whispered, still in shock that day. '*James Quinn Shannon*,' he'd recited to the woman writing it all down and making it official. He'd stood and stared down at the boy for what felt like hours when one of the nurses had gowned and gloved him and handed his son into his arms.

He'd called his younger brother, Quinn, when he'd figured out exactly what this all meant.

'*Hey, uh, I need your help.*'

'*Really,*' Quinn had said. '*Funny, I keep asking you to come home and help me with this brewery, and you keep saying no. Why would I be inclined to –*'

'*Shut up a minute, Quinn, and listen. Carrie…I…we…shit.*'

'*I thought Carrie was long gone. What happened?*'

Ryan recalled the very real sensation of needing to sit down and have a good cry at that precise moment. '*There is…a baby.*'

'*Holy shit. Is she, I mean…wow.*'

'*Yeah. And, no, she is not here. She took off, left my name and number with our…*' He'd had to gulp back emotion. '*Our son.*'

Quinn had blown out a huge breath then done exactly what Ryan had counted on – taken over. '*I'll send Mom,*' he'd said. '*And some money.*'

'*I'll come home,*' Ryan had blurted out. '*I'll work with you at the brewery. I'll do whatever you need me to do – clean, sell, whatever. I gotta get the hell out of here.*'

'*Yeah, I'd say so, my brother.*' Quinn had laughed, making Ryan both relieved and pissed off – a typical reaction to his brother's smug perfection, which had also gone a long way toward calming him. '*And if it took*

Crazy Carrie dumping a kid in your lap to get you to see the light and get your ass home, well, good for her.'

Ryan dozed but woke within the hour, his newly discovered intuition telling him something was wrong. Sure enough, his mother was pacing, jiggling and singing to no avail. Jamie would not calm. Ryan strapped on a carrying device that felt like a military-issue parachute but was really a simple baby holder. He plopped the whining boy into it and went out into the early morning light for the long walk that seemed the only thing that would calm the kid lately. By the time he got back, his mother had the kitchen almost packed and a giant breakfast on the table for them both.

"Thanks, Ma," he said, kissing her cheek before unhooking the straps and laying Jamie in his crib, still in the carrier but finally asleep. He sat, ate his mother's famous healthy start-to-the-day-breakfast and smiled, hoping now that he could really begin his life and stop pretending. The moving truck was due the next morning and he was more than ready to get back home, to his brother's brewery, to start his life over again.

Chapter Two

"Damn it, Quinn, I can't keep up this pace. Not and handle the new distribution contracts and every other thing." Ryan sucked back more Red Bull then focused on yet another busted piece of equipment. The Ypsilanti Brewing Company that he had joined five years ago, bringing along his nascent commercial brewing experience and infant son, was going gangbusters. So much so he could barely keep up. Neither, apparently, could their existing brewing system, if the way shit kept breaking down was any indication.

They needed a bigger brewhouse, more fermentation vessels, a bigger cooler. But more than any of that, they needed more warm bodies. He needed another assistant brewer and a cellarman, and someone to get a handle on sales on the back end now that a half-decent pub manager was in place. They had to find someone who'd work as hard as they did, for next to nothing and no insurance, either, at least until they could wrap their heads around that commitment. He groaned and ran a hand through his hair.

Quinn closed his laptop, stood up and stretched. "I know. I know we need more people, blah, blah, blah. I get it, but you get it, too, right? I can't afford to bring anyone else into this yet. I'm stretched every month paying the five employees we have. We gotta sell more—"

Ryan held up a hand. "We won't sell more, Quinn, not unless someone besides me is managing both the brewery and the sales efforts. Period. And we fire the lame-ass distributor. We have to cut them loose and find a better one while we're at it."

"Ryan, I know you don't want to accept this, but there is no money right now for another employee. Stop asking me. And you know firing a distributor is practically impossible. Stop making it sound so fucking simple." Quinn's dark eyes were hard, angry. Ryan tried to remain calm.

Ryan knew his younger brother—the man who'd once succeeded at everything he did no matter what— could sense failure breathing down his neck. He'd failed at his first marriage, and he was teetering on the edge of something either really great or terrible with this brewery venture.

Another thing Ryan realized about Quinn was that he hated being less than perfect at everything, and these last few years had been a pure exercise in seat-of-the-pants learning curves, mistakes and screwups. All while he attempted to remain a presence in his young sons' lives from a distance. Ryan had never known his ex-sister-in-law very well, but that was his own fault. He'd kept his distance for years, letting a slow-boil jealousy at Quinn's apparently successful life—rich stockbroker with a big house, expensive car and nuclear family—drive a wedge between them. The bonus of Quinn scoring a drop-dead gorgeous wife had served as only the hammer to that wedge. The little that Ryan had been able to drag out of him hadn't given any hint of the real reason for the split other than 'ongoing, irreconcilable differences'. Which was Quinn-speak for 'mind your own fucking business and help me with this brewery instead'. So he had.

He sensed that they were emerging into the light. He had a handle on their strengths and weaknesses, was focusing on three brews they bottled and had plans for one more of them before the year was up. But he needed help, and Quinn needed to make their lazy distributor snap to and start up-selling their product. Traynor Wholesalers was old-school—had too much invested in the macro brews they represented and were a bunch of order takers, not the sales people that Ryan needed to get his new products into the market.

"Are you even listening to me?" Quinn demanded.

Ryan put his hands on his brother's shoulders. It felt beyond strange being the one who was calm, the one who could make the right choices for success, but he was resolved in this thing now. He wanted Ypsi Brewing to take the next step and Quinn was being tight-fisted about another employee when he didn't need to be.

"Take off the bean-counter hat a sec, Q. You know as well as I do that someone who really knows how to sell, who can come up with a coherent marketing plan that encompasses both the wholesale and retail side, will be worth every penny. If we troll around up at Eastern Michigan U, I'll bet we can find a starving MBA grad eager for a paycheck. Right?" He leaned down, trying to catch his brother's gaze.

"Yeah." Quinn shrugged him off, sat and rubbed the bridge of his nose. "You're right." He sighed and stared into the middle distance.

Ryan tried to rustle up some sympathy but found only 'It's-About-Time-itis' with regard to his brother's frustration. "Okay, so I'll post an ad on Craigslist and on our website. I say we see what we get and determine salary value then." He turned to his screen and started fiddling with recipes and checking fermentation temps before heading toward the small lab.

They'd managed to morph the empty auto factory into a twenty-thousand-square-foot brewery, plus three-thousand-square-foot pub that on most nights was standing room only. By the time Ryan had joined the company, infant son in tow, the brewhouse was in place, run by a woman who was now his assistant. She'd happily turned over the reins, declaring herself "unqualified" to be the head brewer. While he was probably even less qualified, he'd jumped in with both feet, using his time spent training at a brewery in Charleston, and between them, they'd managed to crank out some damn good beers.

Ryan was happy with his life, if a little lonely for adult companionship beyond what his brother and the sparse staff provided. But he kept busy and looked forward to each day in his very own brewery, which was more than a lot of people could claim about their day jobs.

"Hey, Fran," he hollered across the brewery to get his assistant's attention. The woman was cleaning out the mash tun after their brew day, the sinewy muscles of her arms flexing as she scraped the spent mash into large garbage bins. He watched her a few seconds, admiring her strength, not to mention the way her jeans highlighted the full curve of her hips and ass.

He shook his head at himself. He knew damn well Francine played for the other team most days, not unlike himself, and they'd established up-front that the knee-jerk flirting they'd been doing during their early days together would never lead anywhere. They had too much to accomplish at Ypsi Brewing to allow for anything else between them. Their relationship now was solid, based on mutual respect, humor and a love of craft beer.

When he glanced at his phone, he realized if he didn't hurry, he'd be late to get Jamie from day care…again. "Shit, Fran!"

The woman propped her arm on the handle of her tool and wiped sweat off her face with the towel she kept hooked in her belt loop. "Go on already—you're late picking up your kid."

"Yeah, I know. Sorry."

She waved him off, her smile wide.

Not for the first time since landing here with nothing but an empty bank account, no place to live and squalling infant in tow, Ryan thanked God for his luck.

He grinned, picturing his son's eager face and bright green eyes. He was pretty much a small replica of Ryan, right down to his temper and apparent need for constant stimulus and movement, which was a blessing and a curse. Ryan shouldered his backpack and headed out, convinced he could find a sales specialist and really get things rolling in a successful direction.

* * * *

"I met somebody."

Ryan looked up from his appraisal of the new fermentation vessel's temperature controls at the sound of his brother's voice. He frowned at the odd look on Quinn's face. The man's first marriage had been one of similar tastes, drive and looks. Ryan had never gotten to know her well during the marriage, but she'd shown her true colors clearly in the last few years, keeping the twins away from their father while demanding ever more in alimony and child support. Ryan knew not having his sons in his life nearly killed Quinn on a daily basis and was only just beginning to understand how awful that must be. His nephews were around this month, however, spending time with their dad while their mother worked on snagging rich husband number two.

The fact that Quinn was owning up to even dating, much less having 'met someone' shocked Ryan to his core. But he determined that playing it cool would be the best current course of action. Not to mention he was jealous. His own love life had seemingly been put on permanent hold for the last five years, but he didn't give it much thought anymore.

"Oh? Who? Where?"

They'd had great response to their call for a marketing director in the last few weeks, and he was working on a group interview, but still wanted to make one more call to the Eastern Michigan Business School. A couple more decent candidates would be ideal before he brought them all in for a group-think session so he could see who stood out from the crowd. *There. That's it. Focus on other things and not your neglected libido.* "That explains the goofy look on your face. I assume you've gotten laid?"

"Maybe. It's Audrey...um...Audrey Traynor. Met her on the job, actually." Quinn ran a hand through his thick black hair. The two of them were about as far apart in looks and personality as brothers could be. Quinn resembled their mother, with night-black hair and bright blue eyes. Ryan was green-eyed with wavy dark blond hair — that same hair that repeated itself on Jamie's head and was in sore need of cutting. Kid could pass for a girl with his soft features and flowing locks these days. His mother nagged him daily about it. Ryan stopped musing, processed what his brother had said then stared at him, open-mouthed.

"Traynor...Traynor Wholesale Company...our distribution partner...the one I want to fire because they suck?"

"Uh, yeah."

"Wow." Ryan put down the clipboard and crossed his arms over his chest. "Nice one. Hope she's worth it."

"Oh, I think she is." Quinn raised an eyebrow and stuck his hands in his pockets. "She wants to have us over for dinner this weekend. She, um, she has a brother at home with her right now. He's a Marine Corps vet, served in Iraq, and he's...a little messed up, at least physically, but she's determined to take care of him until he can get settled."

"A brother," Ryan said, slowly finally realizing what was going on. "A wounded warrior brother. No, thanks, Quinn. I'll take a pass."

"I'm not setting you up with the guy, Jesus. For the record, I still think you should stick with girls, but since you can't seem to make up your mind... Well, I just thought since you haven't been out or anything in a while, and Audrey said her brother was...your type.

Although you should know, he is blind, after a firefight that got him discharged with a Purple Heart and a Navy Cross. He has a service dog that he's trying to get used to plus a new job as an internet security consultant. The shit they can do with computers now — it's like his being blind makes no difference at all in that respect. His name is Cole."

Ryan gaped at his brother. "A blind, gay, pissed-off, computer geek ex-Marine? Gee, Quinn, sounds like fun. Maybe I'll invite my son's drug-addled mother along, you know, to complete the dysfunctional family portrait." He turned away, aware he was being an ass about a guy he didn't even know.

"Sorry," Quinn said.

"Whatever. I'll think about it. Can Jamie come over and stay with the boys and the nanny that night?"

The thought of a man, any man, in his orbit startled him and made him more than a little tingly. He'd spent so much time and energy sublimating these feelings to his new responsibilities. He hardly drank anymore, didn't touch cigarettes or pot, and he ran at least five miles every morning, rain or snow or shine.

His early days in Ypsi, getting the brewery going and running on something like three hours of sleep a night thanks to Jamie, had been a blur and he'd fallen back on some bad habits. But the morning about a week after he'd awoken with a brutal, clanging hangover, lying next to a naked stranger, to the sound of his mother's repeated banging on his apartment door, he'd made a vow of austerity, paternity, maturity and, apparently, celibacy.

He'd never gone without getting laid for any extended period of time, so he'd never questioned it. Sex for a guy like him was pretty easily arranged. He wasn't hard to look at, and he knew what buttons to push for both men and women. Being bisexual had always seemed a bonus.

But right now, at this moment, looking at his brother's happy face, he'd never felt more alone. The slight twinge of horniness at the base of his brain when he thought of the faceless, wounded Cole Traynor made him want to punch something. Words to the contrary spilled out. "I'll go," he called to his brother's retreating back. "I need to get out."

"I thought you might. See you in the morning?"

A shiver passed down Ryan's spine. He was lucky. He had the job he wanted and family he loved. The support Quinn had given him in the last few years meant more to him than he could ever explain or repay. The Saturday morning pancake ritual with his uncle was something Jamie talked about every Friday. It gave Ryan an entire morning alone, and he was always grateful for it.

Quinn's boys were visiting on one of their rare trips to Michigan and Jamie was beside himself. They were great kids and loved their cousin, or at least tolerated him. Ryan shook his head. The least he could do was meet this Cole and his sister, Audrey, whom Quinn seemed gaga over.

What will it hurt?

* * * *

"Daddy! I want to come with you." Jamie did his usual round of whining before realizing he got to have a sleepover with his cousins. By the time Ryan had showered, tugged on dark jeans and a somewhat non-wrinkled button-down shirt, the little boy was standing by the door, backpack full of Legos, ready to go. Nervousness coated Ryan's brain when he kissed the boy's cheek prior to dropping him with the sitter at Quinn's. "Take me with you." Jamie gripped his arm once until he saw the older boys headed toward him.

"Next time, sport," Ryan said, his heart clenching for the millionth time at the sight of his son. He hesitated, somehow understanding this was a pivotal moment but unable to pinpoint why. He smiled at the sitter and climbed back into his car, pointing it toward Ann Arbor and the address Quinn had given him for Audrey and Cole.

He arrived, parked in front of the tidy bungalow-style house and took a long breath. Quinn needed his support, so he was here, nothing more or less. His life was complete. He didn't need anything, including a relationship with a total stranger. By the time Quinn pulled up, Ryan felt steadier—like he could handle whatever lay behind the front door he'd been staring at for ten minutes.

The brothers walked up the steps in silence. Quinn knocked on the door. The smile Ryan saw spread across his brother's face when it was opened by one of the most stunning blonde women Ryan had ever seen made his face hot. He'd met Audrey Traynor once before, but all he recalled from that encounter was fury at her nonchalance about their plight and his utter determination to cut Traynor Distribution loose. At that split second, he remembered her brother, the stiff but model-handsome Marine who'd been in the office that day, on leave or something, visiting his sister.

The woman pulled his brother into an embrace and they exchanged a soft kiss, before Quinn introduced him to her. The whole thing passed like a surreal dream. Quinn frowned at him at one point, but Ryan just grinned and acknowledged that the sensation of hovering over the scene, observing strangers going through the socially accepted motions. He was judge-level sober, but he sensed a wooziness in his brain while something else, something much more interesting, hovered on his horizon.

He stepped into the tidy foyer, his eyes adjusting to the lamplight in the minimally decorated room. It was empty. Ryan blew out the breath in relief. When he turned back to say something to his brother, he heard a low growl.

"Audrey," someone spoke in a rough voice. "The, ah, timer's going off."

Ryan stared, stunned by the sight of the man in the kitchen doorway. A broad-shouldered masculine man who stood with his Ray-Bans on and canine assistant by his side, his face set in a scowl, back-lit from the kitchen. Cole Traynor was dressed in dark jeans and a gray T-shirt. He was, in a word, amazing. He was also furious—so much so Ryan could sense his anger from across the room, palpable and real. But he kept staring, taking in the Marine Corps tattoo that peeked out from under Cole's sleeve and the strong lines of muscle that the shirt did nothing to disguise.

"Huh?" He stumbled when Quinn shoved him with an elbow. His entire body was on alert in a way he'd forgotten. "Oh. Sorry." Ryan let his gaze return to Cole. The other man's brown hair was growing out from its military severity and his square jaw was covered in a light, tidy beard. He oozed a simultaneous 'fuck off' and 'fuck me' vibe that Ryan's neglected libido picked up, absorbed and translated to an embarrassing boner that forced him to shift behind the nearest chair to hide.

"Ryan." The woman stepped in front of him. "This is my brother, Cole." She tugged the handsome, angry man out of the doorway. His shoulders tensed. "Cole, this is Ryan, Quinn's brother."

Cole held out a hand. Ryan stared at it, unwilling to touch him and admit what his every nerve ending was screaming, but realized how rude that must seem. The moment stretched way out beyond anything resembling polite. Quinn cleared his throat, startling Ryan into action. He stuck out his hand. Cole took it without help, somehow sensing what to do, how to reach Ryan's palm. Ryan's life was never the same again.

Chapter Three

Cole

The dream was back. Cole knew it for what it was. Yet he was unable to stop it. He flinched, inhabiting that in-between state of sleep and wake, of before and after, of a whole Cole and a fractured one.

The dream kept coming.

Screaming. Fire. Pain. Over and over again. He heard it a split second after he spotted the seemingly innocuous wire on the side of the road. He started to speak, to warn the driver then...screaming...fire... sand...and pain became his entire universe.

He opened his eyes, expecting the bright, hot, blue sky. And saw nothing. He thrashed around, tried to find his weapon, remembered Dan was in the Humvee behind him and panicked all over again. He couldn't move, couldn't breathe and...shit...he couldn't see. Not to mention that his right leg had been replaced by a flaming ball of agony.

His ears rang, even while the screams of men and women all around him filled his brain. With a huge effort, he finally pulled loose from the safety harness and fell onto all fours, trying to make his eyes and ears function. He scrabbled around on the floor of the truck and connected with what felt like a man's boot. He felt his way up, making contact with the bloodied flesh of the man's leg. He realized too late that the limb was definitely not attached to anything else. He yanked his hand away and brought it to his face. The sickening, coppery smell of blood made him gag.

He sat, blinking fast, but his eyes burned and watered so he shut them and kept crawling, trying to locate the source of all the yelling.

Dan. He had to find Dan.

He called out, picturing the younger man's handsome face. He reached his hand out into thin air then tumbled down to the sand. Yelling and cursing when his knee connected with something sharp, sending a fresh bolt of pain up his spine, he froze when he heard it.

"Cole!"

He rolled over onto his side and groped around, keeping his eyes clenched shut to spare the agony of trying to force them to work, then attempted to stand. The horrific stench of burning flesh suffocated him. He reached out a hand again, hoping to find something to grab onto to guide him back to the truck Dan had been in. "Cole!" The voice was hoarse, weak, but he recognized it.

He and Chief Warrant Officer Daniel Anderson had been together for nearly two years. Dan was from Ohio, career military, and a computer super geek, like Cole. They were both high up on the "need to know" list and were able to manipulate more information between them than was probably healthy. They'd led the small, secretive counterintelligence effort in this particular corner of hell.

Cole was due to rotate back to the States in two weeks, and Dan was going to join him when he finished his tour a year later. Cole was in head-over-heels love with the tall, dark and handsome fellow Marine. And right then, the sound of Dan's voice fading to his left in the chaos was freaking him the fuck out. That, and the fact he still couldn't see, no matter how much he rubbed his eyes. His nasal passages and throat burned, but he ignored it all and dropped to all fours, muscling through the agonizing pain in his knees and hips, half-crawling, half-dragging himself toward the sound.

"Cole," Dan coughed. Cole put a hand on what he hoped like hell was Dan's arm, still connected to his torso, thank Christ. The yelling had mostly stopped, leaving in its wake a terrifying silence punctuated by the snap and crackle of flames and the yammering of a radio somewhere to his right.

"Cole," Dan croaked out, "I'm…shit…" He made a terrifying noise somewhere between a sob and a moan of pain. Cole dragged him up, held him close.

"Shh, I've got it. Help me find the com. I can't fucking see anything."

Dan groaned. The metallic odor of blood filled Cole's nose again, making him want to puke. His hand found Dan's. He tried to remain calm, to remember his years of training. "Your face…" Dan whispered.

"I know how good-looking I am. Now help me find the com." Cole grunted in pain when he started to stand again, his leg singing out a clear tune of torment. He shook, called on his inner reserve of Marine-instilled calm, took a breath and let Dan grab his arm. If only he could just see.

Liz Crowe

"No, go to your left, pull Tanner out of the fire."

Dan's voice guided him to save a couple more of the doomed platoon of grunts that had been their escort, even though the more he tried to rub whatever the hell was in his eyes out, the more they hurt and the darker it got. He stumbled, cursed, limped and finally dragged the last man Dan could see from where he sat out of the blaze that used to be the shit-heap houses they'd been sent to recon. His head pounded and his throat felt coated with sand.

"Dan!" he ground out, crawling again, unable to use his left leg at all. He felt encased in a cocoon of darkness where all he knew was the smell of blood and burning flesh and the sounds of men in pain. Cole found his target, heard Dan's ragged breathing and touched the man's leg. Terror slithered into his brain. His chest ached from inhaling so much smoke. "My eyes," he said, weakly, touching his face and feeling moisture.

"Shh...Cole, it's okay. Just...sit here with me." Dan's low voice set off another wave of panic in Cole's gut. "Please. I want...I need you to put your arms around me."

"Goddamn it!" Cole burst out. "I can't fucking see you."

"It's okay, it will be..." Dan coughed and groaned then put his hand back on Cole's white-hot face. "Sit, be calm, hold me."

Cole sat, pulled Dan into his arms and held him. For how long, he had no idea, but Dan lived only a few more minutes, of that he was sure. By the time the explosion had been reported and a fresh wave of troops arrived, Cole's face was stiff, and he had stopped hurting. Shock had set in. It had taken four Marines to pry his arms away from Dan's body. When he woke, he was covered in bandages in a hospital in Germany. His left leg was in a cast from ankle to hip. He was one of three survivors of a roadside blast that had taken out eight Marines, including Dan Anderson, the man he loved.

He clawed at his eyes, cursed the world for being alive, yelled at the medical staff, refused to eat or drink. None of that changed the fact that Captain Cole Robert Traynor was alone and would never see again.

Cole sat up fast, wishing the nightmare away for the millionth time, once more to no avail. All he'd known for ten years was his life as a Marine. He'd joined after having the rug yanked out from under him when his homophobic father and passive mother got the news about his sexual preferences. Now, after being someone and part of something, he was back to nothing. All his life he'd been what his parents wanted and expected, but when he'd finally been honest, they'd tossed him out as though he was a disposable son, a nonexisting member of their family.

He flopped back onto the pillow, recalling the epic bender he'd gone on after stumbling out of his boyhood home that day. His sister had tried to calm him down. She'd followed him out of the house and down the street, but he'd run from her, ignoring her pleas to return.

He'd decided to need nothing and no one, and the men he'd let pick him up and fuck him that entire weekend at the club solidified it. One of them was an ex-Marine. Cole had poured his guts out to the guy in the wee hours, and he'd made a suggestion that changed Cole's life forever. The Corps needed smart guys, computer-savvy wizards like Cole, especially since the war in Iraq was becoming one of counter-intelligence.

The next morning, with a freshly pounding hangover, he'd opened the door to the Marine recruiter's office, marched up to the cheerful guy in the sharp uniform at the desk and filled out the questionnaire, noting the "don't ask" portion and relishing the supreme irony of his position. While he'd recalled a twinge of regret at that moment, realizing he was doing a completely knee-jerk, up-yours thing, he'd shrugged it off.

The weeks spent at basic training had given him the sort of focus he'd never had. He'd loved it—every miserable, sore, tired, bullshit moment of it. Maybe because he'd known it for what it was. They'd been tearing him down to build him back up into the image of a man he wanted to be. He'd absorbed it all, made it his own and in the process become better. He didn't regret it, even though he was one of the many hiding in the barracks closet.

Lying in his pitch-black bedroom, trying to calm his breathing and pounding heart from reliving yet again the horror of his last days as a Marine, he gulped when the true horror of his new life draped across his brain. His mind would not still, kept sending him unnecessary fight or flight signals. Because now he was home, in his sister's house, with a seeing-eye dog that he didn't want and nothing to live for.

The room seemed to pitch like a massive ship on the ocean, making him reach out to hang on, his stomach roiling and threatening to empty. The ever-present nightmare would not let him go, no matter how hard he forced himself to be awake and to own up to his current reality. He heard a growl, felt the dog's wet nose shoving at him but pushed it away.

"Cole!"

He groaned and rolled over, ignoring the sound of his name.

"Cole, stop!"

He lashed out, flailing his arms, fighting back before the asshole terrorist could lay his stupid coward's bomb and ruin Cole's entire life.

"Please!"

He gasped and sat, felt flesh under his palms then sank back, letting go of whomever he had a death grip on. The dog was bumping his leg, whining.

"Honey, it's just me." He heard his sister's voice, calm, without a hint of fear.

"What is that fucking noise?" He groaned and put a hand on his aching forehead. The *thump-thump-thumping* would not cease. His head spun pretty much nonstop with sounds. The doctors had warned that his other senses would heighten to compensate for the lack of sight, which had proven to be the understatement of the century. He honestly believed he could sense the undercurrent of rain on a sunny day across his skin, could hear people's presence three rooms away, and would swear he could smell breakfast cooking three blocks down the street, although that was likely stretching it a little.

Regardless, it was maddening. The daily headaches from the barrage of extra input were debilitating at best, pure hell at worst. Even his lowest moment in basic training, which he could pinpoint at the end of the first week in the hot stew of Parris Island, South Carolina, when every muscle, sinew and nerve he possessed had screamed in pain, he would take over this infernal pounding in his head.

His VA therapist would invariably ask, '*How is the pain?*'

'*Bad,*' he'd say, rubbing his ears to keep out the cacophony of sounds from the hospital that warred with the nauseating odors threatening to bowl him over.

'*And how do you feel about that?*'

He would clench his fists, force down the urge to punch the useless asshole in the nose. '*I feel like shit, thanks. The side effects from the painkillers and anti-depressants and whatever-the-fuck-else make me dry mouthed, antsy, groggy, madder than hell, and my goddamned head still hurts no matter what pills I take. Anything else?*'

He never stayed for the whole session. He would stand and let his dog pull him out of the room, to the elevator and down to the front door where the piss-reeking van would take him back to Audrey's so he could sit on the couch and hold his aching head in his hands for a few more hours. It was a lovely cycle of do-nothing and talk about it, feel sorry for himself, then be unable to get off his ass because his skull felt as if it was cracking in two, twenty-four seven.

Audrey put her hand on his face, making him flinch. "Cole, it's just Brutus. His tail is hitting the carpet."

"God." He groaned and sat, the animal's head right under his hand. Cole could smell the dog's wet nose. The snuffling noises the damn thing made were deafening. "Beat it." He tried to push the dog away, but of course, he wouldn't go. He sensed Audrey's sigh about a second before she actually did it.

"Here." She grabbed his other hand and put some pills in his palm. He tossed them down and accepted the water glass. "Hopefully these will help." They could've had him on fucking Viagra for all he knew or even cared. "The doctor upped your amitriptyline. Let's hope that will help with the dreams."

"Whatever. They write 'scripts. I take pills." He put his still-pounding head in his hands. "Anything to make this pain go away."

He felt his sister's hand on his shoulder but jerked away. He couldn't stand anyone touching him. "Sorry," he muttered, clenching his jaw and resisting the urge to just lie down and sleep forever. He shied away from that, knowing suicide rates and depression cycles and all that crap would just make him yet another statistical cliché.

This was his life. He had to live it, no matter how viselike the grip on his skull or how much his eardrums echoed and tossed yet more agony into the mix nor how much his nose picked up every random stink between here and Detroit. He sighed, his throat closing up when he pictured Dan, his amazing, handsome face and willing body.

Which made him horny.

Which made everything that much worse.

Chapter Four

Audrey pulled him to his feet and the dog slid under his hand.

"Okay, so Quinn and Ryan are coming over for dinner. I thought you might like to help me pull it together."

"Whatever," he said, reaching out to flip on the lights. Until he realized that the lights were already on, or not, and that it no longer mattered to him. Clenching his fists and trying not to punch a hole in the wall, he recalled all the ruthless talk therapy sessions to go with the drugs. The one thing his group had practically browbeaten into him was the need to work on his anger.

Yeah, like he could fucking do that.

But he put his other hand down and onto the dog's harness and let it lead him out, helping him avoid furniture obstacles and whatever else stood in the abyss between Audrey's second bedroom and kitchen. "Jesus." He clapped a hand over his nose. "Put out that candle, it's killing me."

He heard her blow out the disgusting scent, the residual smoke wafting and dissipating before the air finally cleared, then proceeded to cut onions, tomatoes, peppers and mash garlic for what used to be his special lasagna sauce. "Make sure the noodles aren't too done," he said while soothing cooking aromas suffused his brain. "Put more garlic in the pan. It needs it." Audrey obliged, chattering away about Ryan's little boy, about their parents' beer and wine wholesale company that she now ran, everything under the sun. "Could you…just be quiet a minute," he whispered, putting the knife down and feeling his way back to a chair.

"Sorry." She ran her fingers through his hair. He grabbed her, held on for dear life while a now-familiar wave of depression bowled him over. He swallowed hard, determined not to start crying like a girl.

"Come on, help me over here." She hauled him to his feet then let the dog guide him to the stove where he stirred, tasted and demanded more oregano and yet more garlic until the sauce was right. He sat back down, exhausted and pissed off. The chemical mix of medicines his body absorbed ebbed and flowed and turned him into the walking contradiction he was now—always on the verge of yelling at the dog, his sister—anyone within hearing distance.

Because Cole was a war hero, had saved three of the men in the escort platoon that day, even blinded and with a shattered leg, he was given priority in the assistant dog program. He'd been assigned the animal, along with his Purple Heart and Navy Cross, at a ceremony he barely remembered.

A trainer had given him a grand total of three hours' worth of instruction that he ignored in favor of dozing on and off in between bouts of bone-crushing pain. Thank God for Audrey. She'd taken it all in and demanded that he move in with her, new pet and all. He flinched when he felt the canine head on his leg. "Stupid fucker," he muttered, rubbing the animal's soft ears. He steadfastly ignored the calming sensation he got. The contrarian in him would not accept that petting a dog's head would make him feel better, although it did.

He felt Brutus' vocal cords rumbling on his leg before the growl hit his ears. "They're here," he mumbled, about five seconds before the doorbell rang. Audrey put a cold beer bottle in his hand. He gripped it and waited in the kitchen while she greeted her boyfriend and the man's brother.

Cole had met them once, when he could still see, while on a leave about a year or so ago. They'd been in Audrey's office waiting to talk to her. Cole didn't give two shits about his father's company and ignored all the news he got from it now that his sister was in charge. He had just been there to visit her, recharge his batteries then return to his life, and his lover.

He sat in the kitchen, listening to her talk to them, recalling how striking the two men had been. Quinn was tall, with coal-black hair that Audrey claimed had turned a charming salt and pepper, with bright blue eyes. His brother, Ryan, was slightly taller, with a head full of wavy, dark blond hair, gray-green eyes and even broader shoulders. Cole remembered feeling the distinct sensation of being checked out that day, and he'd liked it. Ryan Shannon was a hot guy, and the few moments they'd stood and talked had made him nervous, given the signals his brain had thrown at him.

By the time Audrey had come out of her office to meet them, Cole had been jumping out of his skin, needing to escape. He'd had no reason to even consider anything but Dan at that moment in his life. But something about Ryan had gotten to him. He had stared at Cole with those green eyes, sending a blatant "let's skip this and find a dark corner, what d'you say?" message that got him so worked up he'd had to drive to Audrey's house and go on a punishing ten-mile run to clear his head.

Of course, now, he was just Cole, the poor blind asshole with a dog and a sad-sack-hero story. He couldn't give a shit who was coming to dinner.

Cole sighed and sipped his beer. He was allowed exactly one serving of alcohol a day on his current medicine cocktail and he never skipped it. An alarm from the stove sounded. He set the bottle down, felt around until he quieted it and decided to join the party in the other room. He stood in the doorway, cleared his throat and informed his sister about the timer.

The testosterone coming off the man across the room was a not-so-subtle cologne, oozing in and out of Cole's brain, warming his libido and making him flinch when someone touched his arm. "Hi." Ryan's voice was low. Cole kept one hand on the dog's harness, the other on the doorframe. Sweat dripped between his shoulder blades. There was an uncomfortable extra beat of silence in the room. Then, drawn by something he couldn't explain, he put out his hand, knowing Ryan's would meet him halfway.

Some sort of conversation resumed and flowed around him. He tried to still the sudden tremor in his hands and voice. "Better take out the lasagna, Audrey," he said at one point then moved to the couch to sit,

Liz Crowe

letting Ryan's warm, somehow malty scent fill his brain. Their thighs brushed together when Ryan stood to get beer for everybody. Cole heard the happiness in Audrey's voice when she and Quinn joked about their professional conflict of interest. He was content that Quinn Shannon did indeed love his sister the way she deserved. Not thrilled, however. No man would ever really be worthy of her. But the sound of her familiar voice, devoid of stress whenever Quinn was around, suited Cole just fine.

He jumped when Ryan put a fresh, cold water bottle against his biceps. "Thanks," he muttered, grabbing it.

"So, Cole, I hear they got the computer set up for you. You'll be starting work next week?" Quinn's voice broke through the erotic fantasy loop Cole had running in his head when he felt Ryan's leg close to his again. Jesus, he was horny. He hadn't even given a half-thought to sex in the past year while he'd recovered in Germany and had then been discharged home to Michigan, to a life of nothingness with a side order of excruciating pain.

"Uh, yeah." He sipped. His headache had retreated to a back corner, still mumbling and threatening to return, but his neck was less tense, thank all the gods. The fact that he felt more relaxed at this moment, sitting next to a near stranger named Ryan Shannon, than he had in what seemed like forever, forced a puff of air from his lips. The dog shoved his muscular body between the men then dropped down on top of Cole's feet as he'd been trained to do, never far away, always on-duty.

He put the bottle down and adjusted the dark glasses that covered his sightless eyes. He tried to form coherent words, but every inch of his skin was on the alert in a way he hadn't been since losing Dan, and his brain wouldn't engage and cooperate.

"Yeah, my brainiac brother's going to be an analyst for an internet security company based in Detroit. He'll work from home but take the bus downtown a couple of days a week. His computer is way cool — with a giant keyboard and a sexy woman telling him what's on the screen. No more of that weird robot voice — it's fabulous," Audrey said, pride evident in her tone. She put a hand on his shoulder. "He picked up Braille in something like two weeks, not that I'm surprised. He's always been the genius who can do anything when he puts his mind to it."

Cole flushed at her words. Truth be told, he was a nervous wreck about the whole damn thing, but the CEO of the company had assured him that it was no sympathy job. Cole Traynor had maintained top security clearance from his work in counter-intelligence. He knew his way around the internet like no one else. Cole gulped back the urge to disparage the whole thing and start a pity party, another thing his therapist had been drilling him about. "Yeah, should be, uh, interesting — especially the part about having the computer tell me what's on the screen. Not quite sure how that's gonna work yet."

Ryan put a hand on his arm. The jolt of sexual energy that shot down Cole's spine from the touch made him gasp. He jumped up, hit the underside of the table with his knees and heard the various cries of dismay at what was likely a huge mess of beer. The dog whined and stuck his head under Cole's dangling hand, propping him up and providing calm at the same time.

"I got this." He heard Quinn moving around beside him. Standing there, the smell of spilled beer up in his nose, his canine companion growling at the guy who'd turned him into a walking hard-on with one touch, he felt like the world's biggest idiot. He put his hand to his eyes, found the glasses and fiddled with them before grabbing the dog's lead. He wanted to walk the hell away from all of them. One thing he surely did not miss were the no doubt multiple and sincere glances of sympathy floating around him. He gritted his teeth and let the dog lead him outside and to a chair. How the animal knew that was exactly where he wanted to go, he had no idea, but he was grateful.

.

Chapter Five

Cole sat at the dinner table, frozen, revved up and miserable for a few minutes before he heard the conversation make its way toward him. Plates plunked down on the glass table top, the delicious-smelling lasagna was doled out, wine poured. He let the conversation roll around him again, keeping silent. He knew he was being belligerent, but he didn't care. He could practically hear his therapist chiding that he would never integrate if he maintained his current fury level — mad at everyone around him who could still use their eyes.

Ryan sat on his left, Audrey on his right. His fork rattled when he put it on his plate. The distinct sensation of a hand on his left thigh made him jump, but he bit back the urge to pull away. "Relax," Ryan said, low and easy. Brutus shifted under the table, but Cole moved his foot, indicating the dog should back off.

Cole's cock resumed its painful exploration along the back of his zipper. He tried to sip water. He took another bite of food then gave up and put his hands on the table. He missed Dan, missed his life and everything he used to be. Cole Traynor had been strong, sure, loud, boisterous and in-charge ninety-nine-point-nine percent of the time. But right now, he felt like a horny little kid—a blind, useless, handicapped horny little kid.

His ears started to buzz with the onset of serious fury. Ryan pressed down on his leg ever so slightly. The buzzing receded. Cole turned his face to the left. The dog leaped up and shoved his body between the two men again, his low rumble sending an ominous and unmistakable message.

"Shit," Ryan said, taking his hand off Cole's leg. Cole tried not to beg him to put it back. The calm he'd felt for a split second at the other man's touch had been odd, but it was also something he wanted.

Cole pushed the dog under the table with a curse and a warning, but the moment was broken. Audrey cleared her throat. Cole picked up his water glass and the conversation that he no longer heard or contributed to resumed.

At some point, the table was cleared. Everyone except Cole had another glass of wine, and he sensed a distinct shift in the atmosphere. His headache was back in its full glory. He pinched the bridge of his nose between two fingers. He heard traffic, kids playing, early onset crickets, the earth rolling on its axis—every goddamned sound in the entire universe pressed onto his eardrums. Which was nothing compared to the scent, that screamed 'Ryan' which had settled into his psyche, nice and cozy and annoying. The malty warmth, with slightly astringent tang that made Cole want to lean over and run his tongue down the man's neck. He clenched his fists on his knees.

"Okay, we're gonna be late, babe. Let's hit it." Quinn's voice broke through the cacophony of noises boring a hole in Cole's brain. His neck tensed and his shoulders crept up around his ears.

Audrey knelt down beside him and took his hand. "We're going to a movie. You okay here with Ryan?" she whispered. He nodded, but he was very much not sure that he would be. The dog whimpered.

"Later, brother," Quinn called out. "Talk soon, Cole. Good luck next week with the new job."

Ryan walked into the house with the couple, leaving Cole alone with his swirling thoughts and pounding skull. Brutus repositioned himself to Cole's left between him and the chair Ryan had just vacated. He put his huge head on Cole's hand. "Dude," Cole said softly. "I think I just figured out why you're upset. And let me tell you now, it's okay. I'm okay. I'm a little...agitated, but it's normal." He rubbed the dog's ears then leaned back and stretched his legs out in front of him, relieving the pressure building once more under his zipper.

He heard Ryan rummaging around in the kitchen, opening and closing the fridge. Cole took a long, deep breath and made a decision. He smiled when Ryan pressed the water bottle to his shoulder but set it on the table that he knew was to his front right. His mind was roiling, but he kept a lid on his urge to suck in a breath when he sensed Ryan pulling a chair up on his other side, avoiding the guard dog. "I don't think he likes me," Ryan declared.

Cole put a hand on Ryan's leg. He heard the other man's breath hitch and would have sworn on a stack of procedure manuals he heard his heartbeat increase. *Don't be ridiculous, you can't hear a heartbeat.* He smiled and leaned back, leaving his fingers trailing along the denim covering Ryan's thigh. "Oh, he's fine, but I think I figured out how in tune to me he actually is."

"Oh?" Ryan touched his fingers, brushed the back of Cole's hand once, then again, making him shiver.

"I think he senses how horny I am. Since he has no frame of reference for it, it's making him nervous, protective."

"Wow." Ryan leaned over and Cole could feel the other man's lips near his throat. "Impressive," he said, putting his hand over Cole's erection.

"Yeah," Cole croaked out. "So, I'm typically not…"

"Shh." Ryan's hand left his cock, made its way up his torso and wound around the back of his neck. "You are pretty amazing."

"No, not really. Just blind. Without a real job. Living in my sister's house."

"But you look damn good doing all of that, trust me."

"You make a point of seducing blind guys you just met?"

"I didn't just meet you. I remember you a few months…before."

Cole shivered again. This whole thing was somehow right and wrong at the same time. He needed a physical connection, bad, but was unsure if it should be with Ryan Shannon. This, of course, coming from his now humming and pain-free brain while his body screeched at him to grab the guy and kiss him.

Cole sighed when Ryan's fingertips touched his newly grown hair. He hadn't had it this long in over ten years. He'd forgotten what color it was. He sighed and raised his face to the cooling night breeze when Ryan's lips found his jaw and made their slow way down his neck, then up. "You are…very attractive." Ryan's words curled in and around Cole's amped-up libido.

He gasped when Ryan slid his zipper down. "Fair warning. I won't last long. It's been a while." His head had cleared, his neck no longer hurt and he felt the familiar, pleasant rush of lust wash through him. "I do need this. But that's all, though, you know? I'm in no position to start a relationship or anything." He gulped as his throat closed up and his eyes watered. "We clear on that?"

"It's clear. I don't need anything more from you. At least not yet, but I think we could both use a nice, hard fuck," Ryan whispered against his neck. "I need you to relax first."

Cole groaned and leaned back, giving into the amazing sensation of Ryan's hand then his lips and tongue on his flesh, letting the man's earlier firm words and no-nonsense commands soothe him. He reached out and threaded his fingers in Ryan's hair. His first thought—that he wished he could watch—was drowned out by the exquisite sensations of Ryan kissing his neck. It was even, somehow, better, this dark place where all he knew was this man caressing his battered and neglected body.

When Ryan's lips met his, Cole smelled the desire between them like a living, breathing thing. Cole gripped the chair arms when the man forced his tongue between Cole's lips, swept into his mouth. He tasted so good, sounded so sweet and sexy—those low noises he made in his throat were maddening and amazing. Ryan pulled him to his feet.

The two men stood, arms entangled, teeth clicking together with urgency when they stumbled inside. "I don't need your mercy fuck," Cole gasped, angry now, on top of the raging lust that was taking over his brain.

"This is no mercy fuck, I assure you. But it will be a good one, if you would just relax and let it happen." Ryan's low, rumbling voice filled Cole's ears, making him sigh with pleasure. "I'm a top. That work for you?" Ryan grunted when Cole yanked his shirt up and off, popped his jeans button and unzipped him, releasing a long, rock-hard cock to Cole's eager hand.

"I can't imagine anything better." And there were no truer words at that moment than the ones he'd said — he wanted Ryan Shannon inside him. Everything about the man compelled Cole to open up, to give, let him take what he wanted.

"I don't have any protection." Ryan hesitated. Cole smiled and the dog bumped up against his leg.

"Check Audrey's room, left side top drawer. She and your brother have been staying here a lot lately, and they forget I can still hear." Ryan drew a finger down Cole's face, cupped his chin and pressed a soft kiss to his lips before walking away in search of a condom. Cole sat, his hand on his own cock, wondering how in the hell he'd gone from friendly dinner with this man to wanting to fuck so bad he could taste the need on the tip of his tongue. The dog whined. Cole grabbed him and gave him a quick ear rub. "Go lie down. I'm fine."

Brutus shoved his nose under Cole's hand once then sighed and padded away. Ryan was in front of him, pulling him up and tugging off his dark glasses. Cole grabbed the man's hands, unwilling for him to see the undoubtedly horrible mess of his ruined eyes.

Ryan sighed into his neck. "Cole, I'm not going to have sex with you if you're wearing these damn things."

Cole's breath caught in his throat. He couldn't do it. This was…wrong. But Ryan kept whispering to him and finally the glasses dropped to the floor. Cole wrapped his arms around Ryan's neck, kissed him and pressed his needy sex against the other man's, loving the roll and press of warm, hard flesh against his own. Music hit his ear, coming from the next-door neighbor, no doubt. Cole let Ryan run his lips and hands all over him. The sensation was exquisite, painful, fantastic and horrible all at once.

A different darkness descended, more intense than the one he'd lived with for over a year. It was accompanied by panic, something akin to a fight-or-flight reaction which kicked in when Ryan dropped to his knees and deep throated his dick. Ignoring it in favour of the extreme pleasure the man's mouth was providing, Cole gripped Ryan's hair, thrust his hips and fucked the man's mouth until he couldn't wait another second. "Now, Ryan. I need you…now."

Ryan rose, his bare skin skimming Cole's on the way up. He kissed him then turned him so Cole could grab the back of the couch. He arched his back, letting go when Ryan kept whispering to him. His entire body seemed to flex, to convulse and spasm so hard he yelled out, not even realizing what he said while he came so hard he almost fell over from Ryan pounding into him.

"Yes," Ryan hissed. "That's it." He sighed and collapsed over Cole's back, holding him close, sweat slicking their torsos.

He shivered, put his hand against his bare eyes, and the familiar panic returned, settling deep in his gut.

Ryan handed him his glasses without a word. Cole shook all over, trying to put them back on. He heard all the noises again, after the blessed relief of silence for the last few minutes. Ryan took his hand, led him around to the front of the couch where he dropped down, collapsing like a marionette without strings. Ryan sat next to him, took him in his arms, kissed his forehead, cheeks, lips. Cole's teeth chattered. He tried to resist.

"Relax," Ryan said into his hair. And Cole did, falling into a near immediate sleep while Ryan held him close.

C h a p t e r   S i x

Lynette

Lynette hated hanging around the university placement office so much. It made her feel like such a colossal loser. Of course, most things did these days. Here she was, shiny, sought-after MBA with honors in hand for the last six months and she still worked at a day care and ran the gantlet of avoiding creditor calls every day. Hell, one of them was practically her best buddy. They all were sympathetic to her plight, even encouraging, but they had to get paid.

She studied the virtual jobs bulletin board again, tucking a wayward lock of hair behind her ear and willing someone to hire her. After an hour of collecting yet more leads and jotting down endless lists of new LinkedIn contacts, she leaned back, pressing fingers to her forehead. Her stomach rumbled and her eyelid twitched while she checked her phone. Ever hopeful for that one elusive call that might be generated from one of the hundreds of resumes she'd sent, and nearly as many interviews she'd endured.

A blank phone screen met her gaze, mocking her eager anticipation.

She was standing to put away her notebook and get the hell out and on her way to the day care center when the secretary waved at her. Frowning, Lynette walked to the woman's desk. She had the phone to her ear and was having a conversation while motioning at Lynette to sit, stay. Her phone bleeped with a text from her mother, reminding her to bring home organic milk and not the stuff full of antibiotics. She typed a quick response before looking up to see the secretary with her finger on the phone's mute button.

"It's perfect," she whispered, leaning in. "Let me hand this to you now, before I have to post it."

Lynette shrugged. She'd been interviewed for more perfect jobs than she cared to remember. The whole thing had lost its luster. It had become a long, daily trudge of disappointment, peppered with anger and frustration now that she'd agreed to let her mother live with her. "Why? What's so great about this one?" she asked, reaching over to take the receiver.

"It's local and so cool, the Ypsi Brewing Company, you know, over in the empty Ford plant?'

"I don't know anything about beer."

The woman waggled the phone at her. "Just take it. Trust me."

"Hello?" Lynette flopped back in the chair, unwilling to even try to sound like she cared anymore.

A deep, masculine voice filled her ear, curled around in her brain and nestled in her psyche. "Hello, this is Ryan Shannon. I'm the head brewer and part owner of the YBC, over here in the old Ford plant."

She stayed silent, not because she wanted to but because every ounce of spit she possessed had dried up at the sound of Ryan's voice. She stood and turned away so the secretary couldn't see her looking like an idiot. After about ten minutes of his talking, her listening and trying to form coherent sentences, she handed the receiver back to the pleased-looking woman.

"Well?"

"I, uh, have an interview, Monday. In a group first with other candidates, then one-on-one with the owners, the Shannon brothers." She picked up her purse, still in a daze from the odd phone call.

Men had zero effect on her. She had barely even looked at herself in the mirror since her life had fallen apart five years ago. Back then, she'd been the prototypical college co-ed, happy and carefree and focused on a future with her medical-school-bound boyfriend. In quick succession, in her sophomore year, her father died of a massive heart attack, leaving behind her mother, who had spent her life being taken care of, and barely enough money in the bank to pay for a funeral.

Her mother had no answers for the 'where is all Dad's money?' questions. The woman had never even written a check in her adult life, in a bizarre throwback of a relationship where Lynette's father had done everything, up to and including nurturing a gambling habit that had left his wife and daughter high and dry after his death. After attending her father's funeral, her boyfriend had pulled her aside, kissed her forehead and said he needed 'space' to 'think about their relationship.' These two things mysteriously involved the intimate assistance of her roommate, it seemed. Last

Lynette heard, they were married. She'd not been on a date, kissed or even held hands with a member of the opposite sex since.

Now, her mother sat on the couch with her cat, watched expensive cable television from the time she woke until she slept in Lynette's small apartment in Depot Town. Lynette was incapable of making her leave. Where would she go? She didn't drink or smoke or even really eat that much, but the inherent frailty that had been enabled by Lynette's father and his over-the-top masculinity proved an impossible barrier to her having a real life.

Lynette sat with her at times, taking in the various news shows and pseudo-news shows, doing her homework and waiting on her mother in an early care-taker role reversal. Other than her constant nagging about Lynette needing to 'find a man' and insisting on organic milk, she barely made a peep.

On the way home, Lynette did her usual prayer to the gods of rust bucket cars and the women who drive them that hers would make it one more day. Realizing she'd forgotten the milk the moment she was unlocking the apartment door, she sighed and shoved it open, needing to process the recent turn of events. She had an interview for a job that would not force her to relocate and drag her emotionally invalid mother with her. And the man who would interview her possessed a voice that had her practically buzzing with something she refused to identify.

She ground her teeth, made apologies to her mother about the lack of milk and jumped in the shower, hoping the proverbial cold water would calm her revved-up libido. Ignoring men in favor of slogging through school and getting top grades while working thirty hours a week had been easier than she'd expected. A few cute guys had tried to get friendly, especially in classes that required group work, but she'd kept it professional, cool to the point of frigid.

She'd had to put one foot in front of the other, daily, for five years, until she had that paper in her hand. The paper that claimed her hire-able with a Master's in Business Administration double focus in marketing and accounting, but that had become about as useful as the stacks of paper on her kitchen counter demanding money she didn't have.

This twanging, nervous jangling of her nerves, replaying Ryan Shannon's voice over and over in her head while she let the thin trickle of water sluice down her face and body, was pissing her off to no end. The guy had a voice made for radio. He was probably some nerdy, bearded, fat guy—which was her mental image of a man who brewed beer for a living. She toweled herself dry, shivering in the super-cooled air. Her mother kept the airconditioning cranked nonstop, yet another drain on her slim budget, but she had no energy to fight it.

She tugged on jeans and a sweatshirt and yanked her rowdy hair back in a ponytail. There were children to be minded and a small paycheck to be earned. Lynette surprised herself at how good she was at this job, how many kids clamored to be with her during the hours they spent away from their parents. She took a perfunctory look at herself in the mirror long enough to take in the slight lines she'd developed alongside her eyes and the worry creases in her forehead. Frowning, she touched them, remembering how many hours she'd once spent rubbing at her freckles, hoping to make them disappear and for her hair to turn normal, not the uncontrollable curly auburn riot that it was. Her flat blue-green eyes stared back at her and a shiver passed down her spine at the memory of the voice on the other end of the phone. *'See you Monday, Lynette. I'm looking forward to it. You sound like a great fit.'*

Chapter Seven

The day of her interview dawned with an inauspicious gloom. Lynette sat straight up, sheets in a tangle around her legs, nerves on fire and her body buzzing with a clearly remembered dream. One where Ryan Shannon, he of the sexy disembodied voice, was holding her, twining his fingers in her hair, pulling her close and kissing her like nobody's business. She passed a hand down her damp neck. Allowing herself to flop back for a few more minutes, she worked her hand into her flannel pajama bottoms.

She rubbed and stroked and pretended she knew what she was doing until giving up. The erstwhile boyfriend in college had been a virgin, too, and between them, they'd hardly figured out more than how to mutually masturbate and had managed to achieve actual penetration only by accident, which had scared her silly. By her own estimation, according to the few pop culture magazines she'd read in waiting rooms, she had never actually experienced true orgasm. Yet one more thing to put on her someday list, she supposed, although at nearly twenty-seven, she figured it would be more likely that she'd discover an oil well in the backyard than her own G-spot.

Lynette groaned and rolled over, pretending she was not the most pathetic excuse for an adult female on the planet. She rose and hit the shower, ignoring her still thrumming body in favor of focusing on maybe, just maybe, landing a job today.

"Honey! I made some breakfast." Her mother's thin voice floated down the short hallway.

Lynette fixed a smile on her face, adjusted the one decent suit skirt she possessed and brushed her usual minimal amount of makeup on her face. She'd given up trying to tone down her freckles years ago and wasn't about to start now, Sexy Voice Man or not. "Coming, Mom, hang on." She ate, let her mother fuss over her hair that she had pulled tight into bun to, hopefully, minimize the shocking effect it sometimes had. "Thanks, Mom, really."

She stood and kissed her mother's cool cheek, took her plate to the sink and stood there, trying to stay calm. She'd been through so many interviews that this one shouldn't be rattling her so much. The thought of getting in front of Ryan the Voice was making her weak in the knees and the eggs she'd just eaten threatened a second appearance.

God, Lynette, you are lame as shit. Get a grip.

She jumped when her mom touched her shoulder. "Honey." She tucked the ubiquitous strand of curly red hair behind Lynette's ear. "Don't worry. You'll find something and hopefully there will be a nice man there you can meet and…"

Lynette jerked away from her, furious and unwilling to guard her tongue. "Shut up about men, Mom. You had a man and what, exactly, did he do for you? Hmm? Die, that's what, after he gambled away every dime he had. Please, do *not* tell me one more time that finding a man is the answer to anything."

She was immediately sorry for her harsh words but, unwilling to back down, grabbed her purse and second-hand leather portfolio. Hesitating a split second before opening the door, she sighed then walked out in to the warm morning, putting on her 'hire me' face one more time.

The Ypsilanti Brewing Company was in its sixth year of business but had already broken more sales records than Lynette could count. In her due diligence research, she'd discovered that jumping on the craft beer bandwagon when he did had been a stroke of genius on Quinn Shannon's part. The guy she'd talked to was Quinn's brother, Ryan, who'd joined the company a few years ago. While the thought of brothers with that same voice made Lynette more than a little wobbly in the knees, she forced herself to focus on the tidbits she'd memorized about the company and the industry in general.

With the market share of malt beverages currently almost fifty percent, the craft brewing business was now more than some bearded dudes in basements concocting random stuff. Lynette knew less than zero about beer generally, didn't even really drink alcohol that much because it was too costly. How she could parlay her expensive marketing degree into some sort of organized, professional effort, like the panty-dropping voice had implied, escaped her even after all her research.

She did have a new working knowledge of how beer was sold in Michigan and how adversarial and challenging relationships with distributors could be for breweries. There were a few names she could drop, like 'Dogfish Head', 'Stone' and 'Bell's.' She'd watched about fifty YouTube videos of beer being made, so at least she could point to a fermenter and know that it was not a mash tun.

She sighed, squared her shoulders and put on a light coat of lipstick. The parking lot was deserted, but the place only had about eight employees, which would account for the few cars in the lot, four of them late model pickups.

A wave of terror made her grip the top of her car. Staring up at the red brick and glass façade of what was once one of the busiest and most successful plants for Ford Motor Company, she forced herself back under control. Which was when she also got her first whiff of a rich, breakfast-y smelling odor. It got stronger as she approached the side door. The amazing smell wafted around her, seeming to hold her in its embrace before rolling out into the warm morning air behind her while she stood in the open door. A man and a woman in rubber boots and heavy aprons were moving around the cavernous space, clambering up and down a metal platform, taking turns stirring a huge copper kettle with what appeared to be a boat oar.

She stood, taking it all in, until a sudden movement to her left made the hairs on the back of her neck stand straight up. "Hey!" The voice that had haunted her since she'd heard it on the phone made her jump, stumble and trip over a thick hose snaking across the middle of the concrete floor.

She cursed and tried to get her feet back under her, but her worn-down heel hit a patch of water and she sensed herself falling, in slow and embarrassing motion, right onto her ass. A better first impression had likely never been made, she reflected on her way down. Her purse went one way and her portfolio the other, scattering resumes, clippings and brochures all across the floor. The final indignity, however, was biting her tongue so hard it brought tears to her eyes and flooded her mouth with coppery-tasting blood.

"Shit." The Voice was at her ear now. Fury at him for letting her wipe out like that made her face redden. She scrambled to her feet and jerked her arm out of his reach. "Hang on there, Red," the man had the nerve to say to her. She blew an escaped tendril of hair out of her face and attempted to tuck it away, straighten her skirt, gather her wits and not burst into tears all at once.

"I'm fine," she ground out, taking a wobbly step away from him. Meeting his eyes was not an option she allowed herself.

"Here, let me…" He gathered up her random papers and shoved them into her folder. The mortification continued when she saw a spare tampon had rolled out of the purse and landed a few feet away. She reached for it at the same moment he did, connecting the top of her head in a very solid way with his nose.

"Ow! Jesus," he muttered, using that damn voice to send tingles along her spine. She grabbed her stuff, stuck her purse on her shoulder and headed for the door. There was no way in this lifetime or any other she would stay in there another minute. "Hold on," he said, muffled, with a towel over his nose. "Aren't you…" He looked down a piece of paper in his hand. "Lynette? Lynette Williams?"

"Yes," she said, giving up on the professional updo and letting her crazy annoying hair tumble down around her shoulders. Fuck this guy and his stupid slippery floor—she needed this job. "That's me. Lynette." She finally looked him full in the face. "Not 'Red'."

He stood, gripping the paper in one hand and towel in the other, staring at her. Her early self-deceiving notions that the man attached to the voice that made her semi-orgasmic was a dumpy, bearded, fat guy with a beer in one hand evaporated, like so much smoke. She narrowed her eyes, realizing that he was blatantly checking her out without even pretending not to. She flushed hot again and acknowledged that she was doing the same thing to him.

Ryan Shannon was six foot something incredible of pure man, with a shock of dark blond hair and the most compelling gray-green eyes she'd ever seen. He rubbed his hand across his stubble-covered jaw at one point during their little moment, perhaps wishing he'd shaved. His broad shoulders were encased in an Ypsi Brewing Company T-shirt, which hugged the lean strength of his torso like a glove. She looked lower, at the light denim jeans and rubber boots then back up, forcing herself not to stare at any one area too long. When they locked eyes again, she had to take a step back at the intensity she saw there.

He cleared his throat, and she was gratified to see that he at least had the decency to blush before turning away to answer a question someone had asked, breaking the connection. She watched his body move, lithe, athletic-looking and… She looked away, horrified for even contemplating the images that had started to flash in her head. Biting her lip, she glanced around, took a very careful step to the side and mentally started the whole thing over again.

Chapter Eight

"So." Quinn leaned back and smiled at her. Lynette grinned, feeling comfortable in this man's presence, at least. He had a mentoring, helpful vibe about him that his brother definitely lacked. "Lynette, you certainly blew away the rest of those folks in the group interview. I'm interested in hearing more about what you think you have to add to our efforts here."

"Well, from what I can tell, you guys are on the verge of taking this to the next level." She crossed her legs, sensing Ryan's gaze crawling all over her but keeping her focus on the other brother, while mentally shooting daggers at Ryan. "I'd say hiring a marketing professional is the right thing to do. It seems you have a decision to make — do you want to be a production facility and make your money on wholesale or to ramp up the retail efforts by expanding the pub, like we discussed in the group?"

She let a beat of silence drag out then leaned forward, never taking her eyes from Quinn's intent blue ones. "What I propose is to come up with a comprehensive plan that would allow you to make it a fifty-fifty proposition. That is, why not grow on both sides of the house? I think it can be done, but it will take a bit more IT infrastructure and more people."

She leaned back and clasped her hands on her lap. She bit the inside of her cheek to keep from turning to glare at Ryan, who sat to her left and was oozing a sort of sexy aura that was making her damp in inappropriate places. She allowed herself a glance in his general direction when Quinn did the same thing, willing Ryan to chime in and not sit there like a lump.

"I told you," Ryan said to Quinn while he kept his smoky gaze trained on her. "More people."

Quinn snorted and stood. "Lynette, I would be honored if you would join us at Ypsilanti Brewing Company as our new sales and marketing director. I'm prepared to offer you a starting salary of thirty-five thousand dollars a year, plus a bonus package based on meeting specific sales targets. We've just added health insurance with prescription drug program that would be available for you to buy into should you require it. I realize that it's not a ton of money, but…"

Ryan rose to his feet, staring at his brother as if he'd just offered Lynette the head brewer's job. "Uh, Quinn, don't you think we should…um…"

Quinn frowned at his brother. "Ryan, she's exactly what we are looking for."

The two men glared at each other. A tendril of uneasiness snuck in under the elation at the actual, real offer. It was small, granted, and she could probably get closer to sixty with her MBA at a larger company.

"I'll take it," she blurted out, causing both men to turn and stare at her. "I mean, if you're both in agreement, that is." She raised an eyebrow at Ryan.

"Seems this Mr. Shannon has some qualms?" She let the sentence dangle, half question, half accusation. Her heart pounded so fast it hurt. Her throat was slowly closing up when Ryan took a step toward her. She could smell the odors on him that would become familiar to her, malt, astringent hops, leather and sweat blended into a slurry of richness that coated her nerve endings. She forced a smile and made herself not take a step away from him.

"What do you drink, Lynette? You know, when you need to unwind?"

Ryan's question threw her for a loop. She bit her lip, glanced at Quinn who was still frowning at his brother. "I don't, actually. It's too expensive."

"Huh," he said, tossing Quinn a look Lynette could not fathom.

"Great," Quinn said, closing up a folder on his desk and grabbing his suit coat. "You won't have to unlearn bad habits. If you will excuse me, I have a meeting at the bank. You can consider this a solid offer, Lynette." He took her hand, clenched it hard. "Just ignore him." He jerked his chin at Ryan, who stood to her left. "For now."

She watched him go, still processing what had just happened to her. She took a breath and faced Ryan. "I'm not always that klutzy, don't worry," she said, hoping to defuse some of the energy hurtling between them. At the same time, she wanted him to step closer, to put his hands on her face, her arms, her back, her… She shook her head. "Anyway, I assume I have some time to think about it?" She grabbed her purse, needing to be as far from Ryan as she could get, like right now. This whole scene was all of a sudden too much for her to handle.

She picked her portfolio up off Quinn's desk, determined to ignore the man standing and staring at her as if she was something nasty on the side of the road. "Excuse me." She had to step closer to him to get by the chairs where she'd been sitting for nearly an hour. "I'm sorry if I'm not your first choice. I need this job, and I'm willing to give it a shot, but only if you stop looking at me like I just killed your best friend." She stood in the doorway, keeping a safe distance between them, and shook her hair back.

Ryan's face reddened. "No, I'm, it's…well." He ran a hand down his face. "This whole hiring someone new was my idea. Quinn didn't want to add any more employees. I'm glad it didn't take him weeks to choose somebody." He looked up at the ceiling, and in that split second, Lynette realized something about the distressingly handsome man she would be working with daily. He was uncomfortable here, in her presence. Maybe even more than she was in his. "You'll be fine. We'll teach you the beer side. You bring a skill set we lack." He smiled, his chiselled face set in calm lines, his eyes sporting a sexy, mischievous twinkle. "Welcome to the team, Lynette." He held out a hand.

She stared at him, mesmerized by the message her brain was receiving but unable to comprehend. She finally had a job and with a man she wanted in ways she didn't even understand. *Well played, Lynette.*

"Thanks." She shook his hand, turned and tried not to run out of the door to her car.

Chapter Nine

"Shannon!"

Ryan looked up from his task and cursed when his skull connected with the solid stainless-steel opening of the giant fermenter. "Jesus," he muttered, rubbing the knot rising on his scalp. If the voice matched the face he expected, his day had digressed from crappy to complete shit. He sighed and turned, meeting the angry stare of Lynette Williams. The woman had been marketing director for Ypsi Brewing Company for exactly six weeks and Ryan bounced from bizarrely obsessed with her to hating her ever-loving guts, when he was not fantasizing about fucking her brains out.

"Yeah?" He forced his gaze away from hers. He knew what was up, but ever since the hot redhead had taken the reins of marketing, Ryan's life had been a living hell, for many annoying reasons, not the least of which she was the sexiest thing on two female legs he'd laid eyes on — ever.

When Lynette had been added to the mix, bringing with her a healthy dose of spread-sheeted, computerized reality, it had turned Ryan into a twitching nervous wreck. His brother had insisted they needed it to get to the next stage and kept forgetting that it had been Ryan who'd convinced him to hire a marketing director — but this particular marketing director was all sorts of infuriating. Ryan figured that this 'next stage' was either going to kill him or make him insane.

He had called the production shots in the brewery from the beginning. Quinn took whatever Ryan and his staff made and sold it, not vice versa. It had worked for them. They'd grown from nothing to one of the most successful new craft breweries in Michigan inside of six years, doing it this way.

Ryan respected the hell out of his brother, with his suave manner, his charming patter, clean-cut suits and the women who'd always flittered around him like moths to a flame — up to and including his model-gorgeous ex-wife and his new girlfriend, Audrey. But he cursed the man daily for hiring this fiery temptress who seemed to think that he would be scheduling his brews around her sales.

She shoved a computer tablet under his nose. "Look at this." Her foot tapped out a familiar rhythm, the *'Ryan is a stubborn asshole and I'm telling Quinn'* one.

He took a step back, trying to get her scent out of his nose. Luckily, she was in full-on bitch mode so he could be pissed and not horny. Besides, he had his own issues, trying to get Cole to answer his calls. The man was an expert at avoidance and Ryan was about to give up, let their smoking hot one-off be just that. He wiped the sweat dripping down his forehead and took the device. A graph flashed red, indicating that they were running low on their flagship hoppy lager.

"Yeah, Lynette, I know. I updated the damn thing this morning." He addressed his next comment to the empty fermenter that had fucked up his last batch of that very beer. He had a service call in on it but believed he'd identified the problem. "I'm sorry."

"Sorry?" She yanked the computer out of his hand, brushing his arm with hers in the process, making him shudder and need some distance. "You're sorry?"

"Yeah. You're deaf?"

"No, you dickhead, I'm not. But 'sorry' isn't gonna cut it this week. I made a huge sale of the Hopped Up Lager, and you know it. I put it here." She tapped the screen, which flipped over to her shiny new sales reporting system that had become the bane of his brewing existence. "You saw it. I know you did because I see you logged into the shared file and —"

"Listen." He turned away from the stainless-steel vessel and glared at her. "I didn't sabotage this thing on purpose. It failed, okay? Broke, blew a gasket, something that I am attempting to diagnose or would be if I weren't occupied being reamed out by you." She blew out a breath, started to speak, but he held up a hand. "Spare me. You're gonna have to short the order. It happens. Jesus."

"Unacceptable," she spat out, tucking the computer under one bare arm. She was parading around the brewery in her sales suit, a tight black skirt, sleeveless silk blouse and the obnoxiously way-too-high heels. Ryan forced himself not to drag his eyeballs up and down her frame as he'd done that first moment he saw her, on her ass on the brewery floor. He refused to give her the satisfaction. "I need five pallets filled and ready in a week. Make it happen, brewer." She barked out the last word, emphasizing his role as opposed to hers. Fury made the edges of his vision redden.

Without realizing he was doing it, he reached out, grabbed her arm and spun her around, even while his brain engaged and reminded him that man-handling her was a big no-no on so many levels he'd might spend his lifetime regretting it. "It won't happen and you know it. Stop coming down here and acting like such a bossy..." He looked away and bit back the word he wanted to use. Her skin was hot under his palm and his body was reacting to her proximity, which only made him madder. She looked at his hand then up at him, her crazy green eyes snapping with something he thought he recognized.

He let go of her, but she didn't move. "Tomorrow morning five-thirty a.m. Be here. Wear jeans, a T-shirt and your hair pulled back. I'm sick and tired of trying to make you understand this process. You are gonna brew with me. To appreciate what we do, so you can get exactly how pissed off you make everybody with your demands."

Her eyes flickered down his chest. "I'm busy tomorrow morning."

Ryan moved directly into her space and let their bodies graze each other. "Yeah, I know. With me." He leaned over her, trying like hell not to touch her. Dear God, he was horny. Since his hookup with Cole, he hadn't had sex in nearly two months. He missed it—he missed Cole. He felt bad for fucking him and running. But, of course, he was now somehow within a split second of laying a tongue-tangler on the maddening, frustrating, hot woman in front of him. He stepped away.

She narrowed her eyes at him. Ryan was highly gratified to see her breathing fast.

Yeah, he would kiss her, but not yet.

"See you tomorrow morning." He grinned at her. "Don't be late."

The click-clack of her heels on the concrete told him she'd left. He put his hand on either side of the fermenter's door and let the press of cold steel calm him. She would be trouble. But he needed it, or something like it. His phone buzzed with a text from Quinn.

I saw that.

Ryan rolled his eyes and responded, *You didn't see shit. Or you're imagining things.*

Quinn: *Leave her alone. I mean it.*

Ryan: *Don't boss me. I get enough of that from her.*

Quinn: *Okay, then fuck her and get it over with. Jesus. You two are worse than a* Moonlighting *episode. And, may I remind you, this was your idea.*

Ryan: *Damn, you are dating yourself, brother. And hiring 'someone' was my idea. NOT her. Oh and 'fuck her and get it over with' is not exactly a CEO-worthy comment, for the record.*

Quinn: *Yeah, well, just do it and clear the air already.*

Ryan: *Maybe.*

Quinn: *Coming to dinner tonight? Audrey's place?*

Ryan winced, recalling the last time he'd been over for dinner at his brother's girlfriend's house.

Ryan: *No, thanks. I'm exhausted.*

Quinn: *Suit yourself. You can't avoid him forever you know.*

Ryan: *Will you butt the hell out of my love life, please, and thank you very much. Jesus. You just got thru telling me to fuck our redheaded marketing director. Now you want me to do what exactly with Audrey's brother? He's the one ignoring me, anyway.*

Quinn: *You should come over. Audrey and I want to talk to you guys about something.*

Ryan: *Fine. Whatever. Are you guys getting married?*

Quinn: *No.*

Ryan waited for the rest of the text, but nothing showed up, so he responded, *Okay. I'll be there. Can I drop Jamie with Tracey and the boys at your place?*

Quinn: *Sure. Seven. See you then. I'd offer to share a ride, but Audrey and I are going out after.*

Ryan: *So, this is more about a set-up for me and her brother?*

Quinn: *No. Maybe. Anyway, see you later.*

Ryan tossed the phone onto the lab table and tried to resume his diagnostic perusal of the fermenter, but his head was a mess. Between lusting over Lynette during the few moments of the day when he didn't want to throttle her, their latest expansion and brew pub chaos and his life as single father, the last thing he needed was another run-in with Cole Traynor.

Memories of Cole's compelling but wounded face and his equally incredible body flashed through Ryan's brain, making him shiver. The man was hot, eager, and had been ready for action the second Ryan had suggested it. Ryan would have kept up the relationship if Cole had been inclined, but he'd made it clear they were not 'lovers', merely fuck buddies, and that only once.

Considering what the guy had been through, Ryan was hardly in a position to argue with him. So he'd left him alone. But Cole's firm, Marine-forged physique haunted his fantasies. Although now, the prospect of hooking up with Lynette, his nemesis, was finally allowing some measure of relief regarding the nonstarter with Cole.

It was probably a good thing Cole had kept him at a distance. The whole thing was such a tangle, especially throwing in the fact that the Traynor kids owned the distributor that Ryan had been on the verge of cutting loose. Now, of course, there were going to have to, or risk accusations of favoritism, thanks to Quinn and Audrey's relationship. He still wasn't sure how his brother and the hot woman he'd fallen for were going to work out those logistics. But it wasn't his problem. Not yet.

He sighed, picked up his phone and sent a text, knowing Cole's phone was equipped with voice recognition software.

Ryan: *Hey, I hear we're having dinner.*

Cole answered nearly immediately. *I hear you're joining us.*

Ryan: *What's the news we're supposed to be getting?*

Cole: *I think they're buying a house. If so, I'm gonna buy hers.*

Ryan swallowed hard. That meant one thing—a guarantee of Cole at pretty much every family event going forward. He put his head on the desk. It was not going to be easy keeping his distance. He pictured the seduction he had planned for Lynette and shoved all memory of the highly erotic connection he'd shared with Audrey's brother out of his head.

He'd gone from four years of virtual celibacy to being faced with two options, equally frustrating and desirable. And the whole thing had his head in a very odd place—one where he could picture them all together which was, of course, ridiculous.

Ryan: *Are they getting married or what?*

Cole: *I don't think so. Audrey's still not ready for that step, but I told her moving in with the guy is over halfway there.*

Ryan: *Well, see you tonight.*

It took a while for Cole to answer. By the time his phone dinged with the response, Ryan had his head back inside the fermenter, trying to salvage some of the day before waving the surrender flag.

Cole: *I've missed you.*

Ryan stared at those simple words and a chill ran down his spine. He sat, trying to decide if and how to respond. Cole had so much bitterness and anger in him. Ryan would give anything for the man to let him in, let him help. But he'd refused, so they'd parted ways, both unhappy and unresolved. Ryan wanted something more, but Cole would not have it and had made that very clear in the weeks following their hot hookup.

Finally, Ryan tapped out a simple answer. *I did what you wanted. I left you alone.*

Cole: *I know. Thanks.*

Ryan: *But I didn't like it.*

Cole: *I know that, too.*

Deciding there was no good way to answer that, Ryan put the phone in his pocket and glanced at the clock on the wall. It was nearly three. He tossed the rag he'd been using to wipe down the sensors inside the fermenter and walked into his office for the weekly brewer's meeting. No doubt about it—a shit day gone to hell and now he had to be around Audrey's brother and pretend he felt nothing for him. Christ, he should have stayed in bed.

Chapter Ten

"I don't care what anyone says, I am not letting that asshole call the shots. He doesn't know what he's talking about." Cole ran a hand down his face. He took a deep breath, the now familiar scents of his home office giving him comfort. His shoulders and back ached when he stretched them out while he sat listening to his boss make excuses.

He'd started working out in earnest again after nearly a one-year hiatus from the gym. It provided him with a huge measure of relaxation that he'd forgotten even existed. He took a deep breath and attempted to temper his usual brusque manner.

"These guys have suffered a massive security breach. A ton of information has been compromised. Banking and credit card information. Big-time shit, okay? He has to understand that." After a few more minutes spent trying to convince the guy on the other end to pay for a stronger firewall, he hung up, unable to tolerate the obtuse politics of this job. Jesus, the military was so much more straightforward. He was the paid expert. People listened to him. He never had to beg anyone to take him seriously.

He pulled his glasses off, rubbed the bridge of his nose and felt the dog bump up against his leg. He rubbed the animal's ears and allowed his brain to drift, the ever-present headache never far from the surface. Muted, thanks to a new daily cocktail of meds. At this moment, right now, today, he wanted Ryan Shannon so badly it made his teeth ache, as the memory of their one night kept washing over him like a warm wave.

He'd woken with a start when Ryan had kissed him, disoriented, sated but with a spinning brain. He got to his feet and felt around for his jeans. Ryan had helped him by pulling the denim up his legs. '*That was pretty amazing,*' he'd said, helping Cole with his T-shirt.

'*Yeah,*' Cole had grunted, short, lame and utterly freaked out. He couldn't do this. He was incapable of even considering a relationship. As much as he was dying to curl up in the circle of Ryan's embrace and sleep, to truly relax in his arms, he wouldn't allow himself to do it.

He was the proverbial wounded warrior. Doped up, blind, dependent on everyone around him even for simple things—useless for all intents and purposes. Apparently, even getting dressed, it seemed. He stepped away from the other man's soothing presence. '*So, you know, that was fun and all, but, I um, well…*' He ran a hand through his hair.

'*It's okay.*' Cole heard Ryan getting re-dressed, resignation in his voice. '*I get it. Fun, but that's it, right?*'

'*Yeah. That.*' Cole tried not to contradict himself by yanking the other man close.

'*So, I'll see you…around.*'

Cole had turned his face away. Had heard Ryan open then shut the front door. The sound deafened him with its finality. *'Wait. Don't leave,'* he'd whispered, dropping to the couch, freshly pounding skull in his hands, the dog shoving its worried nose up in his face. By the time Audrey had gotten home, he had been stretched out in his usual half-asleep state, sounds and nightmares holding him hostage. She'd helped him to his room and pulled the bed covers up to his chin once he'd collapsed there, mumbling about Ryan.

He sighed and took hold of reality once more. Grabbing his encrypted phone, he played back the audio of the text exchange he'd shared with the man in question in his Bluetooth earpiece. Ryan Shannon came with a built-in family. The small boy that he'd raised from a newborn when the kid's drug-addled mother had left him more or less on Ryan's doorstep, was, according to Audrey, a near-carbon copy of his father in looks and temperament. Cole was not about to subject a child to his own personal hell. No matter how drawn he might be to the boy's father.

The meds, therapies, bone-crushing headaches and sudden scary descents into panic and depression — no, he'd keep all that to himself, thanks. Although, it would be nice to get laid again. He sighed and deleted the conversation so he wouldn't be tempted to call him, to really talk. Of course, now it seemed he'd be confronted with Ryan once more, in the oh-so-familiar confines of Audrey's house.

He stretched and cocked his head, listening to yet another odd sound. It had to be the most annoying thing on the planet, this superhero-style hearing he'd developed. In the last six weeks, he had gotten past a lot of the overload moments and was able to carry on conversations even when he could hear the next-door neighbors having sex or arguing. He'd tried to develop it, to embrace and not fight it, to keep it from making him nuts. He'd go on long walks with Brutus and sit by the river, just listening. He did figure out how to discern birds' eggs cracking open in nests nearby from the digging and chattering that went on among squirrels and other rodents.

But this sound was totally new and something he'd spent the last week trying to figure out. It was a kind of *whoosh-whoosh* sound, but with a steadiness, like an underwater drumbeat. "Hey," Audrey called out from the kitchen. "Thirsty?"

"Yeah, I'm coming." He stood, held out his hand and the dog's lead slid into it. "You really are pretty good at this, aren't you?" He smiled when the dog let out a woof of agreement. They ambled into the kitchen and Cole sank into a chair, now comfortable with the house's layout and no longer earning bruises running into furniture or doors. "What's up, sis?" He leaned toward her, hearing it again. "What in the hell is that noise?" He took the water and the pills she handed him.

The noise got louder, then receded when she walked away. He gulped down the meds then touched his earpiece, which had started chirping the name of his boss. He shrugged and silenced the ringer, unwilling to engage in yet more office BS. Audrey moved around the kitchen, getting dinner together, burgers and a couple of salads he'd made earlier using the labels she'd had printed in Braille.

He felt strong today but was getting nervous in anticipation of Ryan's upcoming reappearance in his life. He reached out and snagged Audrey's arm. She gasped when he pressed his ear to her belly. The maddening noise seemed to emanate from her and it was making him nuts. The *whoosh-whoosh-whoosh* filled his ear, like a drumbeat…no, like a heartbeat.

"Audrey." He gripped her hands. "Are you pregnant?"

"What?" She jumped back and he sensed her heart start pounding. He put his hands over his ears. Christ in a sidecar—he could actually hear people's hearts beating?

"Could you… I mean, do you… Shit, I'm sorry. It's not my business." He couldn't help but smile when he sensed her collapse into a chair and burst into tears next to him.

"How can you tell?" she managed after a few seconds of waterworks.

"I hear something that has got to be a heartbeat. It's pretty loud, if you must know. You should go do a test or something."

"Oh God. I can't be. I mean, it's not…" She sighed, letting her sobs reduce to hiccups. He pulled her close, kissed her hair.

"It's okay. You guys should get married anyway. You're great together."

"I don't know. Maybe." She leaned into him. "It's complicated. With the business and stuff. And I'm just getting his kids to trust me."

"Yeah, well, I could be wrong. Go get one of those home tests. I'll hold down the fort if they get here early. Besides, you guys bought the big house, right? Why not start filling it up with spawn?"

She rose and left, trailing that crazy heartbeat noise with her. He smiled, patted the dog, got up and found a glass, drank some water.

Ryan. He was going to be within kissing distance of him again, any minute. The headache was taking up residence in his skull once more.

* * * *

The doorbell rang. Cole got to his feet from his nervous perch on the couch. The dog was at his side, already starting to whine with anxiety matching the level of horny that ran up Cole's spine the second Ryan stepped into the living room. "Hey," he said, "c'mon in."

"Where's Audrey?" Quinn asked, walking past Cole into the kitchen. "Babe?"

"She's at the drugstore."

"What? Why?" The worry was clear in the man's voice. Cole sensed Ryan blow out a breath. The door flew open at that moment, surprising them all.

"Goddamn it, Shannon," Audrey burst out. Cole tensed.

"Uh, what did I do?"

Ryan pulled Cole down on the couch, put a hand on his leg. The combination of lust, worry and a strange sense of rightness surged through him. He could sit here forever, Ryan near enough to kiss. He put his hand on top of Ryan's. "I told you," he said, directing his comment at his sister, hoping to calm her down. He heard Quinn move toward her, knew the man had taken her in his arms.

"What is it, Audrey?"

"You—did you ever go back and get rechecked, you know, after your vasectomy?"

Ryan let out a snort of laughter. Cole smiled. Then in an entirely natural move, put Ryan's hand to his lips, sucking in huge breaths of everything that represented him, but the other man jerked out of his grip and stood. Cole sighed and sat back. His own fault, really. He shouldn't be disappointed. He'd pushed him away, and Ryan was not a guy you had to tell anything twice.

"I, uh, can't remember," Quinn said.

"Well, congratulations. You knocked me up. Jesus."

Ryan laughed. "Well done, brother. I can't imagine a more beautiful woman to knock up than this one."

Ryan kept moving toward the door. He had to get the hell out of here. Cole looked his usual devastatingly amazing — ever longer hair hanging around his face in gold waves. His dark blue jeans and bright white button-down enveloped his amazing physique with an exquisite perfection. His dark glasses were fixed firmly in place. Ryan bit the inside of his cheek to keep from dragging the guy up off the couch and tossing him down on the next available horizontal surface and fucking him until they both begged for mercy.

Lynette, remember, Lynette. You have plans for her tomorrow, plans that will quell this stupid need to be with Cole once and for all. He is unavailable to you. Let it go.

"I'm um, gonna go," he said, shrugging when Quinn shot him an angry look.

"Wait." Quinn pulled Audrey to him and turned to face Ryan and Cole. "Now that we have this added wrinkle, I want you both to know that we bought the house, the big one by the lake. We'll be moving out there in the next week or so. Cole is staying here."

"Alone?" Ryan asked, honestly worried.

"Yeah, I'm a big boy, remember?" The other man didn't face him, directing his clipped words toward Quinn and Audrey.

"Anyway, so, I guess we just wanted you to know and um...then there's this." Ryan's mouth fell open when he saw his brother drop to one knee, grab Audrey's hand and open a small blue velvet box. "Marry me, oh knocked up one?"

She put a hand over her mouth. "You planned this, didn't you?"

"Well, the buying the house part then asking you to marry me in front of your brother bit, yeah. The other...well..." He slid an impressive-looking diamond onto her ring finger. Ryan saw her hands shake, heard Cole's sharp intake of breath and was completely surprised when the man grabbed him and pulled him close.

"Don't go," Cole whispered, his voice low and sure.

Ryan gulped, unwilling to admit how much he loved the feel of Cole's arms around him. "Well, I'll stay for dinner anyway." He smiled when Cole tightened his grip but resolved not to fall into a sex trap with the guy, not again.

* * * *

Later, they lay on their backs, naked and catching their breaths. "You're insatiable, you know that? Not that I'm complaining," Cole said.

Ryan sighed and closed his eyes, letting sleep pull him under for a brief moment. Quinn and Audrey had decamped to his place after a thoroughly annoying dinner show of kissing, grab-assing and sneaking off inside. Cole had declared them banished, shut the door, turned to Ryan and held out a hand. '*Shall we?*' he'd asked and Ryan had not said a word, merely slipped out of his clothes and into bed with him.

Ryan was self-aware enough to acknowledge that he now had a serious dilemma on his hands. He absolutely loved Cole's strong body, firm lips and ass and what they did for him. The undercurrent of emotional vulnerability that was so part and parcel of Cole also tugged at him in ways he couldn't square. Ryan was no caretaker, never had been. His parenting style with Jamie was a combination of buddy-dad on his best days and frustrated-guy-trying-to-cope on his worst. He still didn't really trust his instincts, but he loved his son with every fiber of his being, so it worked.

But now, this thing with Cole threatened to take him places he'd never been and was reluctant to go. The ghostly memory of the hot redheaded woman he'd made an early morning brew date with forced his eyes open. He stared at the ceiling, listening to Cole's breathing even out into sleep. He rolled over, tugging Cole into to the curve of his body, shoving thoughts of her away until a loud, hoarse yell yanked him from a dead sleep, terrified and on alert.

Cole was sitting, hands over his eyes, rocking back and forth, calling for someone named Dan. Ryan touched his shoulder, felt the clamminess of his skin. But the other man jerked away from him.

"Cole," he whispered, but Cole clawed at his eyes, leaving red streaks on his skin and making Ryan worry for his actual eyeballs. He tried to grab Cole's arm, to make him stop, but Cole threw him off with a surprising strength and Ryan had to duck to avoid getting cold-cocked.

"Jesus, man, wake up." He came around to Cole's side of the bed and tried to pry his fingers away from his face before he really hurt himself. "Cut it out." A flicker of fear lit his nerve endings.

Before he could blink, he was on his ass, on the floor, with Cole standing over him, fists clenched, face dark with fury. "Don't fucking touch me," the man said, voice low and leaving no room for discussion.

Ryan held out a hand, realizing Cole was still in a half-dream state. And that he, Ryan, was in danger of getting the shit kicked out of him by a naked, pissed-off former Marine. He eased back, slid up the wall, keeping plenty of distance between them. Cole's sightless eyes rolled in his head, his jaw clenched.

"Cole," Ryan tried to speak softly. "Cole, wake up. It's me. It's okay."

"No, it's not! The goddamn truck is on fire...shit...I can't see, fuck!" He dropped to his knees and clawed at his eyes again. Ryan crawled to him, fear and sympathy warring in his brain. He put a tentative hand on Cole's sweaty shoulder. The pain was shocking when Cole's fist connected solidly with his jaw, then again, with his nose making a sick, crunching sound in his head. He lay back, covering his face, yelling for Cole to wake the fuck up already. The dog burst into the room, nearly tearing the door off its hinges in his effort to get at his master.

Ryan scrambled to his feet. Cole stood, unclenched his fists, his face a mask of agony while the dog whined and keeping close to Cole, his dark eyes fixed up on Cole's face. "Get away from me, Ryan, before I really hurt you."

"No, no, I'm fine. Do you need...medicine?" Ryan put a hand to his bleeding nose and ignored the nauseating sound it made when he touched it, stifling the niggling little voice in his head that reminded him Cole could have killed him with his bare hands. But while he watched Cole crumple to the floor, hands over his face, his body curled in on itself and heaving with sobs, Ryan knew he couldn't just bolt. He had to help. Had to drag the incredible person Cole had once been back into the light of day. The dog whined again, standing over Cole's heaving body, looking at Ryan as if trying to get him to do something.

He grabbed a towel from the bathroom and stanched some of his bleeding, pulled on his jeans, then crouched down on the floor, his hands hovering helplessly over Cole's large, quivering form. It reminded him of his son, when the kid would break down after a particularly dramatic tantrum, spent and sobbing.

He put his hands on Cole's shoulders and tried to get him to roll over onto his back. Cole just curled in tighter, his hands over his ears. Ryan sighed, pulled a blanket off the bed and covered Cole's naked body. Brutus bumped into his hand. But he hadn't felt this helpless since he'd been handed a screaming infant and told it was his responsibility to care for it, that the kid's mother had bolted, leaving the baby behind mere hours after his birth. He got some ice for his nose and fell onto the couch, contemplating how much he wanted to help but how little he'd done so far.

He must have dropped off, because the next thing he knew, the dog was whining and pacing the living room. Ryan watched the display for a minute, then, when the dog hauled off and barked, he jumped up and followed the animal back to the bedroom. Terror gripped him, sending shockwaves down his spine when he saw the empty prescription bottle and smelled the sour tang of bourbon.

Fuck, how long had he slept?

His nose and jaw hurt like a motherfucker, but his chest was tight with fear and dread. "Cole!" He banged on the bathroom door, jiggled the handle, not surprised it was locked. "Open up, you son of a bitch. You are not allowed to do this. Do you hear me?" he yelled, threw his shoulder against the solid oak door, praying the nineteen-twenties-era lock would give. It didn't. He slammed into it over and over, while Brutus started howling like a wolf and scratching at the floor outside the door, shooting him looks of, 'Hey, human, try those useful things you call hands and open the door already, would ya?'

Ryan took a deep breath, put his ear to the door and heard it then. "Go 'way. Leave. Get the fuckout." Slurred to be sure, but definitely still alive. His nose had started bleeding again from his efforts.

"Cole, you asshole. Get up and open the fucking door, I mean it. Open the door!" He pounded on it, sending the poor dog into more paroxysms of howling and pained scratching. The water kept flowing. Finally, Ryan got his wits about him and dialed 911. Then he called Quinn, thinking if Audrey were here, Cole would listen. But they'd gone back to Quinn's house, which was a solid thirty minutes away.

He pressed his aching forehead against the door. When he spotted water oozing out from under it, his vision darkened from the edges. "Cole!" he yelled. "Please don't do this!" He heard the words leave his mouth, then the siren. He ran to the front door after throwing a shirt over his bare torso. The EMT took a look at his squashed, bloody nose and streaming eyes then pushed past him to the back where he pointed, defeated, sore and aching all over. "Cole," he whispered, sinking to the floor, his head in his hands. Blood dripped from his nose to the dark wood.

"Sir!" one of the paramedics yelled from the doorway. "Can you please control this dog? It won't let us near the door."

Ryan jumped to his feet, grabbed Brutus' lead and held him back. He tried to calm the animal while the two men used a sledgehammer to destroy Audrey's guest bathroom door before barreling in. They spoke in low, clipped tones while they pulled Cole's limp form from the overflowing bathtub. Ryan buried his face in Brutus's fur, praying as hard he could remember from his mother-enforced years of parochial school. He heard the paramedics barking orders, trying to revive the man laid out on the bedroom floor.

Time stopped then rushed forward while he held on to Cole's dog for dear life. When Audrey ran in screaming Cole's name, Quinn tried to pull her out of the way. The EMTs were working, doing mouth-to-mouth, chest compressions, hooking up IVs and all sorts of shit. When he saw how blue Cole's fingers were, he tried to drag the dog out of the room with him. But Brutus put all his nearly ninety-five pounds of muscle into staying put, whining and trying to claw his way over to his master.

"Audrey, honey, let them do their job." Quinn tried to keep her calm, but she kept shrieking her brother's name. Finally, she broke down and sobbed, letting Quinn hold her. Ryan watched from what felt like a million miles away while the men tried to revive Captain Cole Traynor, Purple Heart and Navy Cross recipient, but nothing seemed to be working.

One of them put his stethoscope to Cole's chest, yelled for the other one to hook up the oxygen and prep for an on-site intubation. Taking this as a good sign, Ryan gripped Brutus tighter. A tube was inserted down Cole's throat, hooked to an oxygen source and his chest start to rise and fall.

"Oh, God," Audrey whispered. Quinn let go of her. She dropped down to her knees and brushed Cole's hair back from his forehead, murmuring to him, kissing his cheeks, holding his hand. She looked up at Ryan once, anger in her gaze. "What happened? What the fuck did you do?"

Quinn started to step into it, but Ryan held him back. He handed the dog over to his brother and got on his knees next to Audrey. "He half-woke up in the middle of a nightmare. He nearly beat the crap out of me. When he really woke up and realized what he'd done, he just…snapped. I thought he went back to sleep, so I covered him up and left him alone and later the dog came to get me and…" His voice broke. He looked down at Cole's washed-out face. His knees and calves were ice cold from kneeling in the water that had flowed over the side of the tub before one of the medics had turned it off.

Something in him gave way, leaving him exhausted and more aware of how much his nose and jaw hurt than ever. He got to his feet. "I can't do this…" He walked out without another word to anyone, the sound of the dog's howling piercing his eardrums all the way out to his car.

Chapter Eleven

Lynette glared at her reflection in the small bathroom mirror.

"Honey!" Her mother's voice floated out from the kitchen. "Where are you going? Did you make coffee? Can you feed the cat? Lynette!"

"Mom, what are you doing up this early? I have to go to work. Yes, the coffee is ready and I'll deal with the cat later. He was sound asleep on the couch, last I saw." She rolled her eyes at herself, yanked her hair up and tucked it under a cap, then turned, observing herself another minute. Her scalp tingled at the memory of Ryan Shannon's angry glare, his touch, his voice. Jesus, everything about the man did things to her she had no reason to justify.

She blew out a breath. The few tidbits she knew about Ryan Shannon she'd learned through the grapevine at work. He had a kid at home, from some failed relationship or another. Rumors also flew about him being bisexual. Of course, she had exactly zero business thinking anything about him other than work-related aggravation. She was just marking time until she found a real job. She had student loans and the brewery gig had come up quick and she'd leaped at it. It kept her local, which she needed. All the justifications she'd used for the past six weeks crowded her brain. All good for a temporary situation—key word being 'temporary'.

She smoothed her shirt down over her jeans, took a breath and walked into the kitchen. "Honey, really, why so early?" her mother asked.

"I'm supposed to learn the beer brewing process so I can talk about it intelligently." She poured a travel mug full of coffee and headed for the back door. "It makes sense."

"You'll never get a real man, selling beer, you know," her mother called out, always needing the last word at the expense of Lynette's nonexistent love life.

"I know, Mom. I know." She shut the apartment door behind her. The engine of her piece-of-shit car sputtered to life, and she pointed it toward the outskirts of town. She lived only about ten miles from Ypsi Brewing, and the trip over gave her no time to contemplate why she'd even agreed to this ass-crack-of-dawn brewing session.

She sighed and forced the memory of Ryan's huge eyes, his mop of dark blond hair and the amazing span of his shoulders out of her head. He was all man, without a doubt. One who sometimes preferred his own sex when it came to relationships.

He's 'bi', Lynette. That means he can go either way.

She squared her shoulders. She'd been told in no uncertain terms by the bar manager that she wasn't Ryan's type. There was even gossip that he was in the early stages of a relationship with some guy. What she couldn't quite figure out was why every time she was around him, his masculinity — his raw sensuality, if she were being honest with herself — seemed so profound.

She sipped her coffee while driving the few remaining miles to the brewery, berating herself. *It's no wonder you think he's hot. He's the closest thing to a guy you've allowed yourself to consider for, what? Nearly six years?*

Had it been that long?

She sighed and flicked the broken left turn signal manually. Yeah, it had. Six solid years at least since she'd even allowed a second thought about a member of the opposite sex and a good thing, too. She had piled up thousands of student-debt dollars getting her MBA. And now she sold beer for a living, or had at least attempted to for the last few months. There was no time for men, or, would seem, anything resembling a social life. She sat, clutching the steering wheel and pep-talking herself a minute before grabbing her computer, climbing out and unlocking the back door of the brewery.

The burble of fermentation and the *ping-ping* of stainless-steel vats of beer warming up and cooling down met her ears. The smells and sounds were a comforting combination. She stretched her arms over her head, trying to shake the cobwebs out of her brain. She glanced at her phone — only five-ten. She was early, as usual.

She opened her laptop on a pile of malt bags to peruse the sales numbers from the week. But the longer she stared, the more the screen blurred, so after ten minutes she got up and walked into the cooler where their lagers were resting in yet more huge stainless-steel tanks. Kegs with the distinctive Ypsi Brewing label were stacked to the ceiling. She let the cold seep into her bones and get her good and awake, then pushed the doors open, assuming Ryan would be out there.

She glanced around, but the place was still empty. After checking his small glass-framed office that was still dark, she shrugged and decided to make coffee. She sat, watching it burble, while the clock eased past five-thirty. Then she poured a cup and looked at her email. The usual mix of people asking for her ad money, donations for events, and distributors wanting point of sale swag filled it, but it hadn't changed since last night.

Gritting her teeth, she forced herself not to dwell on her lack of a life. Between her loan payments, the rent, utilities and her mother, she did nothing but work and pay bills and placate. She'd found herself in this job, knowing less than nothing about beer but willing to take the salary just to have an income. It had been fun and irritating in equal measure, mainly thanks to the man she'd dragged her ass out of bed for this morning, who was still a no-show.

She sighed, sipped more coffee and stared at the phone clock. Once it hit ten after six she cursed and grabbed her keys. But something held her back. Telling herself it was to put in a few hours of work before heading home, she acknowledged she was waiting for Ryan to show up, pure and simple.

By the time the door flew open, hitting the concrete wall with a bang, she was deep into her pity party, staring at the charts and graphs she'd created to drag the company into a more organized method of marketing. She jumped, looked over and sucked in a breath at the sight of him. His hair was sticking up, his eyes wild, and his jaw sporting more brown stubble than usual. Worse, his nose looked…crooked. And one eye was swollen shut. She clenched her fists under the table and looked away.

"You're late," she said, snapping her laptop closed. "I'm leaving."

"Wait, I'm…sorry." His voice was hoarse, as if he'd been partying or something given the state of his face, all night.

Lynette sighed, tucked her computer into its case and stood. She would not be played, not even by the first guy in nearly a decade that made her wake up in a cold sweat, wondering why she had gone so long without even trying to get laid. She jumped when his hand landed on her shoulder and shrugged away from him on reflex. Her skin was crawling, her brain burning, and she had no reference for how much she wanted him to keep touching her.

"Lynette, listen, I'm…"

She turned, hearing something in his voice that made her hesitate before speaking.

"Are you okay? I mean…your face."

He looked down then walked away from her. "Let's get on with this."

She sighed. *He's gay, Lynette, get a fucking grip.*

"Sure, okay, so, what's first?"

The next two hours were a total blur. She heaved giant malt bags, tested water pH, calculated something called 'plato' and 'original gravity', stirred heavy malt beds, nearly singed her eyebrows off checking the temperature of the wort, measured and weighed hops and let herself get utterly immersed and enthralled by the process. Not the mention the man teaching it to her.

At one point, she looked over at him. He was staring into the dark, one-hundred-twenty-degree sugar water swirling around in the huge vessel. His eyes were haunted and his hands shook as he dipped the long thermometer into the liquid. Something was seriously not right with him. She let him boss her around, watched while he ran the almost-beer through the heat exchanger, supercooling it to less than fifty degrees in a matter of minutes. He showed her how to add the yeast at the bottom of the vessel, frowning when she screwed up and the stuff spewed all over her shirt. "Sorry," she muttered. He cursed and went into the cooler for more yeast in solution.

"Here, damn it, move, let me do it."

She stood, wiping the sweat from her forehead, pissed but unwilling to let on how much. His shoulders flexed and she bit her lip, watching him hook everything up, shift hoses, clamps and other random shit she was only just understanding until the yeast was 'pitched'.

He adjusted the temperature gauges and propped both hands on the vessel. It took her a half a minute to figure out his shoulders were heaving. She put her palm on one, loving the play of musculature under his shirt. To her surprise, he turned to face her, agony etched in every line of his handsome face.

He grabbed her, yanked her to him and buried his face in her neck. She patted his back, nervous and unsure, then took a chance and touched his hair. He felt so flawless in her arms it made her nearly choke.

"Sorry," he muttered but kept holding her close, too close, making her react in a scary, and super-inappropriate, way. She gasped when he tightened his grip, molding her into his tall, strong frame. *Oh, yeah, this is totally bad.* But she closed her eyes, threaded her fingers in his thick hair and let herself have the moment.

He pulled away and stared into her eyes but kept his amazing arms around her. She felt herself sink into him, until his next words. "I think I'm in love," he muttered. "And he, uh, well, he tried to kill himself last night so I'm kinda doubting my existence. And you...you're here and I, I'm...shit. Sorry."

"Oh, well, um..." Lynette spluttered, unable to respond in any coherent way, so she opted for shutting her mouth, disentangling herself and allowing herself time to stare at his wide shoulders, strong arms, large hands at the moment resting on his hips. He was at least six foot three or maybe four, she'd guess, and didn't appear to have an ounce of fat on him anywhere.

And. He. Is. Gay, Lynette, snap out of it. He just told you he was in love, for Christ's sake.

"So, now we clean," he said, startling her out of the fantasy loop in her head—one starring this amazing man and herself. She shook her head and took the metal, shovel-looking thing he held out. "Let's go. This is the really hard part."

Ryan dropped onto a ratty barstool and watched Lynette struggle with the trowel and wet, heavy spent mash they'd created when they drained the sugar water off the malt. He raised an eyebrow when she dumped an entire shovel full of the sticky stuff down her front, but stayed put, let her learn. That was the point of this—well, that and he had planned to seduce her. He groaned and put his head in his hands. When his phone buzzed on the worktable, he nearly fell off the chair.

"Hey," he said, dreading what Quinn was going to tell him.

"Nice disappearing act. What the fuck was that about?"

Ryan sighed.

"What are you, a teenager? Seriously, man, why did you just walk out?"

He could hear hospital noises, and the guilt nearly bowled him over. "Sorry. I, uh, well…"

"You're a lame fucker, is what you are."

"How is he?"

"What do you care? Audrey was ready to come after you and beat you to death. And I wasn't inclined to stop her."

"Quinn, listen…"

"No, you listen. This guy is damaged. We all know it. And you seducing him then bolting when things get messy is –"

"I didn't do that, Quinn. Jesus. He…I…" He put his head down on the desk and let his brother berate him a few more minutes. "Can I see him?"

Suddenly, he wanted that more than he wanted to get the hell away from the whole scene a few hours before. He was running on exactly zero sleep and his nose and jaw were killing him. His whole world was upside down. He wanted Cole, so badly, wanted to help, but something about that moment when Audrey had looked up at him, wild fury in her eyes while she'd knelt over Cole's lifeless form had triggered the sort of flight response he'd not experienced in years. He was not that guy anymore. He couldn't be. He was a father, a responsible adult.

"Ow! Um…help?" He looked up to find Lynette hanging on to the opening at the back of the mash vessel, nearly doing the splits. She had one leg on the pallet holding the garbage bins and it must have slid in all the mess she'd made trying to empty the thing.

"I'll be by later if you think it's okay. He's okay, right?" He kept talking while he walked over to the woman now completely covered in spent malt and grabbed her around the waist with one arm and set her on the concrete. She glared at him and tried to brush some of the grains off her. But he knew from direct experience that was a lost cause.

"Yeah, he's gonna be fine. But I can't promise you that Audrey will let you anywhere near him."

"Fine. I'll be there, I'll deal with her myself." He tucked the phone in his jeans pocket and stared at Lynette. Reaching out, he brushed the trickle of grains off a strand of her deep red hair that had escaped from the hat now sitting cock-eyed on her head. She smacked his hand away and turned around to finish.

He spent a half second admiring her jeans-clad ass, recalling his original goal for today. His body tingled, but his brain was on serious shutdown when the phone buzzed again. He looked at the screen and groaned. Jamie had stayed over with Quinn's nanny and his cousins. And the call was coming from Quinn's house phone.

Quinn's sons were slowly getting detoxed from their spoiled ways now that their father had them more often. Since their mother was gallivanting around with her NFL-trainer boyfriend, never home for more than a few days at a time, Quinn was pushing for full custody. Audrey had eased into her future role as stepmother nicely and, after some initial drama, the boys had settled into their new reality.

"Hey," he said. "What's up, sport?"

"Daddy." The little boy's voice was quivery. "Where are you?"

He glanced at the phone screen and saw it was nearly eleven. Jamie was a stickler for timing and when any plan went awry, he lost it. "Put Tracey on the phone, please."

"No!" He heard running footsteps.

"James Shannon, put Tracey on the phone right now!"

"Here! Want pancakes!" The boy's voice faded.

"Hi, Mr. Shannon." Tracey's voice was chipper. "Sorry about that. He grabbed and dialed before I knew what he was doing."

"I'm sorry. I'm late."

"Yeah, well, I would be okay with it, but the other boys need me to take them to soccer since your brother is…"

"I know." He ran a hand through his hair, noted how fucking messy everything still was in his brewery and tried not to sigh too loudly. He looked up and saw Lynette staring at him then turned away, face flushed with anxiety. He needed to see Cole. He had to pick up his son, and his brewery was a pigsty.

He hung up and calmed his breathing, trying to compile a mental plan of action. He jumped again when she put a hand on his arm. "Hey, can I help?"

"No." He grabbed the hose and started spraying everything down. "Just move out of the way."

"Well, you don't have to be an asshole about it."

He stopped in his tracks. "You're right. I'm sorry. And I'm also sorry for dragging you out this morning, being late, losing my cool, all of it."

"It's okay." She rolled the last of the full bins of malt out the back door to be picked up by a local farmer who used it for his cattle.

"And for the record..." He kept talking, blaming exhaustion for the extreme truths he was about to spill. "I had plans to brew with you but wanted more. I wanted to seduce you, if you must know. You're hot. I was lonely. I had ulterior motives and I'm sorry for that, too." He switched off the water and ignored her gaping stare. "So, now you know."

"Uh, okay." She took her hat off and he had to force his eyes away from the tumble of hair that flowed down her back. Her shirt was wet, too, which didn't help. "I thought you were...um...that I wasn't your type."

"I'm bi. And now I have to go pick up my son. Can you just..." He waved around, feeling helpless and stupid, not even positive he'd just spilled so much of his own truths to this woman.

"Tell you what." She crossed her arms. "I am a certified caregiver, I mean, I worked at day cares all through college. I was an ace babysitter. And it sounds like you need to go visit...um..."

He narrowed his eyes at her, contemplating it. "Jamie is a handful. He's a couple of handfuls with some left over, if you must know. I'm not sure that would be fair to you."

"Someday, I'll tell you about the summer I spent with twin three-year-old boys whose favorite thing to do was to smear their shit on the kitchen floor, just so I could clean it up."

The laugh felt good and suddenly the air was clear between them. He put a hand on her arm, felt her flinch then relax. "Okay, you win. I'll pay you the going rate. But I'm not really sure how long I'll be." He texted her

Quinn's address and his. "Thanks, Lynette. That's really great, especially considering, ah, what I told you and all."

She leaned back on the worktable and the look in her eyes made him shiver. "No worries. For all you know, I had the same plans for you." She winked and, before he could blink, had whipped off her damp shirt. The black sports bra highlighted the creaminess of her skin.

Ryan gulped and looked away. "Uh, yeah, so that's cheating." He tried to paste a neutral look on his face.

She grabbed a spare brewery shirt from the swag closet and tugged it over her lush, too-tempting torso. Ryan shook his head. *Cole, remember? The guy you fucked last night? Lying in a hospital bed right now?* The memory of the other man's flesh under his hands, and utter agony on his face later, made Ryan's eyes burn. He needed to get a grip. "Thanks, Lynette."

"No problem, Ryan," she tossed over her shoulder. And something about the way she said his name made him want her all over again.

Jesus H. Christ. Shannon, you are a mess. Or perhaps merely a sex-crazed idiot.

He hosed down the rest of the brewhouse and grabbed his keys. He had to see Cole. Get some things straight with Cole's sister. Then he needed to sleep for two days. The fact that he was turning his only son over to a woman who for the last two months meant nothing more to him than a potential sexual conquest didn't give him much pause. Something about her oozed confidence and he needed backup. Hopefully it wouldn't be a terrible mistake for everyone concerned.

Chapter Twelve

Lynette followed her smart phone's GPS and found Quinn's house in the middle of a neighborhood of gargantuan brick homes. She whistled to herself when she pulled into the semicircular front drive of the biggest one on the street, glanced at the number to confirm it and got out. She tucked her sunglasses on her head, brushed off her sticky jeans and walked up to the huge oak front door. After ringing the doorbell a couple of times, she crouched down to peer in a sidelight, bracing herself for a bratty, miniature Ryan.

A huge pair of watery green eyes met her stare. The little boy had his nose pressed to the glass and his face was fixed in an unhappy frown. She put her finger against her side of the glass. He shrieked and jumped back, giggling. Lynette saw a pair of identical dark-haired twin boys who looked an awful lot like the man who'd hired her appear behind the still laughing kid. They grabbed him and yanked him away from the door, yelling what sounded like 'stranger danger' and 'Tracey!'

She stood up when the door opened. "Oh, hi, you must be Lynette," the girl said, smiling. The little boys peered out from behind Tracey's legs but the mini-Ryan marched around the trio and tapped her leg.

"Yes, I am," she said to the nanny. She knelt down. "And you must be...SpongeBob."

"No, silly. I'm Jamie."

"Huh, well, I'm supposed to be picking up some kid named Bob so I think I'm at the wrong house."

The boys laughed. Jamie cocked his head and looked so much like his father at that second Lynette blinked. He reached out and touched her hair. "What color is this?"

"Burnt amber. I'll show you, once I find this Bob kid." She stood up and pretended to look around.

By the time she had Jamie home, eating fruit she found by rooting around in Ryan's kitchen, she had him convinced they could color his hair like hers with a crayon. He munched on carefully cut-up grapes and apples and kept pulling strands of her hair out from under her hat, rubbing them between his fingers in awe, babbling a mile a minute.

While he ran into the family room, she checked out the pictures taped to the refrigerator's grubby stainless surface. Running a finger across the ones that featured Ryan, noting how good the man looked in pretty much every single one of them, she smiled when she felt a hand on her leg.

"So, are you ready to read now? Or do we need to use the burnt amber on your hair?" She picked the boy up and tossed him over her shoulder. He seemed small for a five-year-old, but that just made him easy to carry around. He giggled his way down the hall, pointing to his bedroom—a breathtaking mess of army men, matchbox cars, plastic dinosaurs, clothes and books. "Wow. Too bad we don't have magic wands to clean this place up."

She tossed him on his unmade bed and tickled him a minute before standing and succumbing to her inner neat freak. "Okay, let's play a game. I'm going to race you to see which one of us can pick up the most toys...ready...set...go!"

The kid was full of energy, and the room was tidy in no time. He talked nonstop, and once she'd helped him spread up his Lego-land sheets, he fell over on the floor. She sat, anticipating a tantrum, but he just looked up at the ceiling, closed his eyes and fell sound asleep. She gave him a few minutes then tucked him under a blanket on the bed and left the room.

She sent a quick text to Ryan, letting him know Jamie was settled. Even while convincing herself that it was a really bad idea the entire time she was doing it, she eased into the dark room across the hall from Jamie's. She tiptoed around the unmade bed, touched the soft sheets, noted that the father was as bad a slob as the son and ran her hand over the smooth, black surface of the dresser.

An amalgam of junk littered the top—dollar bills, coins, various receipts, Chapstick, an expensive-looking watch, a couple of dirty T-shirts and books about brewing. She smiled at a picture tucked into the mirror. Two small boys stood with their arms around each other's shoulders, one dark, one light—Ryan and Quinn Shannon at age ten or eleven. Born eighteen months apart, classic Irish twins. She grabbed it and held it close to her eyes. Then when her phone buzzed with a text, she jumped and put the photo back, then exited the forbidden room, berating herself the whole time.

"Hey," she answered, hoping Ryan didn't know she'd been snooping and realizing how stupid that was. She dropped into a dining room chair. "All is well."

"Okay. Cool. Thanks, a lot." He was quiet. Lynette could hear people and random hospital noises in the background.

"Is everything okay...you know...with...?" She trailed off, unsure what to say. This day had taken such a bizarre turn. His words about seducing her still rolled around in her brain.

"His name is Cole and he is resting now. Stomach pumped, the usual shit, I guess, I mean when you try to OD on Vicodin and bourbon."

"Wow." She let the unasked question hover, suddenly so nervous she had to get up and pace. Ryan's presence permeated his house. She could smell him, sense him in every corner. She opened the sliding door and stepped out onto the brick patio.

"Yeah, it sucks. Sorry you got dragged into this mess today. Seriously. Not my intention."

"Huh, well, maybe better considering your actual intention for today if that was indeed the truth."

He chuckled, making her shiver. "Touché, Red."

She sighed, pacing around his back yard. "Well, take your time. I'm good. Jamie's fine. But I may impose some cleanliness on this nasty pit you call a house. And don't call me Red."

"No, no, please, don't make me feel even more guilty by cleaning up. Jesus."

"Too late."

"Fine. Whatever. You are turning out to be too good to be true, but fine."

"Just take care of…"

"Cole."

"Yeah, Cole. I'll be here. Oh, bring some beer home." She hung up before realizing that calling it 'home' might be a tad forward.

Ryan stared at his phone, not quite sure how to take Lynette's last request until he realized that the thought of going 'home' to her didn't sound that bad, and not for his typical reasons. He leaned forward on the ugly blue hospital waiting room chair, elbows on his knees. The stress and lack of sleep, plus his busted nose, were helping morph the headache he'd been nursing into a real temple crusher. His vision was even getting blurry.

He gripped his phone and willed last night back. Wishing he'd done more than just jump the poor kid's bones, as pleasant as that had been. He leaned back and tried to relax the knot of muscle in his neck. Guilt flooded every corner of his psyche. He should never have pushed Cole into bed again. He obviously hadn't been ready for it.

Now something about his perception of Lynette had shifted. Or perhaps it was him, but whatever it was, he looked forward to seeing her. If for no other reason than he could drink some beer and finally relax after the barn-burner bullshit he'd been through these last twenty-four hours.

Audrey dropped into a chair next to him.

He turned to the lovely blonde woman who was going to marry his brother. "I'm really sorry. I mean, I don't know what got into me, but…"

She stared straight ahead. Ryan recalled Quinn's words about his fiancée—that the woman was eight thousand layers of stubborn, wrapped in intransigence, all tied up with an ornery string. She'd have to be, having built the most successful wine and beer distribution operation in the state out of her father's one-time disaster of a company. He sighed and looked out onto a sea of faces in the VA hospital waiting room.

"Okay. I know this may be hard for you to believe, but I didn't do anything to him. We, he…well, this is the second time we, you know." He blew out a breath. She maintained her silence. "I have no excuse or reason why I bolted. It was wrong, lame and everything in between. And I'm sorry. That's all I have. Take it or leave it. But I'm here now and really want to help him, if I can. I…care about your brother, Audrey…a lot."

He spotted Quinn come around the corner carrying cardboard cups of what passed for coffee. His stomach churned at the thought of it. When Audrey started talking, her voice was monotone, as though she was reciting her times tables. Ryan listened and tried to find some thawing toward him in the words.

"Cole was the star of the football and the track team in high school but had no really close friends. He went on dates, but no girl was around more than once or twice. When he graduated, we had half the class at our house for his party, but we never really knew him, I guess. By the time he was halfway through his junior year of college, he decided to come out to our parents. And they told him to get out of their house. To never come back."

Ryan leaned back, wanting to know more, but not really. And hating himself for thinking that. He took a cup of the swill from his brother and they sat, listening to Audrey give her flat-voiced monologue. "We weren't close growing up. But when he told my parents, there wasn't a big fight or anything. Our father just stood up, opened the door and told his only son to leave and never come back. And I hoped…well, I don't know what I hoped."

She sighed and put her face in her hands. Quinn reached out to touch her, but she jerked away. "No, don't." Quinn shot Ryan a what-did-I-tell-you look. "He was at loose ends since our parents stopped funding his college tuition and somehow ended up at a Marine recruiting center. They figured out quick he was a math and computer savant and sent him straight to officer training after basic. When my parents were killed in a car accident two years after my father disowned him, he didn't come home for the funeral. It was…shitty. After that, we started talking more regularly. Then he ended up in Iraq, met Dan and…"

She turned to fix Ryan with an angry look. "Cole falls in love fast and hard. And I will not let you fuck around with his head. Do you get me, Shannon? I don't care whose brother you are." She stood, shrugging Quinn off when he tried to join her. She gripped her elbows, shivering in the too-cold room. "He's all I have. My blood. My family. And you can't just walk out like that and then show up here and claim that you care about him."

"Hang on a second." Quinn started to protest, but Ryan put a hand on his brother's knee. Quinn glared at him.

"Let her finish," Ryan said quietly.

"I won't let you hurt us," she spat out and turned and walked to Cole's room, shutting the door behind her.

"Nice. Now I'm in trouble, too? Fuck." Quinn checked his phone. "Tracey says Jamie went home with Lynette? Is that my firebrand marketing director?"

Ryan nodded, words frozen on his lips.

"I don't know what in the hell you are getting yourself into with her or with my future brother-in-law, but so help me. Ryan, I will fucking strangle you with your own shoestring if you screw this up for me. I love that woman with everything I have and I've worked too hard to lose her because you can't decide which goddamn team you bat for."

Ryan stood and started for the elevator. He was shutting down, could barely see or hear. Audrey's words had cut a hole in his gut he couldn't justify. *Cole.* He wanted to see him so badly, but Audrey had said no. He'd sat for hours in the ice-cold waiting room, tried to be supportive and now was going to leave without even laying eyes on him. A hand on his arm made him turn around. His brother's gaze was pure ice fury. "Stop walking away."

Ryan jerked his arm out of Quinn's grip. "Stop lecturing me. She won't even let me near his room. What the fuck am I supposed to do here? My son is at home with a woman who was kind enough to volunteer to help me out. I want a shower, a beer and a nap. I don't need to hear any more from either of you. I'm an asshole. I get it. Let go of my arm."

Quinn blinked and stepped away. Ryan turned to push the ground floor button on the elevator and got a glimpse of Audrey guarding her brother's hospital room like a mama bear over a nest of cubs. He sighed. All he wanted was sleep so he could think straight and maybe fix this, or at least make it less shitty.

He drove home in a daze, barely remembering the journey. Jamie was tucked into Lynette's side, poring over a stack of books on the couch, when he opened the front door. "Daddy!" The boy jumped into his arms. Ryan held him, smelled his fresh-bathed little boy and let tears slip from his eyes. Lynette rose from the couch, patted Jamie's back and put her lips way too close to his ear.

"I'll go. You guys rest."

"No!" Jamie yelped and tried to reach for her. "Lynette, stay."

Ryan put a hand on her arm. "Yes, please, Lynette. Stay."

Chapter Thirteen

Cole put out his hand and was soothed by his dog's presence. He scratched Brutus between the ears and listened to the emails being read to him from the computer. He leaned back in his chair and contemplated the latest dilemma presented by this new client.

"Jake!" he barked out, grabbing the water bottle never far from his reach. "I need the Trillium report."

"Got it," his new business partner said, just over his left shoulder.

Sounds still assaulted him, but he'd learned to filter them, thanks to a different drug regimen and a better therapist. The ten days he had spent essentially a prisoner in the VA hospital had taught him a lot. Mainly that the self-pity bullshit needed to stop. So, he tried.

And, now, a month later, he sat in the house that his sister was slowly vacating while she moved her life into a new phase—one married to the brother of the man he still obsessed about. While he had taken his best clients and opened his own internet security consulting firm that consisted of him and Jake Lowery, a fellow Counter Intel vet.

"Here, Cole, listen to this." Jake leaned over his arm, hit something on his keyboard and a fresh report poured into his ears. He tried to absorb it, but he was having one of those days. The days he dreaded, when the memories of Dan, of the time they'd shared and then the horrific carnage that had taken the man from him rippled through him like an undulating serpent. His head was pounding, reminiscent of his early days post-surgery. The dog whined and pushed his huge head onto Cole's leg. "You okay?" Jake put a hand on his shoulder.

Cole shrugged, drank more water and repeated the mantra. *One hour ahead, one day ahead, one week ahead, it's all you have to do. Enjoy what you have.* And he had a fair bit. His sister, Audrey, was getting married in a few weeks and he loved teasing her about the shotgun he was bringing. He truly looked forward to being an uncle.

But Ryan Shannon haunted his every moment, awake and asleep. He had told the therapist about him—about their two intense physical encounters and his own suicide attempt after the second one when he'd woken from his sleep/dream state and sensed Ryan's body beneath him, heard his strangled cries for him to stop.

The sick part was that he even remembered what Ryan looked like, from the one brief time they'd met and that hurt the most. The memory of faces had to be one of the worst things on a long list of things that sucked about being blind.

God, he wanted to see Audrey again, even Quinn, so he could stare into the man's face and make sure he was going to do right by his sister. He'd give anything to open his eyes and…just fucking see.

He sighed and rubbed the bridge of his nose. He felt tense all over. He needed release. Required a physical connection. Frankly, jacking off blind was even lamer than if he were sighted.

"Cole?"

"Yeah, sorry, Jake. Let's talk about Trillium."

After he and Jake shut things down for the night and the other man had left, Cole sat, absorbing all the night sounds that swirled in his ears. He was marking time and hadn't been tempted to do anything stupid for nearly a month, but it was a close-run thing every day. Every minute that he did not hear from Ryan made it worse. He worked, of course, nearly around the clock, but the empty space that begged filling stayed that way.

Audrey's ring tone made him jump. He stuck the Bluetooth device in his ear and absently rubbed his dog's giant head. "What?"

"Well, I'm fine, Cole, thanks for asking. How are you doing today?"

"What do you want?" He rubbed his neck. Ghostly memories of Ryan's lips and voice made Cole's skin pebble with repressed lust, frustration and embarrassment.

"I need your opinion on something." Audrey kept her voice light, but Cole had gotten even better at hearing stress between her words.

"Not more wedding crap, please."

"Sorry. It's all-consuming right now. And it keeps me from ripping fresh assholes at work. This pregnancy thing sucks. And I have to plan a wedding in December, which was just stupid. Why didn't you talk me out of that?"

"Yeah, so what's the question?" Cole's heart sped up at the thought of a niece or nephew—one he would likely scare with his creepy sunglasses and protective dog.

"It's a food thing. I'm wondering if we should try and feed all hundred and fifty guests a meal or just snacks and beer."

Cole sighed, settled back in his seat and helped his sister sort out the latest nuptial dilemma. Her being pregnant was a bit of added strangeness, but Cole was happy for her. While he'd never figured his sister as being particularly baby-crazy, he chalked it up to just another female mystery he didn't want to solve.

After he hung up, Brutus made a snuffling noise and put his head on Cole's leg again. "Yeah, I know, dude." Cole scratched the dog's ears. "This whole thing is wild." Half-thankful for the animal and half-frustrated at the fact that he needed him in the first place, he touched the computer mouse and more emails were read to him by the sexy feminine, only slightly computerized voice.

He dictated some answers and leaned back, sipping from the water bottle. The dog pressed against his leg, a comfort when he admitted it, which wasn't often.

"What the hell am I supposed to do?" Brutus bumped his hand, indicating he had heard him. "Seriously. I still love…I mean, I miss, oh fuck. I need to get out of here." He stood, and his canine eyes slipped beneath his hand to guide him out of the house and down the sidewalk. After some fresh, cool air, he felt a little better, but the thought of Audrey and Quinn's wedding still made his gut churn because it meant one thing — Ryan would be back in his world for good.

.

Chapter Fourteen

Ryan groaned and stood, trying to stretch out some of the tension he'd developed in the last few days. They were working on a few new brewing concepts, and he was tearing his ever-loving hair out trying to work through the complexities while getting his brew staff on board.

On the plus side, he wasn't constantly knocking his head against the bright red brick wall of Ms. Lynette Williams. They had relaxed into a much less confrontational means of communication, and he'd promised her a beer school session tonight. He had a bunch of classic craft styles gathered and was going to have her over to do some sipping and talking about how they compared and contrasted with what Ypsi Brewing made.

He rubbed his hand down his face when he spotted her across the brewery. The deep red of her long hair was hard to miss. Well, that and the luscious sway of her hips, currently encased in a silhouette-hugging slim gray skirt and light blue silk blouse. He swallowed hard.

They were friends. All was well. He had no reason to think there would be anything else between them, but his libido was rising to an occasion he had no business contemplating, so he turned away from her and refocused on the familiar frustrations of running his brewery.

When he looked up from his latest round of projections for the year, making the determination that his brother was going to have to loosen the purse strings and buy him another hundred-barrel fermenter, the place was nearly deserted. He glanced at his phone. "Shit, fuck, hell...shit!" He was thirty minutes late to get Jamie from day care—again. The boy had recently discovered that the world actually did not revolve around him, and it made the evenings challenging since he took out his five-year-old pent-up frustration on his father. Many nights they would simply collapse and sleep on the couch, healthy dinner, pj's and teeth brushing be damned. Ryan cursed every morning they woke up this way, realizing he was the worst sort of parent letting that happen.

He tossed his backpack onto the back seat of his Jeep. Just when he was about to call the day care to apologize for being tardy again, he looked down to see a text from Lynette sent over an hour ago.

I got him. See you at your place?

He smiled and relaxed, then shook it off. Lynette was a friend to him and to his son and nothing more. His scalp was tingling by the time he pulled into his driveway. The sight of her in jeans and a brewery sweatshirt, sitting on his couch with his son on her lap, made a strange warmth steal through him.

He grabbed the kid when he ran into Ryan's arms. His life had been so unfocused for so many years, and while he was grateful that something as drastic as becoming a father had set him on a better path, at times it overwhelmed him in the extreme.

"Hey, dude, sorry I was late." He swung Jamie's slight form up onto his shoulders. Quinn had initially wanted him to get a paternity test, but he didn't care. Being Jamie's father had given him purpose, a focus he'd never had. They didn't do everything by the book, especially in the early years when he'd been happy to obtain a few hours of sleep a night even if it meant the infant slept in his bed. Jamie had not exhibited any signs of being born to a drug-addicted mother other than being below the size curve. He was smart, verbal, walked early and if anything was developmentally advanced. Between Quinn and his boys and his mother who was flat-out obsessed with the kid, he never lacked for family attention.

"Daddy, I want Lynette to pick me up every day."

"Not an option, but I'm glad she was there today." He smiled at her, ignoring the voice in his brain that screamed at him to take note how perfect this moment was. He didn't want her like this—he didn't require domesticity, but dear Lord, she looked positively edible sitting there, her bare feet tucked up under her, sipping a milkshake. Her grin was infectious. "Can you grab some of the cases out of the car?"

She rolled her eyes and rose, unfolding herself inch by glorious inch. Ryan's mouth dried out at the sight of her, but he distracted himself hustling Jamie into the kitchen. *Do not fuck up a potentially great friendship. The last thing either of you need is to complicate things at work by getting in each other's pants.*

He threw some steaks on the grill and tossed a salad and Lynette made what she claimed was magically addictive, potentially orgasmic macaroni and cheese. The smell of it bubbling away in the oven was, indeed, mouth-watering.

When Ryan came in from the patio with the food, he stopped and watched her, sitting with Jamie at the tall kitchen table, coloring and having an in-depth conversation about a potential winner in an Optimus Prime versus Batman smackdown.

She grinned at the boy and tucked a lock of her curly auburn hair behind her ear. She looked straight up at him, catching him gawping at her. He arranged his face into serious lines. "Son, don't ever pit anything or anyone against the caped crusader. It's an unfair fight. Let's eat."

They opened beers for themselves, a precursor he claimed to the classroom session coming up later. Jamie inhaled the food, with the only potentially awkward moment coming when he asked "Daddy, what is or-gas-mic?"

Lynette giggled, but Ryan looked right at her when he spoke. "It's an amazing word, Jamie, full of mystery and potential danger. But all you need to know right now is that you have two more bites to go and then it's bath time."

The kid grinned through a face covered in melted cheese and Ryan's heart nearly burst open at the sight of him. He had never been given to overly emotional moments. But ever since he'd taken the small, mewling bundle from the doctor's arms in South Carolina, he had to watch it or he'd be turning into an Oprah-watching, tear-spewing, emo-man.

Lynette stood and took their empty plates. "Hit the showers, boys, I don't have all night."

Ryan looked up, surprised.

"What? I have a date later. After beer school, don't worry."

"Oh, uh, sure." Ryan plucked his son from the booster seat and carried the giggling kid to the bathroom, ignoring the small pulse of jealousy that threatened to make him say or even do something utterly stupid. He dropped Jamie into some bubbly water, washed his hair, sang his favorite bath time songs then scooped him out.

"Daddy! I want to play more!" the boy protested loudly. But Ryan was on a mission.

"Listen, son, I need to spend some time with Lynette, okay? We're doing some beer stuff. I'm gonna read to you then put on *Toy Story* in your room. Does that work?"

"I want Lynette to read to me. I want Lynette to live here all the time. Lynette!" the kid yelped, making Ryan wince.

Lynette spoke from behind him. "Remember, Jamie, there's no need to yell. You get more attention from people if you use a calm voice." Her voice did anything but make Ryan calm. He pulled Jamie's pj's on him and mumbled something about walking the dog. He pushed past her, handing over the boy who wanted her so badly.

"Daddy! Did we get a dog?" Jamie's voice echoed in Ryan's ears. He made his way to the kitchen, berating himself for having invited her over. He obviously had no self-control whatsoever. And he'd never in his life felt so conflicted.

Cole still haunted his every dream. Visions of the man's incredible form and handsome face covered by Ray-Bans, him yelling incoherently and beating on Ryan's face, his pale body on the gurney while the EMTs tried to revive him — it was all a long, lusty nightmare Ryan truly wished he could get past.

Given that they were about to become brothers-in-law, it seemed inevitable their paths would cross. But Ryan had gotten the message loud and clear. Cole wanted no part of him ever again, and if he did, Audrey seemed poised to pounce and keep him away. The whole steaming pile of shit was maddening, and he had only the guy staring back at him from the mirror to blame.

But Lynette, with her smartass sense of humor, quick mind, gorgeous hair and pert figure — she was here, now, with him. He sensed that he had reverted to flirt mode, acknowledged his desire to seduce and keep her here tonight, away from whatever date she had. He placed his hands on the counter, counting backward from twenty. It helped.

Then he spent some time lining up the beer bottles, organizing them into taste categories and noting he'd picked some pretty heavy-duty Belgians plus several Imperials and double alcohol brews. It didn't matter. They'd only be tasting, he justified, pouring some pretzels in a bowl then locating a bunch of clear glasses.

By the time she wandered back into the large kitchen, tucking her hair up into a messy bun on top of her head, he felt like he had a grip. He popped open a couple of classic India Pale Ales. "Okay. Sit. Taste and learn."

"You got it, Sensei," she said, pulling out a notebook and pen.

He held up the first glass, stared at it then launched into his 'hop forward' speech while she sipped and took notes. After an hour, they'd worked their way through the IPAs and were on to malt forward beers, like amber ales and their own Ypsi Brewing California Common.

The more he drank, the more he wanted her. At one point, he had to grip his knees under the table to keep from reaching across the small distance between them and running his fingers down her neck and his thumb across her full lips while she tasted and kept writing in that stupid notebook.

"So," he said, his voice cracking with tension. She looked up. A tendril of springy red hair dropped out of the holder and slipped across her face. He reached out and tucked it away. She narrowed her eyes and leaned back just enough to let him know his touch was not welcomed. "Right, sorry. So, let's move on to these." He pulled the three Belgian beers he'd chosen closer, trying to cover his embarrassment. "We don't do this style at Ypsi nor do I plan to." He paused, pondering his one-time dream of crafting nothing but sour, crazy, off-the-wall ales.

She put a hand on his, yanking him back to the present. He stared at her hand then up at her. Her eyes were full of concern. "You okay? How's Cole?"

"Oh, uh, he's okay. I think."

Lynette nodded, munched a pretzel, never taking her eyes from his. He shifted, his skin and nerves reacting to her uncomfortable proximity. "I have to wonder how it will work."

"How what will work?" He poured them each a healthy sample of La Fin du Monde, one of the finest examples of a Belgian triple known to man. The cloudy yellow liquid was rich, layered and amazing. He drank it way too fast considering it was nine percent alcohol. Nervousness had the best of him, and that was annoying in the extreme. "You mean Quinn and Audrey? Well, if they don't kill each other, I think they'll make a fine couple."

"But how can they be together? She owns the company that distributes our brews in Michigan. Isn't that some kind of, I don't know, insider trading kind of a thing? And with Cole and you...well, hell, you guys are worse than a Lifetime movie. Whoops!" She nearly knocked over her glass of the beer and blushed. Ryan stared at her.

She's drunk and maybe more nervous than I am.

He smiled and leaned forward on his elbow, missing the table by a good two inches. Which resulted in him smacking his chin on the hard wood surface. "Fuck!" he yelled, cupping his jaw while Lynette laughed so hard tears ran down her face.

Chapter Fifteen

Lynette's ears buzzed and her head spun. While she knew damn good and well she could thank the beers she'd been drinking for the last nearly two hours, she also had to admit that being here, with Ryan, having such a great time with him was turning her on, period. She had gone so long without a man's touch, she'd moved beyond missing it. Kind of like when a person reached that point in a diet where they didn't even really miss food anymore. Not a fun place to be, nor healthy, but there it was.

Ryan stomped over to the freezer, grabbed a bag of frozen vegetables and put them under his chin. She snorted and tried to stop laughing but it was too much. He was so incredible—talented, funny, great with his son and sexier than any one man had a right to be. She had no business here. She had to leave.

She stood when a burst of anxiety nearly split her in half. Tingling in places she had forgotten existed but for their daily functionalities, she was terrified and horny in equal measure.

"I gotta go," she said. Her hair kept falling out of its tie back so she gave up and yanked the flimsy band out so it tumbled around her shoulders. When she stood up and looked at Ryan, his mouth was literally hanging open. She grinned, slid her feet into her shoes and started for the kitchen door.

"Wait," he croaked. "Lynette. Don't go."

She turned, knowing full well the effect she was having but unsure what to do about it. "I am not going to sleep with you, Ryan Shannon." Her throat ached with a combination of fear at what was about to happen and worry that it might not.

In a flash, he was in her personal space, his full lips inches from hers. She swallowed hard when he slid one hand up her arm and tangled the fingers of the other hand in her hair. He smelled boozy but she knew she did, too. "I'm not sleepy," he whispered.

The room did a slightly nauseating one-eighty when his lips met hers. She stood, frozen, let him part her lips with his tongue, but she couldn't seem to move her arms. Her body wouldn't cooperate and do the thing she knew she wanted to do — grab him, wrap herself around him. He broke away, his breathing ragged, cradling her face in his large hands. "I don't know what it is about you. I'm prepared to screw up a great working relationship right now, just to feel your skin against mine. In fact, if that doesn't happen in the next few minutes, I may spontaneously combust." He stepped away, hands on his hips, looking down at the floor.

She backed up, stumbling when her backside met the countertop. Her thighs trembled and the pulse between her legs matched her heartbeat. She bit her lip. "But…" she said, knowing that with this man, complications would be the name of the game. "Cole." She spoke softly, understanding and figuring this for just one more close shot at something special she would miss.

He looked up at her, his gaze intense, then turned away. She walked around him and sat, raising the glass of La Fin du Monde. The end of the world indeed. "I applied for a marketing job with Ford," she said between sips. "I have an interview next week."

Ryan dropped into the chair across from her and picked up his glass. "Well, I remember you once yelling at me that the beer job was just a stopgap. That you wanted to be in...how did you put it? Oh, yeah, 'grown-up marketing' someday." He glowered at her.

She matched his frown. "Well, anyway, I have huge student loans, and it's not like you guys are paying me the big bucks."

"Good luck to you then, hot shot." He raised his glass and knocked back the liquid in one gulp.

He's as nervous as I am.

She put her glass down. "Tell me about Cole, Ryan. You probably need to get your head around how you feel about him. I'm a good listener. Talk to me."

He sighed and poured another small portion of the rich brew for them both. "There's nothing to talk about. Cole is...damaged, wounded, in more ways than one. And I have no business even considering anything about him."

She frowned, sipping and forcing herself not to get distracted by the way his jaw clenched when he talked or by her extreme need to kiss him there, to taste his skin just once.

"He's Audrey's brother. Did you know that?"

She nodded.

"Yeah, I guess everybody knows everything, don't they?"

She nodded again but stayed silent.

"Well, he's blind from an attack about ten days before he was slated to rotate back home from Iraq. His lover, Dan, was among the Marines killed that day." He put his elbows on the table, hitting the mark this time. "About three months ago or so, I went to his and Audrey's house for dinner. We, uh, ended up, you know."

"Fucking."

Yeah, I get it and the mental image I have of it is pretty hot.

Lynette put her hand to her lips, hoping she hadn't actually said those words, shocked to her very soul that she'd thought them.

He cleared his throat, his face reddening. She let him continue. "So, after that, nothing really happened. No communication, not for my lack of trying, mind you. I ended up there again, the night Audrey and Quinn got engaged and found out she was pregnant. Jesus H., what a daytime drama, huh? I can't believe I'm telling you this."

He got up to pace. Lynette leaned back in her seat, pulling one knee up to her chin, watched him move around the room with a casual grace, yet agitated beyond belief.

"Quinn and Audrey left. And we went at it again. It was..." He stopped dead in his tracks and put his hands on the counter. They shook but his voice was without a tremble. "He was...is...amazing on so many levels. He's strong and vulnerable at the same time. Incredibly smart and mature, but naïve and trusting. But he lost it that night. Woke up in a weird dream state and started hitting me. I mean, using the full force of his Marine-trained self into beating the shit out of me in his sleep." Ryan touched his nose, which was still slightly crooked.

"When he came to, or woke up or whatever, he had some kind of breakdown. I…I covered him up, tried to talk to him, but he wouldn't listen, so I left him alone. When I woke up on the couch, his dog was having a conniption fit. Cole had taken a bottle of painkillers and a fifth of bourbon into a full bathtub behind a locked door." He turned and glared at her. "You heard enough yet, or should I go on?"

Lynette got to her wobbly feet and put her arms around Ryan's waist, holding him tight. He was stiff at first, resisting her, but then he seemed to crumple and grabbed on to her for dear life. Their lips met, tongues tangled. She wanted him so badly she was willing to overlook a crucial piece of his emotional pie—that he was in love with someone else.

She leaned back as his lips found her neck, kissed there then stopped him when he started to reach under her shirt to her bra clasp. "No, hang on. I need to tell you something, too."

He cupped her ass, held her against the unmistakable press of his erection. "Seriously, Ryan," she gasped when he reached up and grabbed her hair again, bringing a sharp edge of pain to the many sensations coursing through her.

"If you tell me you're a virgin, I won't believe it," he mumbled around her skin, licking, kissing, teasing her so much she thought she might orgasm without him even touching her below the waist. Her hips angled when a slow meltdown began in her lower belly, one she'd had no frame of reference for and that scared and thrilled her all at once.

"No, but I am, I mean, sort of…" She threaded her fingers in his hair as he eased his hand up her shirt and flicked open her bra with one practiced twist of his fingers. "Like a born-again virgin. I mean, I haven't had sex in so long I… Oh, Jesus," she groaned when he leaned down to flick his tongue across her nipple. She didn't even remember the shirt coming off. "I'm rusty at best. The guy I, um, well, I don't even know if…shit…Ryan…and if it's possible for a hymen to grow back due to general disuse…ah, God…yes." She hissed, shivering almost uncontrollably by now. His lips, teeth and tongue were all over her breasts and nipples. He shoved his thigh between her legs, grabbing on to the counter to steady them.

"You're in great hands, sweetheart," Ryan whispered. He popped her jeans button, unzipped her and had them down around her ankles in seconds. He put his foot on them, helping her step out. His mouth found hers again, kissing her so hard the room darkened around her. "Allow me to introduce you to the amazing, dangerous mystery of orgasm." He grinned into her lips and Lynette let herself own a half second of sheer bliss—visions of their night together, with dinner, Jamie, the beers, all blending into a stupid little domestic fantasy. She shoved it out of her head.

"Okay, I'm game." She squealed when he picked her up and plunked her on the kitchen counter, shoving aside paper towel holders and other crap in his way. He kissed his way down her neck, to her breasts, sucking one nipple then the other so hard her back arched and she shook with the need for release. She put her fingers in his thick hair. "Just this once, you understand, because we both need it. No other reason."

"Nope, no other reason, but it's gonna be epic. And I for one cannot wait to see just how redheaded you really are." He grinned, holding her gaze while he stripped off her panties, leaving her totally naked on his kitchen counter.

"You won't be disappointed, I don't think — Oh. My God…" She exhaled when he found his target between her legs. He kept his lips on hers, kissing, caressing her mouth, gentle and earnest and amazing, while continuing his fingers' dance against her sex. He rubbed, then stroked, then slid some combination of fingers inside, stretching her and making her gasp.

"Now, let's see if I can't find…oh yeah, there it is." He went deep, pressing high up when his lips found her nipple again and his thumb kept contact with her clit. The combination made her cry out, slap a hand over her mouth in case it woke the kid. Her hips bucked toward him and her arms wrapped tight. He held on and stroked and sucked her until her every molecule seemed to shimmer, hover on the edge of something amazing.

She finally gave in to it, groaning and clutching him, letting herself drop right into the abyss. She sighed and he held her tight, letting her ride out the climax as long as she wanted.

"Christ almighty, Shannon. I think you should bottle that and sell it. Forget all this cascade hops, Bavarian malt crap." She shivered when he pulled his fingers out of her, put them to his lips and sucked. She watched, elated, embarrassed, sated but wanting more. He put the fingers against her mouth and she stared into his eyes and tasted herself on his skin. "I've never...um...well, never mind. My turn," she whispered, reaching down to unzip him and take his cock in her hand. It was hot, smooth, rock hard. The tip was soaking wet. "I want a taste." She rubbed her thumb across it, making him shudder. He leaned his hands on either side of her. She put her fingers in her mouth, absolutely loving the salty male-ness of him.

She'd not had much exposure to the male anatomy. And had very limited sexual experience. When the groping, equally ignorant boyfriend tried to go down on her, he'd been terrible at it, then insisted she suck his cock and she'd nearly thrown up gagging. It had done nothing but convince her the whole act was overrated. She'd gotten excellent grades, worked two jobs and dreamed about how her future doctor boyfriend would learn the right moves and use them on her while she turned into a domestic goddess and they lived happily ever after.

Until right then, that moment, when she heard the most amazing and unlikely words coming from her mouth. "I need you inside me so badly I'm...I don't want anything else. We can be friends. I know you love Cole, but please, dear God, fuck me right now."

He picked her up, kissing her the entire time. She wrapped herself around him. He walked them down the hall and into the room where she'd snooped around. He dropped her onto the bed, yanked his shirt off then fell down beside her, tugging her up and on top of him in one motion. "Okay, your redheaded wish is my command. But I want you to set the pace." He grinned and pulled her down so his lips were level with her nipples. He teased, licked, sucked and bit down on her flesh, digging his fingers into her ass until she tossed her head back and came yet again in a rush of lusty energy, her clit grinding against his shaft. "Uh-huh. That is exactly what I'm talking about."

He pushed her up so she was sitting. "Let's see how this feels. Shift your hips." When she was about to do it, to have his amazing girth inside her, he stopped. "Wait, shit." He reached across to his bedside table and grabbed a condom. She decided to ignore how many rubbers were in there in favor of continuing along their current, pleasant trajectory.

She moved back on his thighs, opened the foil with her teeth and rolled the latex down his cock. "What does this thing feel like anyway?" she asked, more than a little fascinated by how huge he was even sheathed in rubber.

"Like I'm wearing a girdle. It sucks. But it's necessary. I mean, I'm clean and I'm sure you are but I've done the parenthood thing enough already." She smiled and moved forward, going up on her knees and sighing when he pressed against her. "I'll go slow," he whispered. She was shocked to feel tears against the back of her eyes. "Lean down here. Let me kiss you some more."

She did, dropping forward so her hair formed a red curtain around their faces. He cupped her chin, then her neck, pulling her down and laying one of those amazing kisses that she could get addicted to on her. His slow, easy personality combined with the edgy energy made for the most amazing of all kissing techniques. Ryan was firm, in control, yet gentle, probing, and she rolled her hips so he slid into her one delectable inch at a time. He grabbed on to her, swept into her mouth with his tongue and thrust his hips just enough, making her cry out and break away when a surprising pain shot through her.

"Lynette," he whispered against her cheek. "Relax. Let me in. It's okay. I won't hurt you, I promise."

She angled her hips down, arching her back so he could reach her nipples and suck her flesh until her skin flushed and the orgasm crept up on her and smacked her upside the head, making her grip his entire length so hard he grunted.

"My turn on top."

She nodded, moving, already feeling him between her legs, as if he were meant to be there. But no, he wasn't. He loved Cole. But he was here now, fucking her so hard she thought her head would fly off.

She gripped the headboard, lifted her hips high, biting her lip and watching his face as his hips rolled and he moved in and out of her, setting his own rhythm.

"Faster," she said, putting her hand to his face and wrapping her legs around his waist. "I can tell you want to go faster."

"I don't want to hurt you…oh, Jesus."

She slid her hands around his neck and tugged him down so she could kiss him while he came. His body contracted, and his left leg look shook, just once, like a little spasm. She sighed when he pulled out and dropped to his side. She stayed still, legs bent, arms out at her sides. Her every nerve ending sang with happiness even while her brain clouded over.

She must have slept, because the next thing she remembered was hauling her ass out of bed and stumbling to the bathroom, the twin urges to pee and drink a gallon of water making her head pound. She leaned on the marble countertop and stared into her own bloodshot eyes.

Oh hell, Lynette, what have you done now?

"Lynette!" She jumped and grabbed a towel when she heard Jamie's delighted voice. "You had a sleepover? Can you make pancakes? I'm hungry!" He took off at a full run down the hall toward the kitchen. She peered into the bedroom. Ryan was sprawled on his belly, his muscled ass and legs bare. His snores made the windows rattle.

She sighed. Fuck buddies seemed logical, useful and even fun on the surface. But when she found a pair of his shorts and a T-shirt to put over her nudity—remembering a second too late that her clothes were still on the kitchen floor—a little pinging sound started up in her brain. She touched his broad shoulders and shivered, remembering the drunken intensity of the night before. He rolled, put his arm over his eyes. She avoided looking down at him for a half second then shivered at the sight of his impressive erection. "Shit," she muttered and got up, headed for the door.

"Hey," he said from behind her, his voice rough. "Thanks." She refused to glance back, anger at herself making her teeth ache.

"No, thank you. You were the master of the highest orgasmic order, I'll grant you that." She tried to be flippant. But something in her resisted this next scene, told her to get her clothes and get out. Jamie and his dad could come up with their own breakfast. She walked down the hall, noticed the little boy curled up on the couch with a book, found her clothes and threw them on, tossing Ryan's into the laundry room. By the time she walked out of there, Ryan stood dressed in nothing but boxer shorts that were nicely tented. He smiled at her, held out a hand and she slid into his arms. The kiss was gentle, but her lips were raw from the night before. She moved away.

"I need to go home," she said, wanting him to ask her to stay.

He turned to fiddle with the coffeemaker. She waited, willing him to say more. But when he didn't, she grabbed her purse, gave Jamie a quick hug and empty promises to see him soon over his protests and ran to her car before she talked herself out of escaping.

She dropped her keys, cursed then climbed behind the wheel. Sitting for a minute trying to catch her breath, she let the slow reality of what she'd done seep into her bones. Her skin tingled. She was pleasantly sore between her legs. And her heart ached for the potential of a ruined relationship in advance.

Her mom was sitting in her usual spot on the couch, staring at reruns, when Lynette came in. "Where have you been, young lady?"

Lynette tossed her keys and purse on the small dining room table. "None of your business, Mom." Her head and heart pounded from alcohol and stress. The last thing on the planet she needed was her mother nagging at her.

"I had no idea if you were alive or dead."

Lynette turned slowly, crossing her arms over her chest. She wanted nothing more than an hour-long shower, a gallon of water and a three-hour nap. But she had a ton of work to do, assigning values to her new marketing graph system and squaring it with the point-of-sale computer they'd just set up in the pub. "Mom, I am twenty-seven years old. I don't have to report in to you."

"Don't you take that tone with me, young lady. I'm your mother and I deserve respect."

"Yeah, Mom. Sure. Fine. So here is what happened. I picked up Jamie Shannon, the five-year-old son of

Ryan, who is part owner and head brewer where I work — remember? The brewery? Because I knew he was running late and we had a beer school session that night. So, we ate dinner together. I learned about beer. We drank too much. Then he fucked my brains out until we passed out. And now I need a shower. Okay?" She stomped away, leaving her mother open-mouthed with shock.

"Honey! You had a date! Congratulations!"

Lynette bit back a retort and slammed her bedroom door and leaned on it, useless, girlie tears slipping from her eyes before she willed them to stop. Resolute, she pulled her phone from her pocket and sent Ryan a text.

Thanks for the fun time, but we shouldn't do that again. Okay?

She hit send before she lost her nerve.

* * * *

Ryan stood at the kitchen window and watched Lynette make a mad dash for the car. He groaned and looked down at the sink. *Goddamn it, Shannon, you've scared her off. You and your fucking horny self went too far too fast and now what? No more friend. Jesus.*

He swallowed hard, watching her struggle and curse and drop her keys. His gaze took in the pleasant curve of her jeans-covered ass. Now that he'd had a taste of that, he wanted more. He watched until her car had screeched down the quiet morning street, figuring out how he'd get back between her legs again when his phone rang.

It was Cole.

He ignored it and went to find Jamie. "Let's go, pal. I'm taking us out to breakfast!"

"McDonald's!" Jamie squealed.

"No, IHOP!" Ryan matched his tone.

"Yay! I love you, Daddy!" The boy bounced up and down on the couch. Ryan caught him in midjump and ran down the hallway with him, wondering just how much he'd screwed everything up with one, amazing, unforgettable night.

Chapter Sixteen

By the time he'd wrestled Jamie into clothes, Cole had called again so Ryan gave up ignoring him and hit redial.

"Hey, uh, sorry to bother you. I need to talk to you about something." The other man's voice was low, and it set off a cacophony of memory in Ryan's slightly hungover brain.

Trying to shove the vision of Cole's incredible physical presence out of his head, he grabbed his keys and opened the kitchen door so Jamie could run out to the car and climb up in his car seat. The whole thing with Lynette had him tied up in knots, even after the monster orgasm, which usually set him on an even keel for a day or two. "Sure. You okay? I mean…"

"Yeah, but Audrey isn't."

"The baby?" Ryan slid behind the wheel and started the car.

"Daddy! No talk and drive! Dangerous!" His son's voice made the rapidly developing headache worse.

The silence on the other end of the phone drifted on a while. Ryan sat, keeping the car in park.

"Sorry, I'm interrupting," Cole finally said. "And the baby is fine, as far as I know."

"Don't be ridiculous. We're going out for breakfast, anyway." His gut turned over at the thought of seeing Cole right now but knowing he had to do it. "Give me a few minutes."

He made the trip from his house over to the southeast corner of Ann Arbor then sat in front of the house where he'd had his world rocked so hard, on so many levels. He tried to get up his nerve to get out, gripping the steering wheel. "Daddy. This isn't IHOP" Jamie piped up helpfully after waking from a car ride–induced catnap.

"Yeah, I know, buddy. It's a friend's house. Can we go in a minute? I just need to talk to him about Uncle Quinn."

"Okey-dokey," the boy agreed.

Ryan hauled him out of the safety seat and set him on the sidewalk. Cole was on the porch, Brutus by his side. The sun slanted across the front of the house, catching the gold in the man's hair. Ryan sucked in a breath at the sight of him, barefoot, dressed in dark jeans and a Marine Corps T-shirt that hugged his newly recovering muscles.

"Dog!" Jamie screeched after getting one look at the huge creature and racing up the sidewalk to the steps.

"Jamie! Stop!" Ryan ran after him, terror in his throat at the thought of Brutus' potential reaction to the boy-shaped torpedo headed right for him.

But the dog sat, calm and still, letting Jamie practically climb up on his head, while he talked a mile a minute. Ryan stood a few steps down and watched.

Cole seemed more nervous than the dog, flinching at one point when Jamie touched his hand.

"Hey, mister, can I walk your dog? I'm a good dog walker!"

Alarmed when the kid started climbing up Cole's arm like the man were a jungle gym, Ryan started to speak. But Cole merely bent his elbow so Jamie could swing from it still patting Brutus' head. "No, son. Brutus has to stay with Cole. That's his job."

"Why?"

Ryan recognized the stubborn edge that crept into his son's voice and braced for a scene. Cole smiled then, and Ryan relaxed. Cole kept his arm bent, making Jamie giggle when he raised it and brought the kid to eye level with his own sightless ones. "He's my eyes. I need him to help me see."

To Ryan's utter horror, Jamie reached out and snatched Cole's Ray-Bans off. "No, don't!" He grabbed the sunglasses and tried to hand them back to Cole. But the other man kept his smile fixed in place, and Ryan suddenly realized how flawless his face was even with the fading burn marks. It seemed odd that such a pair of striking, beautiful eyes would simply no longer do the work they were designed to do.

"It's okay," Cole said, palming the glasses. He hunkered down next to the dog, and Jamie dropped down beside him. He put a large hand on Brutus' head, and Jamie mimicked him. "Hi, I'm Cole."

Jamie grinned, making Ryan's heart leap into his throat like it usually did at the sight of his son's eager smile.

"You're Jamie, I'm guessing." The boy nodded, seemingly mesmerized by Cole's face. "So, Jamie, the deal is, I'm blind. I got hurt in the war. Brutus is with me all the time, no matter what. And he helps me do what I need to do so I can — "

"What's a war? Does he take baths with you?" Jamie interrupted, reaching out to put his small hand on the fading pink scars that streaked across Cole's forehead. "Do you need some Band-Aids? We have some ambiotic cream in the car, don't we, Daddy?"

Cole laughed. The sound was music to Ryan's ears. In all their intense time together, he didn't think he'd ever seen Cole smile or laugh without it being seductive or bitter. "No, I take showers. But he stands right outside the door, waiting until I get out. And I had a lot of Band-Aids once, but I don't anymore. Thanks for offering, though. And I'll let your dad explain about war another time."

"Wow. He's a really smart dog." Jamie looked at the animal with renewed interest, crouching down and staring right into the Brutus' eyes. "Can I walk him?" Brutus made a funny chuffing sound.

Ryan sighed and reached down to pull Jamie away. "Sorry. He's a little single-minded sometimes."

"Like his dad, I guess." Cole got slowly to his feet, making Ryan swallow hard when the recent memory of his last night with Lynette filled his brain. "Tell you what, let me sit over here in the chair, your dad and I will talk and you can walk him down to the corner and back."

"Really?" Jamie jumped around, until Ryan put a calming hand on his shoulder.

"You sure, Cole? He doesn't have to. I know it's important that he stay with you."

"Nah, it's okay. We have an understanding now. Hang on." Cole turned and Brutus led him to a wicker chair. He sat, pulled the animal to him and seemed to have a whispered conversation while the dog looked at him with intense concentration. "Okay, Jamie. He's all yours for a while." Jamie squealed with delight and grabbed Brutus' lead. The dog's tail whipped back and forth, but he looked back at Cole as if asking, "You sure about this, boss?"

Seeming to sense the animal's hesitation, Cole pointed, kept his voice firm. "Go. I'm fine."

Then without another sound, Brutus let the small boy walk him down the steps and the sidewalk. "Amazing," Ryan said, watching the animal that had fifty pounds on his son walk alongside him while Jamie chattered the poor animal's ear off. He looked back at Cole and bit back the urge to touch him. "So, what's this about Audrey?"

"It's all this wedding stress. She's drained and, when she was over here yesterday, crying for an hour over a fucking florist. My sister does not cry over flowers, Ryan. Are you getting any of this crap from Quinn?"

Ryan ran a hand down his face. "Uh. No. I mean, I assumed the woman did all the fretting and details. I don't think Quinn's mentioned anything about the wedding other than asking me for a couple of bartenders for the reception."

"I figured." Cole leaned forward, putting their knees within touching distance. "Can you tell him that he needs to step in and either take over some of it or tell her to stop stressing over stupid crap like what color ribbons to put on the bouquets? Seriously. I'm worried about her."

Without thinking about it, Ryan reached over and put his hand over Cole's clenched fingers. He heard the other man's sudden intake of breath and his own heartbeat sped up at the contact. The sudden impact of what was about to happen to their odd relationship configuration hit him between the eyes. "Sure," he said quietly. "I'll talk to him. You look good. Feeling better?"

"Some, yeah. Working out again. Jake, my work partner, helps me with that." He sat back, taking his hands out from under Ryan's.

"Oh. Well, that's good." Ryan had a sudden vision of a giant, well-formed 'partner', doing what he wanted to do to Cole right now. He shoved it away. "I mean. You know."

"He's not fucking me, though. I know you want to ask." Cole's voice had taken on the familiar hard edge Ryan remembered.

"None of my business," Ryan insisted, clutching his knees.

"I'm afraid I might beat up another guy in my sleep, I guess." Cole's voice got softer.

"Lucky for him," Ryan said, suddenly angry. "Okay, well, if that's all, we should get going." He stood, but Cole reached for his hand, stopping him.

"Sorry. I'm working on not being such a bitter asshole. Or so I'm told. I don't know why I said that about Jake. It just sort of popped out." He sighed, making Ryan's head pound harder.

Cole leaned forward, resting his head against Ryan's shoulder. The movement was not sexual in the slightest, totally unlike their previous encounters, but spoke of a connection Ryan wanted more than anything. Ryan allowed himself a split second of joy, touching Cole's soft blond hair. It was a sublime moment of comfortable dependence, because Ryan wanted nothing more than to comfort.

He looked out and saw Jamie still man-handling the huge dog up and down the sidewalk. He kept stroking Cole's hair while the other man leaned into him for a few quiet minutes more. A bright, crystal clear vision of the gorgeous redheaded woman who'd rocked his world the night before shot through his memory, making him shiver.

Cole moved away from him. Ryan grabbed both of his hands and turned so he was facing the other man. "Don't cut me out of your life, okay? I know we had some intense moments but—"

"Well, we are going to be uncles to the same kid in a few months." Cole smiled that sweet, somewhat innocent smile again, and Ryan's heart leaped into his throat at the sight. "So I guess we—"

Ryan leaned in and touched his lips to Cole's rough cheek, startling them both. "I want to be your friend, Cole, if you will let me. But that means not being flippant and bitter all the time. Let me in some. Let me know how you're really feeling."

Cole's smile turned more ironic than Ryan cared to see. "Friends, eh?" Ryan held on to him when he tried to move out of reach.

"Yes, Cole. Friends. Let's keep our relationship...on a different level. Because I think you need a friend more than you need a fuck buddy. You can trust me when I tell you I would gladly be that for you, too. But I don't really think it's good for you or for me." He let go of Cole's hands.

Cole lifted his glasses up, and Ryan was struck all over again by the angular structure of his face and the deep green of his eyes. "I want to see you," Cole said. "So badly."

"You can," Ryan said, taking Cole's hand and holding it to his own cheek. "Feel me, hear me — that's what you do."

Just when he was about to ruin everything by kissing the guy, his son shrieked, making both men jump to their feet. Ryan heard Jamie giggling like a maniac, lying on his back on the grass while Brutus nuzzled and licked him all over. He sighed and put an arm around Cole's shoulders — a friendly arm — something to comfort a man who needed it.

"He's a good kid. You're lucky," Cole said, keeping distance between them.

Ryan kept watching the boy, his miniature if you looked at photos of him at that age, only nearly two pant sizes too small. "Yeah, he's pretty amazing, considering his mother was a meth addict by the time he was born."

"Wow, that's tough. Is he…okay? I mean, other than being kind of small?"

"How do you know he's small?"

"Audrey told me."

"Oh, right. Well, against all odds it seems, he's normal, although he'll never play forward on the basketball team. I mean, I'm nearly six-five, but his doc tells me he'll only be about five-eight or so at most. But he's healthy as a horse. Speaking of, I gotta feed him soon or he'll turn into one of those gremlin things when they go bad, you know?"

Cole laughed and the sound made Ryan's entire body prickle with something he refused to identify. He put a soft kiss against Cole's cheek and stepped away, then turned at the last moment, allowed himself a long look at Cole's firm jaw and firm military torso that hid

Liz Crowe

a truly fractured soul. "Want to join us? IHOP? Death by pancakes?"

Cole tilted his head and held out a hand so Brutus could slide back under it. Just when Ryan was sure he'd say yes, he spoke. "No, thanks. You guys have a good time. And be sure and talk to Quinn, okay?" He turned and let the dog guide him back in without another word, leaving Ryan with his whirling, confounded thoughts.

He got Jamie strapped back into his seat and looked down on the console to see Lynette's text. He stared at it so long, trying to process what it meant, that he jumped when Jamie kicked the back of his seat. "Hungry, Daddy! Pancakes! Now!"

He shut his eyes and visions of Lynette's amazing, sexy perfection floated through his brain. Her lips, laugh, voice, all of it. That incredible way she rolled her hips and flexed around his cock. But even more, the moments when he'd watch her with his son.

Ryan ran a shaking hand down his face. Of all the split-second decisions he'd made — including fucking Jamie's mother enough to create the small human currently beating his heels against Ryan's seat — he was damn close to regretting the one he made last night, when he'd kissed Lynette for the first time. Not because it was a bad encounter, but because it was so right. And now, he had told Cole he wanted to 'be friends'.

God, I have shitty timing.

"Hang on, son. Hang on. I promise, we are going straight there. Just give me a minute." He tapped out a reply to her.

No. Thank you. I had a great time. And yes, you're right. I promise to keep it all business from now on.

Chapter Seventeen

"Holy shit, yes! Oh my God...Ryan." Lynette shuddered, digging her fingertips into his shoulders while he held her up against the wall of his pitch-black office. The smell of their lust combined with the usual brewery odors of malt and yeast made him groan and bury his nose in her neck. He licked the sweat he found there, loving her taste, feel and her words in his ear.

Three days after their first encounter, they'd hosted a beer dinner and kept their distance for the entire time, the chilly air between them almost visible. After she'd bid the last of the one hundred people goodbye, he'd escaped back to his office and tried to get his bearings. She'd looked like a million bucks in a sleek, simple green dress, that thick, amazing hair cascading around her shoulders. He'd nursed a near hard-on the entire two hours and it was pissing him off completely.

He'd sat, staring at emails without seeing them until he figured she'd left. When her hand touched his shoulder like he somehow knew it would, he jumped up, grabbed her arms and pinned her against the wall.

He shoved his tongue between her lips and yanked her skirt up without a word and she offered no protest. If anything, she ripped at his clothes with equal gusto.

"Come," he commanded, whispering in her ear. He shifted her legs up higher around his waist, giving him an even better angle. She groaned when he pressed deep, giving her clit contact with his pubic bone. His own orgasm hovered, but he wrestled it back.

She looked up and let her hands drop to his shoulders, her breathing calmed. He tilted her face down and stared at her. "Just this once more, okay?" he croaked.

"Yeah," she whispered, biting his earlobe and yanking his shirt up. She ran her hands up his chest, flicked her fingers across his nipples, making him shudder. "Handy, having condoms in your desk drawer. You do this a lot?"

He sighed and pulled her away from the wall, carrying her and kissing her neck until he found the desk. Keeping their bodies connected, he leaned over her. She dropped back to her elbows. "If I told you I brought them in today, just in case, what would you say?"

She bent one long leg up against his chest, drawing him in deeper. "Jesus, Red, you are like...some kind of addiction." He closed his eyes, kept thrusting his hips and let her lean up to bite down on his nipple. He groaned when she tightened her inner muscles around his cock. "Gonna come," he whispered. "Kiss me."

She raised her lips to his. He tasted her while his vision dimmed and the orgasm roared up his spine and exploded across his brain. They stayed there, clinging to each other, their heartbeats calming.

"I'd say you were a liar," she said, rearranging her dishevelled dress and hair.

"Huh?" He rubbed his face, still addled and buzzy from the orgasm.

"I'd say if you told me you brought those rubbers in today, just in case, I'd say you were lying."

"Oh, well, I'm not," he said, tugging the condom off and wrapping it in a tissue before flopping into a chair. He grabbed her hand so she couldn't walk away and drew her down to his lap, kissing her nose, cheeks and lips. "Come home with me tonight."

"No," she said, snuggling into his embrace. "No more sleepovers. If we're gonna fuck with some sort of regularity, that's fine. But I have zero interest in anything more."

He leaned back, narrowing his eyes at her. "Well, that's different," he said, putting his thumb over her lips.

"How's that." She bit his finger with a grin, then jumped up and found her shoes.

"A woman who just wants to fuck. Maybe I want you to sweep me off my feet, romance me, buy me flowers?" He smiled, but his gut was churning.

"Sorry, doll." She patted his cheek. "I never promised romance." She leaned down, giving him a lovely view of her lush breasts. "You don't want that from me, remember? You have someone else in mind for sweeping-off-your-feet duty. Or had you forgotten about him?"

Something in her voice made him stand and grab her arms. "For your information, Cole and I have come to an understanding. We are friends and nothing more. Not even with any benefits." He let go, his face hot with fury and something resembling embarrassment.

"Oh," she said, lightly but with an undertone of something he wanted to latch on to.

"What are you doing December twentieth? Around four?" He leaned back on the desk where he'd just fucked the lovely woman now standing in front of him. "Got a nice dress?"

"I don't know. And why?" She matched his pose.

"My brother's getting married, and I would like for you to accompany me. As my – "

She breached the small distance between them and put her fingers over his lips. "Don't say it." She replaced her fingers with her lips briefly. "I'll come with you to the wedding. But it's not a date. Got it? Just friends. A favor because you can't find anyone else." Her eyes were hard.

"Fine, whatever." He shrugged away from her. "Good luck tomorrow."

She gave him an odd look. "Um, thanks. What for?"

"Your interview? Real marketing job with deep-pocketed auto company?" His chest hurt when he looked at her but he forced his voice to stay calm and noncommittal.

"Oh yeah, that. Thanks." She turned, opened his office door and walked out without another word.

Ryan sat for nearly thirty minutes, trying like hell to square his thoughts about the woman – and the man – in his life. And honestly wondered how in the world he could ever be happy with either one of them given his own inability to decide, as his brother so eloquently put it, which goddamned team he batted for.

Chapter Eighteen

Ryan smiled down at Jamie, dressed in his suit, standing beside him and Quinn while they waited for Audrey to make her appearance at the back of the chapel. The little boy tugged on his trouser leg, whispering loud enough for the first three rows to hear. "Daddy. What are we waiting for? I'm hungry. You said there was cake. Can we have cake now? Is Santa coming? You said he might! Remember?"

The crowd tittered. Ryan patted his son's head and leaned into Quinn's ear. "Uh, is everything okay?" Quinn frowned at him, shot his cuffs and shrugged at the justice of the peace, who smiled. Stress oozed from his twin brother's pores. "I'm gonna go check on things."

"Yeah, thanks," Quinn said, keeping his eyes trained to the back of the room. The rehearsal had gone off without a hitch, the dinner was fun and relaxed. Nothing indicated that Audrey was having second thoughts. But she did look more stressed around the edges than Ryan cared for, although he told Cole she looked 'just fine'.

Ryan had been unable to tear his eyes from Cole's date for that night. Jake was a solid wall of handsome muscle, charming to a fault to everyone and attentive to Cole in a way that made it crystal clear to Ryan their relationship had passed beyond the business partners stage. He'd shot Ryan a couple of funny looks, and Ryan mentally cursed for not insisting that Lynette come with him to that stupid event, too. She'd begged off, telling him going to a wedding was bad enough — she hated the damn things and was not about to drag out the agony by going to a rehearsal for it.

He let his eyes pass over the man in question, sitting near the back, dressed in an impeccable dark blue suit, his long brown hair held back with a small strip of leather. The guy met his eyes and nodded curtly before training his eyes to the front that was still devoid of a bride. Ryan spared a second of admiration for the elegant simplicity of the Michigan League room Audrey and Quinn had chosen. It was lit by about a million candles, with simple red roses tucked into holiday-style greenery arrangements along the strip of white that led up to where his brother stood nervously running a hand through his hair.

Ryan couldn't fathom what sort of planning and detail had gone into such a simple-looking setup but he knew one thing — if Quinn's fiancée did not appear soon at the back of the room, the guy was going to lose it. His son slipped his small hand into his uncle's, making Quinn flinch then look down at his nephew, a smile playing around his lips. Quinn's sons were there, too, providing a bit of moral support.

Ryan's heart pounded when he snuck into the back room. He saw Audrey in Cole's arms, her shoulders shaking. Cole lifted his face when Ryan shut the door behind him then motioned him closer.

"Shh, Audrey, listen, it's going to be fine. Please. You love him. There's no reason to be so upset. Since when do you break down like this? I mean, come on." Ryan could tell that Cole was having a tough time keeping a rein on his own stress. The two of them were not helping each other at all.

Ryan made his way toward them, while Cole rubbed his sister's back. Her sniffles sent a shaft of anxiety to Ryan's brain. "What's up in here?" he asked, keeping his voice light. "There are approximately a hundred and fifty people out there waiting to see you but one in particular who's sweating through his tailor-made tuxedo. Because I'm the best man in the general vicinity, I was sent to determine the state of the bride's condition."

Audrey shrugged out of Cole's embrace and turned toward the window where snow was covering the campus of the University of Michigan with a soft white blanket. Her shoulders and hands shook. Ryan stood next to Cole. "What's up?" he whispered.

"I have no idea," Cole said, looking helpless and pissed off in equal measure. The dog was whining and bumping against Cole's leg, as if trying to get him to fix whatever was wrong with Audrey.

"Will you guys stop staring at me like I'm a circus side show?" Audrey demanded. Ryan took a breath and watched her pace. She was breathtakingly gorgeous in her classic cream-colored figure-hugging dress that left no doubt the woman was pregnant. But it worked for her. She looked lush, full, sexy, if about to shatter into a million pieces. "I mean, shit, you know what I mean."

Cole sighed and sank into a chair. "Honey, what is it? Everything is fine. The reception is set. I know you must look great. I—"

She whirled around, her fancy updo starting to wilt, her eyes full of tears. "I don't know. Don't you get it? I'm a fucking basket case. I can't even enjoy this day—my day—I cry at the drop of a hat and the thought of walking out there and doing this is making me want to claw my skin off."

"Uh, yeah." Ryan glanced over at Cole, who mouthed "Get Quinn," at him. He nodded and shot Lynette a text to get Quinn back here and bring Jamie, too. Within a few minutes of Audrey pacing in silence while Ryan and Cole stood shoulder to shoulder watching her, the door flew open.

"Audrey, what in the hell in going on?" He stepped back when she flew at him.

"Damn you, Shannon. I don't want to be pregnant. I mean, I'm glad and I...shit." She pounded on his chest a minute, then gripped his lapels and hid her face in his chest.

Quinn looked over her shaking shoulder at Ryan, who shrugged and tucked his hands in his pockets. Lynette lurked near the door, Jamie hanging on to her hand, his eyes wide at the outburst. He smiled, noting how amazing the lovely redhead looked in a simple shimmery gray dress.

"Shh, baby, listen. It's this wedding. I knew we shouldn't try to do all this crap. I hate it, and it's made you insane," Quinn soothed, his eyes wide and confused.

She yanked herself away from him. "I thought you wanted it. Why didn't you tell me you hated it?" She stood, chest heaving, glaring at him, her face flushed red. "How can we possibly be married if we can't even communicate about this?" She sank into a seat, face in her hands.

Quinn shoved his hands in his pockets and looked around, worry evident in every line of his face. She glanced up, her hair escaping its many clips. "We can't even communicate about this?" Her last, repeated words were loud, and Jamie clapped his hands over his ears.

Quinn set his jaw, took Audrey's arm and drew her up to her feet. His brother pulled the hysterical woman into his arms. "You're right, my love." He kissed her hair, tilted her face up and brushed her tears away with his thumbs. "I'm so sorry." He put his forehead to hers.

Cole touched his arm, and they started to make their way out to give Quinn and Audrey some privacy. Ryan moved toward the door and heard words that made his heart clench with happiness for his brother and no small amount of jealousy that he couldn't find the same kind of soul mate.

"Listen to me," Quinn said when he and Cole passed them, paying no more attention to all the family in the room than he would a fly in the window. "Audrey Gail Traynor—I love you. I want to be with you forever. With our family." Quinn touched the swell of Audrey's belly. "And I vow right here and now to never keep anything from you again. These last few weeks have been a nightmare—and now I know why. Because neither of us were being honest. I would have eloped with you—anywhere you wanted. But I thought you wanted all this." He waved his hand around. "All I want is for you to be happy."

She nodded and put her hand to Quinn's cheek. Cole gripped Ryan's arm. The dog whined. "I love you, too. And I'm sorry to make such a stupid scene at my own wedding."

Quinn chuckled, kissed her forehead and held her close. "Are we back on here, sweetheart? Or do I tell all these people to hit the road?" Ryan asked.

She turned to him and Cole, wiped her eyes and smiled.

"You joining this family, or have you come to your senses and decided to bolt before it's too late?" Ryan asked.

She grabbed her brother, tugging him close. "No, I think I'm all in, Ryan. Sorry." She closed her eyes a split second.

"Audrey, are you sure you're okay?"

"No, I'm not sure," she said, her voice a high and thin. "I need to sit a minute."

Quinn eased her into a chair. She blew out a breath. "Um, water?"

Lynette handed her a bottle. Jamie jumped on the dog. Cole frowned. "What the fuck is going on? I can tell something's wrong. I hear it…Audrey, the baby…"

She leaned back, her eyes closed, holding the bottle to her flushed face. Cole crouched beside her and she grabbed his hand. "I'm good. Baby is fine. I just haven't eaten today—too nervous. Feeling a little lightheaded."

Quinn put a hand on her shoulder. "Anybody got a granola bar?"

"There are some over there." She motioned toward a leather bag on the floor. Lynette grabbed one and handed it to her. "Thanks," she said. Cole frowned and rose, backing away from Lynette so fast he stumbled over a chair. Brutus growled, grabbed his hand in his huge jaws, shaking off Jamie, who promptly burst into tears.

"Okay, then." Ryan grabbed his son and took Lynette's hand. "I'm gonna go remind people we are here for a wedding. That work for you, drama queen?"

Audrey gave him a thumbs-up.

"Lovely." She turned the thumbs-up into a middle finger. "Yeah, that's the sister-in-law I want." He tugged Lynette out with him, ignoring Cole completely. Unfair perhaps, but if he didn't get the hell away from the man, there would be yet another scene, and he figured that could wait for another day.

Cole gripped the dog's lead and felt Audrey put her hand through his arm. "I love you," he said, leaning over to kiss her cheek. "I'm sorry."

"What for? I'm the one causing the problems today." She shivered. But he could hear the comforting and now familiar *whoosh-whoosh* of her baby's heartbeat. Now that he was used to it, all the extra-sensory shit like hearing things no one else could was not so bad. He patted her hand when the music changed.

"Um, is this right?" He shifted from foot to foot, more nervous than he'd been in a long time. The string quartet and piano were playing something, but not quite the song he expected. "Audrey, seriously." He muttered, then laughed. "Al Green? Jesus."

She leaned into him. The strains of *Let's Stay Together* became clear. "Let's go. Walk me down the aisle, damn it. I need to get to my man."

He kissed her. "I wish I could see you right now. I know you are beautiful, but…"

"Shh, Cole." She put a cool palm against his face.

"No, I'm sorry for being this huge pain in your ass. Something you have to worry about all the time."

"I worried about you anyway, you dummy." She bumped him. "You're no more a pain in the ass than you ever were. And I'm glad you're here with me today."

"Me too," he said and felt a rush of fresh air against his face. Brutus pulled him forward and he heard the sighs and "ahhs" of the crowd as he walked his sister down the aisle. At one point he hesitated, getting a whiff of it again—the sweet smell of honey. The same odd scent he'd caught when Ryan's date, Lynette, passed near him to hand Audrey a granola bar. It had nearly bowled him over then, and it was now, too.

"You okay?" Audrey whispered, letting him stop a second.

"No, but what else is new?" He gulped and kept walking, cursing fate that had taken his sight, blinding him not only to his sister's wedding day but also to the woman Ryan had brought who smelled so tantalizing.

Brutus stopped, indicating they had reached the end of the walk. He felt Quinn's hand on his arm, then gripping his. "Thank you, Cole. I promise I will take good care of your sister."

He nodded, unable to form words at that moment, kissed Audrey's cheek and let the dog lead him to his seat. The ceremony was simple and heartfelt and before he knew it, he was standing, clapping and getting jostled out to the aisle again.

"Hey." Ryan's voice hit his ear, making him want to turn and pull the man to him, to kiss him so hard they'd both collapse from the effort. "Nice job," Ryan said. A strange sort of anger and sadness gripped him, choking off words. He felt Brutus dancing around beside him, sensing his anxiety. "C'mon." Ryan's hand was on his elbow, propelling him forward and out of the crowd.

Then he sensed Jake was on his other side. "Cole, the car's this way." He let the other man turn him from Ryan without a word, but the honey-like fragrance he'd smelled when Lynette had been so near him lingered around Ryan like a fog. He frowned, and Jake led him away from the man he wanted, even more than he wanted to have his sight back.

Chapter Nineteen

Lynette stared around at the happy group at the reception. Beer rock stars abounded, befitting the nuptial celebration of two of their own. She'd met more famous owners and brewers than she knew what to do with, up to and including Austin and Evelyn Fitzgerald. Fitzgerald Brewing in Grand Rapids was one of the breweries she'd studied before her interview and their story had stuck with her. Turns out, Quinn and Austin had gone to college together — even been fraternity brothers — and they'd let Ryan come out and brew with them during the early days when he was getting his feet under him.

The two men were talking now, Austin holding a gorgeous little toddler girl who was doing her level best to break free of her father's arms and hit the floor running. She smiled, ever charmed by little kids, especially the rambunctious ones, and looked around the room. The tables were gorgeous, yet simple, with cream-colored tablecloths, red roses in the center and rich white china and crystal at every place. But in a nose-thumb to convention, the food was a mash up of gourmet and beer snacks. Everything from the huge pretzels with beer cheese made from the Ypsi Brewing India Pale Ale to burgers that were actually sliders of lamb with rich blue cheese were on hand. It was classy to a fault, but over the top, including the five medium-sized ice sculptures of beer steins that graced the buffet.

She sat back, sipping her beer and watching the party unfold. She should so not have come here, especially not with a Shannon brother. She closed her eyes a split second, relishing the way she felt — sated, enervated and tingly with anticipation all at once. She and Ryan had been fucking around nearly daily, unable to keep hands off each other, and her body was beginning to adapt and want more, which Ryan was eager to accommodate probably more than was necessary.

The words 'just this once more' had become a sort of code for 'come over here and fuck me'. Which they had done — in his office, between fermenters, at his house and once, memorably, in her own tiny office while she was trying to conduct a conference call with her on-the-road sales staff.

She caught Jamie when he ran past her, already high on an unlimited supply of cola and cake. "Hey, mister, come sit with me." She loved this kid. There was no doubt about that. His endless supply of positive energy was contagious. Ryan stressed over his parenting skills, but she had reassured him more than once that such a happy, comfortable-in-his-own skin little boy did not occur by accident.

"Lemme go. I want to see the dog." He squirmed out of her grasp.

"No, Jamie, don't bother him." She startled when a warm, wet, distinctly canine nose shoved her arm. "Hey," she said, smiling and scratching the boxer between the ears.

She looked up, taking in the full Marine dress uniform of the man attached to the animal. The crisp, formal clothes seemed to hang on him. While it was obvious that at one time he had been bigger, his classical, masculine V-shape was breathtaking. His shoulders were broad but not bulky, his jaw firm, if clenched with stress that marred it. His golden-yellow hair was thick and touched the collar of the uniform jacket. She bit her lip and dispelled the sudden erotic loop of imagery—Ryan and this man, naked, together. "Hi," she said, holding out a hand. "I'm Lynette."

His face turned to hers, and his smile was so incredibly sexy and innocent at the same time her heart hammered. He held on to her a few seconds longer than was polite. She tugged but he wouldn't let her go. "I hear your heartbeat," he said quietly.

"Oh, wow, that's…um, cool." She had no idea what to do with her arms, hands or heartbeat. Jamie was all over the dog, who was panting and wagging his tail like mad. The party flowed around them, getting louder by the minute. Suddenly, Lynette wanted to be alone or more precisely she wanted to be alone with the man in front of her. He wore his emotional pain like a medal on his uniform, and something about him compelled her to want to help—or possibly it was because Ryan still loved him.

Wow. This could get messy.

She squared her shoulders and stuck with what usually worked best—brutal directness. "You must be Cole."

His grin faded slightly. "Yeah, I guess I am the only blind ex-Marine with a dog date here, huh?"

She leaned into him, determined to keep to the direct path she'd set for herself. "It's okay. I know about you and Ryan."

"Really. Well, tell me then, Lynette." He put his lips near her ear. The overwhelming compulsion to put her hands on him made her knees wobbly.

She gripped the chair back to keep herself from collapsing. The party noises ramped up around them, but she barely heard them. She was too mesmerized by Cole's face, voice and the warm hand in the small of her back.

"Tell me what you think you know about me. And Ryan." His lips tickled, making her break out in goose bumps. She turned her head and caught Ryan staring at the two of them from across the room.

"I know he loves you," she said, then took Jamie's hand and was about to lead him away before she said or did anything she couldn't take back with the sad-faced, ridiculously handsome blind man in the Marine uniform.

But Cole gripped her arm, lighting a small fire on her skin. The dog snuffled around her leg, whining as if sensing his master's distress. "The hell you say," he said, his jaw tight. "Besides, he has the smell of you all over him right now. I don't know if it's your perfume or shampoo or what, but you smell like rich, sweet honey. And I can tell he's been dipping into it. Not that I blame him."

"I don't wear perfume and I use unscented shampoo." She tried to stop trembling at his innocuous yet sexy words. She ran a fingertip down his face, unable to resist.

"I'm not interested in your type." But his low voice and the warm proximity of his body — something he'd initiated — said otherwise.

"You say that now," she whispered, shocked at herself. How she'd gone from practically celibate to caught between two smoking-hot men more interested in each other escaped her understanding. But she was full-on horny now. And knew who could help her out. Something about Cole's vulnerable strength made her want to weep, to hold him to her breast and to climb all over him and fuck him silly at the same time.

Jesus, woman you are out of control.

Without exchanging any more words, she let Jamie pull her away. "Where's your dad?" she asked, when he stopped in front of the giant buffet of beer-friendly finger food.

She spotted Quinn's sons hovering in the corner and took Jamie over to them. They led their cousin straight over to the chocolate fountain. Lynette resisted the urge to stop them, realizing the kid might as well OD on sugar. It was a party after all. She looked around. Ryan was nowhere in sight. And she had never needed him more.

Ryan frowned. A shiver slithered down his spine. He sipped, chatted with the owners of a couple of large Midwest breweries and tried to keep a bead on his kid, his date and Cole. This whole scene was beyond imagining. He couldn't wait until it was over. He supposed he'd be taking Lynette home, to his house. Quinn and Audrey were leaving for their honeymoon in a couple of days — Munich, then Belgium, then France. He shook his head at their beer geekiness. The boys were headed back to the west coast to their mother's, and Ryan felt at loose ends, as if this were the precursor to everything changing in a way he wasn't sure he wanted.

The band was setting up, ready to launch the mild cocktail party to the next stage. That weird tingly sensation hit him again. He looked around, ignoring the people in front of him, seeking the red hair of one and the blond of another. He ended the conversation, wandered back to the bar and had them pour him another mild lager. He was trying to keep it cool, to be the sober one.

A hand on his waist that then dropped down to his ass made his cock press against the back of his zipper so fast he gasped and stepped away from her. "Cut it out," he muttered into his beer.

"Ryan," Lynette whispered, setting his every nerve ending on edge. "I need you."

He pulled her close. "No, you don't." But he knew what she meant. He grabbed her hand and tugged her away from the crowd, finding the steps down to the basement underneath the club where Quinn and Audrey were holding their reception. His body was crying out, fairly screaming for contact with her—especially since catching her and Cole with their heads close together a few seconds ago.

They were both so beautiful, so incredible, yet so terrifying. He felt like a marble bouncing between them, yet pulled equally in both directions.

Now, he no longer heard the band or the conversations or pretty much anything but her voice in his ear. This sex-soaked journey they'd embarked on was alarming to him on some level. Wild, awesome, hot as hell, but yet, lacking something he wanted from her.

"Jesus, Red, what's gotten into you?" He shoved her skirt up, needing to touch her, to taste her. She smiled and handed him a condom from her purse. Experiencing a half second of frustration at the interruption, Ryan wondered just how she would feel without the thin latex between them. But he'd declared this a hard-and-fast rule. Her adaption to it was admirable.

"You have, Ryan. God, help me." She sighed. He ran his thumb across her lips and stroked into her warm, welcoming grip, shoving her hard up against the wall. "That's it, baby. That is exactly what I want." She gripped his hair, yanked his face to hers and kissed him, pulling him over the orgasmic edge fast.

"Shit," he grunted, gripping her ass and pumping into her. "You are...ah, God."

She smiled, threaded her fingers in his hair. "Lucky me. I remembered your condoms."

"Yeah," he said, burying his face between her breasts. A sweet scent filled his nose, something he'd noticed before around her but that seemed even more intense right now in this illicit hidden space under his brother's newly married feet. "Lynette," he whispered.

"Huh," she said, lifting herself up and off him, zipping him back up and adjusting her dress. "That's me."

He tossed the used condom in a nearby garbage can, his face flushed and his heart pounding. He stopped her from fidgeting around with her hair, held her face and stared into her eyes. "You are going to kill me. Or something."

She bit his lower lip and slipped out from under his touch, like she always did. "Something, I'd hope. So you're around for more." She took a few steps away.

He leaned in the doorway to the storage room, trying to recover and get a grip on his roiling emotions. "Oh, uh, hi, Cole."

Ryan tucked his shirt back in, reassembling himself fast, then looked up and saw him, the man he believed he loved, standing with a look of disbelief on his face.

"You know that honey smell I told you about upstairs? It's even stronger now," Cole said, leaning into Lynette but keeping his face turned to Ryan. Ryan started to say something but the sight of Cole's strong, firm, uniform-clad form close enough to Lynette to reach out and hold her close had rendered him utterly speechless. Cole went on. "Sorry to interrupt. But your son is throwing a fit worthy of a pop star diva up there. I was sent to find you. I guess I can thank my dog that I got to catch the last bit of your quickie."

He put his lips near Lynette's neck, and she trembled. Cole licked his lips, then turned and walked slowly back up the steps. Ryan stood, mouth gaping open. Lynette scratched her nose and fiddled with her hair. "Wow," she said, not looking at him.

"Yeah," he said, walking past her. But she put a hand on his arm.

"You need to clear the air with him. For both of your sakes." Her eyes were sad and Ryan felt all kinds of shitty.

"Lynette, I..." He tried to summon the guts to say what he was feeling at that moment—to be honest, like they'd declared they would be. They had no emotional connection, at her insistence. But what was washing through him at that moment was nothing but a raw, aching need to watch Cole kiss Lynette. But the words required to describe that sounded selfish, not to mention depraved.

She touched his cheek then climbed the stairs, leaving him alone with his ragged, tumbled thoughts.

.

Chapter Twenty

The band was getting ready, and Cole realized he would have to do the first dance with Audrey, in lieu of their long-dead father. He sighed, gripping the dog's lead tight and accepted the beer that Jake put in his hand.

He had a brief flash of memory, so incredibly bright and painful he had to put the drink down before he dropped it. Dan's face, dark, handsome and open appeared as clearly as if the man were right next to him. He pictured him, the night they'd met, when the guy was transferred into Cole's counter-intelligence unit. They'd been in crisis mode, and Dan had sorted out a huge network snafu that had threatened to take their entire surveillance program down for several hours.

Cole had sworn off relationships at that point, having been burned by the last guy he'd cared about and had been fighting a very strong compulsion to jump between the legs of a fellow IT grunt — a distinctly female one — that had made him doubt his sanity.

But Dan's amazing mix of tall-dark-handsome, computer savvy, dry sense of humor hotness had him floored within hours. They'd danced around each other a while, always wary of being caught. But when Cole had gone on a well-earned shore leave in Southern France, he'd been thrilled but not really surprised when Dan had appeared at his hotel room, six-pack of beer in hand. They had not left the room for nearly two days. And Cole had been able to not only disperse the odd moment he thought he could find sexual satisfaction with a woman but also to fall deeply in love with the younger man.

"Dan," he whispered, hating the way his soul darkened when he thought about what had happened. The reception music faded. He could no longer feel the dog's head under his palm. It was like a black hole had opened up and consumed him, right in the middle of Audrey's big day.

He cursed and rubbed his temple. The headache that usually trotted in on the heels of this kind of slide into depression crouched in the corner of his psyche, preparing to pounce and turn him into a quivering mass of no-fun-at-all.

"Do you want to leave?" Jake's voice was at once a comfort and an annoyance.

"I can't leave," he said, flinching away from the hand on his shoulder. "Sorry," he muttered, picking up the beer and draining it, wishing he could just be alone — or better yet, with Ryan. Or possibly even with Lynette — she of the mysterious honey smell and sultry voice, commanding Ryan to come inside her just a few seconds before. He lifted his face when he sensed Audrey standing next to him.

"Hey, handsome. Let's dance." She pulled him to his feet. He went, reluctantly, after telling Brutus to stay. "Thanks." Audrey leaned on his shoulder while music swirled and he could hear people muttering about 'that poor man' and other bullshit. He swallowed the fury that threatened. "You okay?" his sister asked.

He nodded, determined not to ruin this for her with his usual melodrama. They moved around the dance floor and strains of *Stand by Me* floated through his brain.

"I love you, Audrey," he said, his throat closing. "I'm so glad you found happiness."

He held her close, comforted by the under-the-radar pinging of the baby's heartbeat. He frowned when the familiar *whoosh-whoosh* seemed to take a little jump, get faster. Before he could focus on it, he felt a hand on his shoulder. He stepped back, handing Audrey over to her new husband.

"Hang on," Audrey said, taking his hand to lead him to his seat. But he shook her off.

"No, go on, dance. I'm fine." He stood a moment, alone, his own heartbeat pounding so loudly it drowned everything else out. He realized he was frozen in the grip of a sudden panic attack. Why had he brushed her off? He'd actually believed he could find his own way off the dance floor to a seat?

No, he couldn't even manage something that simple on his own. He put a trembling hand down to his side, but his dog wasn't there. He lifted his arm, but Jake didn't appear. Then he felt her, Lynette, the girl who smelled like honey. She slipped into his embrace as if she'd been there her whole life. He sighed, put one hand on her hip and threaded fingers of his other with hers.

Cole had lost his virginity to a girl in high school. It had not been unpleasant, but quick like most male deflowerings were. She'd been a couple of years older than him, a friend on the track team. They stayed friends, and she'd told him he should open his eyes and own up to the fact that he was probably gay. He'd had a few more female sex partners during the years he spent in college. But by his junior year, he'd been unable to sleep, compelled by something he could not name, when he'd met and fallen for a much older man.

He shivered, recalling long-buried memories of his first true male sexual experience and his subsequent obsession with the handsome, erudite and very married calculus professor. When Dr. Grant Patterson had called their torrid affair finished because he felt Cole was getting 'too attached' Cole had experienced the first of what he'd learn were near suicidal depressions.

He had loved Grant with everything he had but later came to terms with what it had been—his true deflowering, an honest sexual awakening that had left him breathless and horny every waking moment, but nothing more. Afterward he'd been firmly convinced that 'gay' was the word for him. Not 'bi' or 'curious' or in any way anything other than a man who loved men.

But right now, this minute, with the lovely Lynette in his arms, every inch of his skin was on fire. He could hardly breathe for the sweet essence that emanated from her pores. He shifted so she couldn't feel just how turned on he was, frowning when she molded herself back against him. "Cut it out," he whispered in her ear, letting his lips touch her flesh just enough to allow a taste to coat his tongue. He moved his hand around to the small of her back and held her close. If she wanted to feel his erection, then that was her choice.

The small sound she made deep in her throat — a sort of sigh crossed with a deeper, sexier sound — nearly made him come unglued. She turned her face so he could feel her breath on his skin while they swayed into the next song, to music Cole no longer heard. "Cut what out?" The hand she had on his shoulder moved closer to his neck. "You are really good-looking," she whispered.

"No, I'm apparently a unicorn, or at the very least an optical illusion. The man who claims he loves only men but gets turned on by you. Go figure."

"All that hotness and a sense of humor, too. Nice." Her fingertip grazed his neck.

"This is the strangest thing that's ever happened to me." He heard his voice break. But he kept his nose near her hair — anything to keep smelling her. He moved his hand a little lower, relishing her soft curves, the light-as-air feeling in his arms. So different from what he believed he wanted and so absolutely right, at this moment.

"Oh?" She cupped his neck and slipped her fingers in his hair.

"Yeah, using a slow dance to grope is not part of my repertoire, under normal circumstances."

"You're hardly groping, Cole. Believe me."

He flinched when her lips touched his jaw. But the contact was soft, not urgent, amazing and pleasant and just about all he could take. He needed to push her away, but in some kind of contrarian move, he lowered his face and their lips met. He kept it soft, clamping down on the urge to press further. Then he broke the connection, leaning into her ear once more. "You smell so good. And you feel…" He held her close. "Perfect. I wish…" He blew out a breath.

She put her head on his shoulder when the song ended, then stepped away from him, still holding on to his hand. "What do you wish?" she asked while they made their way off the dance floor. He put his arm around her shoulders. The contrast between her and all the men he'd had was startling. She felt slight, like a bird, crushable. But a sudden thought flashed over his brain — a vision, if that were possible — of him, and her, of them. The mental picture of her slim bare legs on either side of his hips, her lips on his, his flesh indistinguishable from hers made his cock throb and his head pound in time with it.

He sat quickly, put her hand to his lips and kissed it then released her. But she must have knelt down on the side opposite the dog that had quickly bumped his nose against Cole's thigh. Her hand was on his other leg, her lips way too close to his ear yet again. "Tell me what you wish, Cole."

He reached up and touched her face, loving the soft flesh under his palm. "I wish I could see you."

"You are seeing me," she said, covering his hand with hers and bringing it to her lips. He allowed his fingertips to graze her cheekbones, her nose, the long line of her neck.

Then with a quick kiss to his cheek, she was gone, trailing that intoxicating honey aroma with her. Cole shivered, trying to square a long-buried need and attempting to understand why he even felt it for the woman that Ryan had brought to his sister's wedding — one who he knew from direct experience Ryan was satisfying in his own way.

Cole didn't know what was worse — being jealous of Ryan's relationship with her or of Ryan's easy comfort with his own bisexuality. He groaned and put his head down, ignoring Jake once again when the man put a comforting hand on his shoulder.

* * * *

An hour later, Ryan was exhausted. Still tingling from the quickie with Lynette, his brain was entering shutdown mode after the long, emotional slog of the day's events. Jamie was draped over his shoulder, stripped down to his dress pants and T-shirt, snoring away a sugar crash. Nursing another beer, he handed the kid over to Tracey and stood, stretching out the kink in his lower back.

He'd observed the Lynette and Cole dance floor show and was still trying to process how he felt about it. Surprised that above all the alpha-male possessive clamor that had rattled around in his brain at first, the sight of the man's hand sliding down from her hip and the way she curved into his long, lean frame had turned him on so much he had to duck into the men's room and breathe deeply for a few minutes.

They were, in a word, beautiful, moving together in time to the music. Their bodies fit like pieces of a puzzle he was dying to get his hands on. He gnawed on the inside of his cheek, forcing the memory out of his brain lest he tent his tux pants all over again. He wanted them to do more, willed them to kiss, and when they had, he'd nearly come apart at the seams.

The band shifted gears and took on a funky beat with *Boogie Shoes*. Lynette walked by, tugged his arm, and they ended up on the dance floor for the next few songs. He laughed, watching her shimmy and shake, and at one point he held her close, bit her earlobe and felt her shiver. "Nice work with Cole. It was quite the show."

She turned her head, grabbed his neck and kissed him with an embarrassing ferocity. He was in tune enough to her signals by now and could practically feel her nipples hardening against his chest, could smell her lusty energy all around him. "Maybe," she said, after loosening her lip lock on him. "You like to watch?"

"I don't think you'll be terribly surprised to hear this, but yes, I do." He reached back and cupped her ass, drawing her closer.

"Hmm...well, in the meantime, I think we should probably call it a night." She danced away from him, shaking her hips and looking over her shoulder. He stood, hands in his pockets, and watched her move away until something else caught his eye. He did a quarter turn and spotted Cole sitting with that cover-model-slash-business-partner-slash-fuck-buddy Jake. Their faces were close. Jake was talking. Cole smiled, and the sight of it made Ryan's heart clench. When Cole took Jake's hand, he had to look away. What in the name of all that was holy was he even thinking?

Entertaining some kind of perverse fantasy about putting together the two people he cared about, who possessed him in body and spirit—so he could watch them fuck?

Jesus. You are one sick bastard, Shannon.

The back of his neck got prickly so he turned around on reflex and looked at Cole again. The other man had his sunglasses off. The bright, clear green of his sightless eyes knocked Ryan's breath out of his lungs. He would swear that Cole could see him, really truly see. Cole stood, settling his Ray-Bans back in place, his dog at his side. The two men made their way over to where Audrey sat on Quinn's lap.

Ryan's smiled. His brother so deserved this after all those years of insanity at the hands of his ex-wife. But his smile faded as he watched Audrey's brother approach them, Jake's huge possessive hand on his shoulder. Audrey jumped up and gave Cole a hug. Quinn shook his hand, then Jake's. Then the men walked out, together, and Ryan was left with his fantasies, one in particular of landing a hard left hook to Jake's firm jaw.

"Hey," he yelped when someone wrapped arms around his waist from behind. He drew the sexy redhead around to his side. "You temptress. Look what you've done to me with your dance floor seductions." He held her close, trying to quell the now crystal-clear vision of Cole, between Lynette's legs, moving up her body and sliding into her while Ryan stood behind them.

"Nice," he said, when she put her hand right on his cock. "Slutty. I like it. Let's get the hell out of here."

Chapter Twenty-One

Cole woke, sat up and rubbed his face. No matter how many mornings he faced, it was always the same thing—the quick terror of darkness accompanied by frustration, then gloom when he remembered no matter what he did, his eyes would never cooperate. Brutus snuffled around next to him, pushing at his hand and whining.

"What is that noise?" Jake grumbled on his other side. Cole sighed and swung his legs to the floor. He honestly didn't recall agreeing to a sleepover but he'd been so down lately, more than usual after the wedding and strange encounter with Lynette, that he didn't have the energy to argue about it. "Cole, here. It's your phone." He jumped when Jake poked his shoulder with the clanging device. He didn't recognize the ring so at least it wasn't Audrey, or Quinn, each of whom had an assigned tone.

"Yeah?" he croaked into the phone. "This had better be pretty important." He felt Jake's hand on his bare shoulder but moved away from him at the sound of Ryan's voice.

"Hey, yeah, it is. Sorry."

He jumped to his feet, knocking his big toe against the bedside table and cursing while jumping around and trying not to panic. "Shit. Is it Audrey? What's wrong?"

"No, no, it's not her. Relax. You okay?"

"What the hell is it, then?" He sat back down on the bed and rubbed his sore toe.

"Something's gone wrong at the brewery. We had a power outage around midnight and the generator kicked in, but I can't get the main computer to fire back up."

"So? Call your IT guy."

"He's on vacation. Listen, Cole, if I don't get the brewery back online, I have something like a million gallons of beer that will spoil. Can you...I mean, I can come get you."

"What the fuck do you think I can do about it?" He kept his voice gruff, but his heart was lifting at the thought of being pulled into Ryan's orbit again, even if it were over an easy computer fix.

"I don't know. Crap, I'm fucked. Never mind. I'll figure something else out."

"Hang on, hang on." Cole stood and stretched. He heard Jake's soft exhalation and knew immediately the man was not happy. At that moment he realized something—he had to cut off his physical relationship with the guy. It wasn't fair to him. Jake was a top-notch business partner, finding them high-level security computer problems to solve, not to mention the money to fund their daily expenses.

But he, Cole, had to grow up and stop relying on Jake for sex. He put his arm down and the dog slid into his grasp. "I need a quick shower. And will need a ride."

"I'll be there in a half hour. Thanks."

* * * *

After a stressful hour spent with Cole trying to get Lynette to relay all the messages the server kept burping up on the screen while he attempted to reboot, the computer finally made the reassuring little singsong indicating that the operating system was back online. She handed him the phone so he could talk to Ryan, who was down in the brewery, anxiously waiting the fermenter indicators to flash back to life.

"Okay, you should be good," he said, shifting to the right in a vain attempt to get away from Lynette and her delicious scent. It was subdued in the wee hours of the morning and held a subtle overlay of Ryan. He had no doubt where the two of them had come from, roused from their activity when the security guard called about the power cut.

"Yep, they're all flashing back to life, thank God — no, thank you, Cole. Seriously."

"Eh, it's fine. Easy."

"Okay, I'll be up in a few minutes. I need to reset everything down here, make sure the bigger fermenters cool down properly."

"Sure, whatever." He handed the phone to Lynette and leaned back, letting his fingers graze the reassuring fuzz of his dog's ears. The animal made a concerned noise. He knew why. The sudden realization that he was alone with Lynette — she of the amazing scent, now layered with the definite Ryan one—had him sending anxious signals. Like he had the first time, when Cole had been so totally turned on by Ryan, Brutus was tracking his anxiety and wanted to get his master away from what was causing it.

He sighed and forced his brain to be calm. But Lynette's silence made him beyond nervous. He reached for the cup of coffee she'd brought him, sipped, set it down and tried to figure out how to get the hell away from her before he did something he would regret—something he didn't even really understand at the moment.

"Oh shit," he groaned when he felt her hand on his neck, sliding up into his hair. She lifted his sunglasses off. Her lips covered his without a word. He let go of his death grip on the chair arms and gathered her close, sucking in huge lungsful of her sweet, sultry scent. Her small tongue probed between his lips, forcing them apart, and he wasn't surprised to find she tasted as good as she smelled.

She settled herself onto his lap, reminding him once more of the differences he had not given much thought to in the last fifteen years—the way a woman felt under his hands, soft, curvy and light was a stark comparison to what he usually liked.

Oh yeah, then why the fuck is your cock so hard it could cut diamonds right now, genius?

Jesus H. Christ, he wanted her. Wanted inside her, all over her, wanted to keep kissing her forever. His mind spun, trying to process, to stop him from this…thing…this female he had no business wanting but did so badly he was about to come in his shorts like a teenager.

He slid his hand up her back, found her ponytail holder and tugged so he could bury both hands in her soft curls. She broke the kiss and leaned closer so his lips found her neck. He nibbled and licked, moaning as she ground down against his crotch.

The noise she made, deep down in her throat, the same one she'd made on the dance floor, floated into his ear. Her essence took on a spicy, sexy note. Funny, how he never suspected that a turned-on female would smell so…fuckable. The word nearly made him laugh.

"Oh," she sighed when he ran his thumb across one rock-hard nipple. Her back arched and she must have yanked her shirt aside, or off, because before he knew it, his lips were sucking, his teeth tugging, at the most delicious flesh he could possibly imagine as he cradled one firm globe.

He moved from one luscious nipple to the other while she kept rubbing against him, her hands in his hair, the heat of her pussy making his cock ache beneath the shorts he'd thrown on after the shower. "Goddamn it," he grunted when she slid her hand down his chest, shifting back ever so slightly so she could touch him. Her small hand was cool on his aching shaft. "Don't," he whispered into her skin, moving back up to find her lips. "Seriously, I mean it." But his words meant little. His hips moved of their own accord, thrusting and seeking more serious contact.

"You want me, Cole?" she whispered, her teeth grazing his earlobe.

"What? You can't tell?" A sudden rush of painful lust shot through him, making him tremble. He gripped her hips, holding her still. "But I need to ask you something," he said.

"What?" She bit his lower lip, keeping up her hand action on his cock.

He turned his head toward the door. "How do you feel about him watching us?"

She jerked away, leaving Cole panting in the seat. His brain buzzed when the loop of fantasy ran through him once more — one starring the lovely woman who'd been on the verge of hand-jobbing him to climax and the man he'd sensed hovered in the doorway and who'd been there for at least the last ten minutes.

"Uh, sorry." Ryan's rough voice betrayed how he felt. Cole's face flushed. He stood, grabbing the dog's lead, furious indignation mingled with embarrassment replacing all the lusty energy he'd been riding for the last few minutes.

"I don't know what you people are playing at, but the last thing I need is any more brain fucking. Got it?" He let the dog lead him to the door, to an elevator and down. The funky, malty brewery smells he'd learned to associate with his sister enveloped him. Weird, burbling noises, combined with metal pings and clanks, made Brutus skitter closer to him, bumping against his leg and nearly shoving him over.

He ached with a need he refused to admit and his chest burned with a combination of humiliation and fury. "How the fuck do I get out of here?" Then it hit him. Even if he could find his way out, he had no way to get home. Because he was blind and helpless, at the mercy of people who could do normal things, like drive a car.

He shook and backed up until his ass connected with something that felt like a chair and he sat, his face in his hands. The one thing he'd felt confident about — the core truth of his own sexuality that had forced him away from his family, made him hide his real self just so he could let the military form him into something new, he'd never doubted. He'd clung to it, recalling in a breathless rush his time with the professor, with Dan, his rough and raw encounters with Ryan and more recently Jake's gentle, careful lovemaking.

But images and memories of the women he'd fucked, their light, curvy, welcoming bodies, long hair, distinct, tantalizing odors shoved all that out, made him grit his teeth. He yanked the sunglasses off and willed his eyes sighted and himself whole again. Maybe he wouldn't have all this conflict if he didn't feel so useless. Complex, distressing emotion boiled through him. He clenched his fists. The dog bumped against him, whining.

"Stop it," he muttered. "Just leave me the fuck alone." He stood, the restless energy of an unconsummated erotic moment making him antsy. He sat, then stood again and let the deep dark reality of his dependence—his stupid goddamned handicap—suffuse him.

When a masculine hand landed on his shoulder, he leaped up and gripped the arm attached to it. "Take me home," he demanded. "Now."

Ryan must have opened a door not a foot from him. Cole set his shoulders and let the dog lead him out. The ride home was quiet and tense beyond belief. Cole sensed Ryan's need to speak but hoped he would stay quiet. He did.

Ryan parked, keeping the engine running. Cole startled when Ryan touched his thigh. "Don't fucking touch me." But his voice was low, soft and when he lifted his face and found Ryan's lips, it was exactly what he wanted.

Chapter Twenty-Two

Lynette's face boiled as she looked from one man to the other. Cole sat, chest heaving, shorts tented but with fury etched into his face. Ryan stood in the door, hanging on to the doorjamb, his jaw set, but eyes unreadable. Cole's words about being mind-fucked had stabbed straight into her gut.

She stood, staring at Ryan—the man she would swear she loved, if she'd let herself admit it. Why she'd felt compelled by the young, handsome, wounded Cole Traynor, she had no idea. It made her sick to her stomach, but there it was, nonetheless.

"Oh, I'm, um…shit. I didn't mean to…" She gripped her elbows, willing Ryan to come to her, hold her and tell it was okay. Assure her that she had not taken utter advantage of a hot, blind guy just to prove something.

"I don't know what you think about him, Lynette, but he's right. You can't just jump him like that. It's not how it…" He looked down. "Just leave him alone, okay? I won't bring it up again. He can't…he won't...we shouldn't do this." He turned and headed for the stairwell.

She dropped into the chair Cole had vacated, still feeling him beneath her, still tasting his lips. Tears pressed against her eyes, but she forced them back. No crying. She was not going to cry over this. She needed to gather her wits, to process her thoughts, to sort through why she'd done what she'd done.

He'd been focusing and doing his job, while she'd attempted to help by relaying what was on the screen so he could figure out how to fix it. All the while she hadn't been able to take her eyes off him. His shoulders were broad, not quite as a wide span as Ryan's but compact, suitable to his shorter frame. And the soft gray Marine T-shirt had highlighted his biceps and the obvious fit condition of his torso. She'd sat, staring at him, loving the heat of his proximity even while he'd cursed and hollered at her to give him every detail of the messages on the recalcitrant computer screen.

His thick golden hair had grown even more. It brushed his neck, with a slight curl at the end. His dark stubbled jaw had begged for her fingers. He'd bitten his lip, working the computer keyboard quickly and efficiently. She'd kept reaching for him then retreating, reconsidering her every move. The dog had kept his eyes on her, ever his master's guardian, but hadn't growled at her.

When she hadn't been able to stand it another second, she'd moved without any thought involved, taken off his sunglasses and kissed him. She'd been determined only to taste, to try, to let him know how she felt, but the whole scene had progressed and she'd found herself stroking him, unable to get enough. She blushed with the memory and her skin prickled in every spot where he'd touched her.

She got up and started pacing, running her hands through her hair. She wasn't trying to mess with him, no matter what either man thought. She wanted him. More than she'd wanted anything. Catch was—she wanted Ryan, too, and not just for a fuck buddy anymore. Their hours together at work and outside it had become so comfortable she'd lie awake most nights watching him sleep or, if she were home alone, wishing she were watching him sleep.

Ugh. What a fucking mess you've made, Lynette. And now, you've potentially screwed up what you thought you had with Ryan because all up with your horny bullshit.

She sat, but would not allow herself a cry—that was one thing she would not do. No man was worth her tears—of that she was certain and she'd made that particular vow to herself years ago. She was not about to break it now no matter how tempting it may be. She rose, turned out the office lights and headed downstairs, wondering just how she could face Ryan the next day, or Cole, ever again.

* * * *

Ryan tried not to think, attempting to let his emotions lead him, while Cole clutched at his shoulders over the truck's console, a desperation to his movements that Ryan recognized at once. He pulled away, swallowed hard, then got out of the truck. Cole met him halfway before he made it around to the other side, shoving him back against the truck's hood and forcing his lips open with his tongue, gripping his hair, his ass, everywhere he could.

Ryan groaned and pulled away. He held the other man's shoulders, keeping his focus on Cole's face. Once he had a modicum of control, he lifted off Cole's sunglasses. "Relax. It's okay. It's fine. I'm sorry. She…I…well, that was sort of my fault back there."

"What?" Cole's hands shook when he ran them through his hair. Ryan cursed himself for the millionth time for putting this vulnerable man in such a difficult position. He should walk away from it — from Lynette, for whom his feelings were becoming complex enough to terrify him — from Cole, whose very presence right now brought out urges Ryan had to fight with every ounce of his willpower. He was going to ruin everything if he didn't watch it and bring two innocent people along for his selfish ride.

He held Cole at arm's length. "I planted the idea with her, about you. I could tell you guys had a moment on the dance floor at the reception and, um, well, I told her I thought it was kind of hot. And she's sort of a sex convert these days."

"What the fuck are you talking about?" Cole leaned next to him, shivering in the cold night air.

Ryan took a breath and leaped into the void, hoping like hell Lynette wouldn't kill him for what he was about to reveal. "Lynette was what you might call repressed. Sexually speaking. She didn't have bad experiences. Just no good ones, and after a while didn't seek them out. She worked, went to school and worked, in that order. Dating and sex and relationships weren't on her agenda."

"Yeah, and you were just the guy to help her out with that, I take it."

"Apparently." Ryan took a deep breath. "You make me sound like I'm some kind of predator, but I assure you it was mutual. She needed, I needed, we both give and get. And it's...well, it's nice."

"Super. I'm happy for you guys. Now if you'll excuse me." Cole gripped the dog's lead and started to push away from the truck.

Ryan grabbed his hand. "Wait. Cole, I need you to hear this. Don't judge her. She's not trying to fuck with your mind, I swear it." Cole held out his hand. Ryan handed him the Ray-Bans. "I want you to know. I would, I mean, I'd like...oh hell." He relinquished his wavering self-control and tugged the man close, kissing him long and deep, making them both breathless in the near dawn of a freezing Saturday morning.

Cole pulled away, reached down and cupped Ryan's erection. "Yeah, I know what you want. I can tell what you'd like. But I don't, okay. It's too much for me. I don't want...her. I mean, I can't." This last was choked out, making Ryan frown at the emotion he heard in Cole's voice.

"I think you do." He ran a finger across Cole's cheek. "And I don't blame you. She is the most amazing woman on the planet, hands down, period, end of story. And our relationship isn't about love. More about friendship and, um, mutual satisfaction, I guess. So, if you change your mind..."

Cole planted his feet and poked a finger into Ryan's chest. "That is the dumbest, most asinine horse shit I have ever heard. If you actually think that about her is one thing, but to let it pass your lips like you really mean it? You disappoint me, Shannon. And don't worry. I won't change my mind." Cole's stomped up the steps to his house. Ryan watched him go, a bright burst of possibility making his knees weak. He grabbed his phone and sent a quick text to Lynette without even thinking.

It's okay. He's fine. I'm fine. Get some sleep. Let's talk about next steps.

Later, giving up on sleep, he sat sipping coffee in his kitchen, thinking about what Cole had said and picturing Lynette for the rest of the morning. He dragged himself up and into the car, needing to pick Jamie up from his mother's where he'd left him in the middle of the night to deal with the emergency. One look at his son's face and hearing his happy declarations when he jumped into Ryan's arms smoothed his rattled nerves and gave him fresh resolve.

Chapter Twenty-Three

Cole's hands shook and his face burned, but the rest of him was ready. More than ready — he was locked and loaded and needed to fuck something. Bad. That was the sum total of this little adventure, he repeated in his head for the thousandth time — fucking, screwing, getting off, pure and simple, nothing more. And he deserved it, every last breathless, pleasant minute of it.

The room was chilly, but it felt good against his skin. He reached down, but the dog wasn't there. A small thrill of panic lit the base of his spine. He couldn't get anywhere without the animal. He held out a hand, started to open his mouth, to ask for a ride home, suddenly not ready anymore. He replayed the last few days in his head, still not believing he'd experienced it.

Lynette had come to his house two days ago, just shown up on his porch uninvited. They'd sat outside in the cold — she'd refused to come in — and talked for what felt like hours. She'd given him her side of the 'Ryan is my fuck buddy' story and he still hadn't bought it. But she'd gotten him talking, too, about Jake and how he wasn't involved with him sexually anymore because that just felt cheap and crappy.

He'd asked her point blank about the 'sex convert' stuff Ryan had alluded to and she'd confirmed it. Her heart had pounded like a kick drum whenever she talked about Ryan. Cole had known her emotions were ruling her, and he'd cursed Ryan all over again for being such a blind shithead to the whole thing.

Cole had told her about the professor, about the few women he'd been with and a little about Dan. But that subject remained a fresh wound he'd refused to prod too deeply.

She'd stood, given him a soft hug and brush of her lips to his jaw. '*I'm sorry for jumping you like that in the office. But I'd love it if you could consider my – our – offer. We won't do anything you don't want to. But honestly, Cole, I – we – feel strongly about you and want you to be happy.*'

'*And you think engaging in a three-way with you and Ryan Shannon will accomplish that?*' He'd hated the sound of his own voice right then.

'*Well, yes.*'

He'd sensed her move away from him. Anger, combined with no small amount of lust, had rolled around in his gut. '*I don't do girls, not anymore,*' he'd declared, his hand gripping the chair back.

'*I'm not asking you to do girls, Cole,*' she'd said from a few feet away. '*I'm inviting you to make love to me and Ryan together. But I understand if you'd rather not.*'

And now, here he was. Cole lifted his face and let a breeze cool his burning face. And then he sensed her nearby. No, right next to him. Her hand took his and her lips pressed against his jaw. He tensed, a sudden flight reaction prickling his nerve endings. He pulled away from her, turned and stumbled against some random stupid piece of furniture. "Where is my dog?" he demanded, regaining his footing before he landed on his ass. "Goddamn it, Ryan, get me out of here."

Silence met his ears. Silence tinged with a distant, pounding heartbeat. He put his hands on his hips. "Sorry," he said for the millionth time. "I thought I was ready for this. I'm obviously not. I should go."

He turned and Lynette was there, filling his nose with the sweet essence of her, his arms with the light, perfect sensation of her. He tried not to respond, attempted to stop the rushing blood in his ears and the straining behind his zipper.

"Shh," she said, her lips close to his. Her cool palms stroked his face. He clenched his jaw, but her lips trailed along there, loosening it despite his determination not to allow it. "It's okay. Relax."

He put his hand on her hips, ready to push her away, to end this stupid setup or seduction scene or whatever the hell it was. It was starting to irritate him, all this effort for a simple physical act. One he was more than ready to perform granted but unable to justify all of a sudden.

When he heard music waft in from somewhere, he leaned down and touched his lips to her bare shoulder, shivering when he wrapped his mind around the fact that she was totally naked. Now that she was closer, he smelled her, all of her — the honey of her skin, the spicy tang of her need just below that. "You should know something about me," he muttered, his lips near her flesh.

She ran her hands down his front, unbuttoning his shirt slowly, delectably, pressing her lips against every inch of skin that she bared. "Uh-huh, what's that?" she asked when her fingers reached his belt, unbuckling and unzipping and undressing him in slow, careful movements. He grabbed her hands when she reached for his straining boxer shorts. She stopped and stepped away, taking her tantalizing scent with her.

"I'm not into this because of you. I want…I need to see…I mean, try…I'm…oh dear Lord, just come back over here, would ya?"

His brain shut down when she molded her soft, lithe form into his. He ran his hands down her back, her ass, then back up, adoring the feel of her, the sensation of her breasts pressed against him, the distinct warmth between her legs. He licked his lips. "I'll bet you taste just like you smell. Like honey, heavenly." His voice was rough, his entire body a raw nerve ending.

"She does." Ryan's voice rolled through him. He felt the man's hand on his shoulder, trailing down his back to his ass. "And one of her favorite ways to come is at the end of your tongue."

Lynette made her little moan and sigh, and Cole sensed Ryan's hand low, touching her, stroking her sex. Her chemistry changed then. He smelled it, felt it in his arms when she moved, arching her back and making that intense noise down in her throat. He sucked in a ragged breath.

Was he ready for this? Did he want…her? Or was he just humoring Ryan because he wanted him so badly he would sometimes wake up crying out the man's name in the night?

And now, he was here, too. Ryan's hard, masculine body pressed to his back, the soft, voluptuous curves of Lynette at his front. "Feel her," Ryan whispered into Cole's ear. "Like this." He took Cole's hand, placed it between her legs. Raw lust curled up in his brain, nestling in for the long haul. He groaned, leaned into kiss her, sweeping into her mouth with a firm thrust of his tongue when his and Ryan's fingers found the hard flesh of her clit.

"Keep stroking her there," Ryan said, his other hand now gripping Cole's cock. Cole didn't know if he was coming or going — was the giver or receiver of pleasure. "Relax, Cole. Don't think about it. Just feel," Ryan commanded, biting his earlobe. He ground his long shaft against the cleft of Cole's ass.

"Jesus," Cole muttered, running his lips down the sleek line of Lynette's neck. She wrapped her arms around him, held on tight when he stroked her then slid deeper, the velvety folds of her body pulling him, calling to him. The grip of her sex around his finger was tight, different from what he was used to but one of the most erotic things he'd felt in a while.

"Cole," she whispered, shuddering into him and lifting a leg around his waist. Ryan grabbed it, held on to her, keeping his delicious friction up and down Cole's cock. "Make me come…ah…" She tensed, then he felt it — the pulse and spasm of her on and around his hand. "Yes…" she hissed, arching her back and angling her hips closer.

"Lovely Lynette," Ryan muttered. He dropped her leg and stepped back from Cole, leaving him cold, bereft and throbbing with unmet need. He put his trembling hand to his lips and sighed with satisfaction at the taste of her on his fingers.

"I told you," Ryan said, taking his hand and guiding him a few feet to the right. "She's here, lying on the bed, her nipples are hard and ready and that sweet pussy — well, you've only felt a little of what it will do for you."

But Cole stopped, frozen, panic making his throat close. He shook uncontrollably and his brain started a familiar slide into terror.

He wanted this. More than he'd wanted anything since losing Dan. But he wanted them both, and that just felt selfish and wrong. Panic gripped him and he sensed withdrawal on his horizon.

Lynette bit her lip when Ryan led Cole to the bed. She still tingled from the knee-jerk orgasm she'd had, coming practically from the sheer presence of the men, Ryan holding her leg while Cole stroked and kissed her. But the smaller man was shaking more than she liked, so she sat up, put her hand on Ryan's arm and mouthed the words, "Back away a minute."

He nodded and stepped into the shadows of the candlelit room. She pulled Cole down to seated and handed him a glass of water. His unseeing eyes shone in the dim light, his amazing, thick shaft pressed up against his belly, but his hand trembled when he handed the empty glass to her. She put it down and sat next to him, running her fingers through his hair, light, easy, attempting not to throw him down and straddle him and in the process scare him to death. He took a deep breath and smiled at her.

She cupped his chin. Her heart hammered against her chest. She was turned on beyond belief, but something else nibbled at the corner of her consciousness. She was not this girl, and how she'd gotten to this point was simultaneously thrilling and mortifying.

Something about Cole—his innocent smile, his poor ruined eyes, his odd juxtaposed strength and extreme vulnerability—made her pause. Maybe this wasn't right. She leaned her head on his shoulder. He shifted and put an arm around her. His lips touched her hair.

"We don't have to go any further, Cole. If you don't want to. I...I'm feeling a little predatory right now. Don't get me wrong. I want you." She let her fingers trail along the inside of his muscular thigh. Her skin pebbled in reaction to his shiver and a pearly drop of fluid appeared at the head of his cock. She forced herself to take her hand off him. "Maybe we've done too much too soon."

"Oh, hell no," he said, his voice low and raspy. "I don't think I've ever wanted anything more." He ran a finger along her jaw, tilted her face up and kissed her, parting her lips, meeting her tongue and pressing her back on the bed at the same time. She sighed and put one foot on the bed, letting the cool air caress her from tip to toe.

"Lynette," he sighed into her neck. He cupped a breast and caressed her nipple. "I am pissed off beyond belief that I can't actually see you but believe it or not your smell has me so turned on I...I'm afraid. I can't be what you need me to be. I'm...oh..."

She gave in to the moment, let it carry away any of logic or rationale and just kissed him, pulled him over on top of her and wrapped her entire self around him. If she angled her hips just right, she would have him and she wanted it so bad it hurt. But he propped up on his arms, the strange green of his sightless eyes seeming to bore into her, intent and sad. He started at her jaw, licking, nibbling, making her shiver, then worked his slow, delectable way down.

"Oh, dear God, I love these." He cradled the curve of one breast, tugging and sucking so hard on one nipple she pulsed in immediate response. She threaded her fingers in his hair and closed her eyes, an odd sensation pressing behind them as if she could actually cry from the perfection of the moment. But she was no crier, so she focused on the exquisite sensation of Cole's lips and hands instead.

"Nice," said Ryan's soft voice near her ear. She opened her eyes, looked at him and held out a hand. He threaded his fingers in hers. Cole nibbled his way down her torso, palmed her hips and lifted them to meet his face. Ryan rolled in next to her, his long cock pressed hard against her hip.

He kept holding her hand. "That's right, Cole. Right there. She is so incredibly sensitive." He brushed the back of their joined hands against her nipple. She let go and cried out when Cole's lips found her clit. He sucked hard, elongating her flesh, tickling it with his tongue before he let go, making her gasp and tilt her hips higher, needing him back where he'd been.

He flicked his tongue downward and stroked along the edges of her pussy. She gripped his hair, felt Ryan's strong hands on her nipples, pinching, tugging when Cole latched on to her clit again. She draped her legs over Cole's shoulders with a sigh of pleasure. His hands dug into her ass. Ryan leaned into suck her nipple. Her vision dimmed. The room narrowed and her back arched.

She opened her eyes and drew in a huge breath. She smelled man, all around her, all over her. She released Cole's hair, touched her face and drew her fingers away wet, startling herself. But right then, tears seemed like the only reflection of the extreme emotions that gripped her.

"Lynette," Cole whispered. He climbed up between her legs. "Don't cry." He covered her lips with his at the same moment he thrust into her. She had no idea where Ryan went and that moment she didn't care. She gripped Cole's neck, tasted herself on his lips and tongue and met his every movement. They went slow, easy, but there were only two people in the universe — her and the amazing man above her. He broke the kiss and buried his face in her neck as his hips moved faster. "Don't ever cry…" he said, so softly she barely heard him.

She wrapped her legs around his waist and he spread her, going deeper with each movement. He stayed close, allowing her constant contact with his pubic bone. She gripped his ass when yet another orgasm hovered. She arched up, letting it take her. "Cole, oh God, yes."

"Shit," he muttered. "I can't…I'm…oh…" He shook all over, his strong arms holding him up over her. She stared at his face, loving the beautiful look there. "Lynette," Cole said, his voice breaking.

She pulled him down, trying to stop the stupid girlie tears, but then just let them flow. They felt natural, like a part of this moment. He shivered, dropped onto her.

"Oh God, I'm sorry," he said, struggling back up.

"Shh…no, no, it's fine. I love it. I love the way you feel." She sighed and held him to her breasts. "That was…"

"Amazing," he mumbled, then propped up again, kissing her and running his tongue along her lips then into her mouth. "I could kiss you all fucking night."

"I wouldn't tell you no," she said. The tears kept rolling down her face, no matter what she did. He touched her wet cheek.

"I said, no crying." He rolled to his side and propped up on one elbow, all the while keeping his fingers on her face, her neck, her breasts. Then to her utter mortification, she let loose and sobbed while he held her close, crooning and making shushing noises. She had no idea why, but it felt great, cathartic, and as much a part of the moment as the connection they'd just shared.

By the time she'd gotten hold of herself, she had no idea how much time had passed. He felt complete, holding her, kissing her hair. She sat up, rubbing her nose. "Where's Ryan?"

Ryan stood and watched his long-held fantasy unfold. Saw Cole drop down between Lynette's legs, bury his face in her pussy while Ryan stroked her nipples, teased her until she came in a frantic rush of erotic energy. Then, that moment when the man climbed up her torso and dove into her, his strong ass moving, her lean legs wrapped around him, their age-old dance of sexual satisfaction filling his brain, something in him snapped. He sat back, stood, rubbed his eyes.

Cole was whispering to her. She was about to come, Ryan could tell. She arched up, cried out his name. Ryan clenched his jaw. He backed farther away, stumbling over a chair, still watching. "Wait," he whispered. "You didn't put on a..." He groaned and sat, fisting his cock and giving it a couple of quick tugs. Cole's back arched, his head went up and he called for her, his body shuddering in the grip of climax as Ryan groaned and covered his belly with his own fluid.

He sat, breathing heavily, frozen in place. Cole stayed over her. They kissed and he heard a sob and sat up. *Lynette? Crying? No way.* But yes, her shoulders shook and Cole rolled to her side and held her close, kissing her hair, telling her it was fine.

Ryan stood, a kind of bizarre fury hitting him between the eyes. He knew it for what it was — jealousy. He acknowledged it, walked out of the room and stood in the kitchen, holding the edge of the sink and counting to twenty then forty. He looked up at the ceiling.

This is what you wanted. Remember?

"Ryan?" Lynette's voice floated out of the bedroom.

He'd spent a fair amount of time discussing this night with her. They figured that Lynette should be the one to invite him over, tell him it was merely for sex, but only if he wanted it. He'd agreed, to their surprise, and Ryan had held back the urge to ask about Jake. None of his business and besides, 'this was about sex,' as they kept insisting even to each other.

He looked out over the dark lawn and had a terrifying epiphany. He wanted more from Lynette. He wanted to be with her every morning, every night, to hold her hand and take walks. He closed his eyes.

Get. A. Fucking. Grip. She does not want any of that from you.

And now? He sighed, ran a hand down his face. "In here," he said, fixing a neutral look on his face after wiping off with a towel and tossing it into the laundry room.

"Come on in here." Cole's voice sounded strong, stronger than he had heard it in a long time. "We're lonely."

He smiled and stood in the doorway. The two people he adored were sitting in each other's arms, gloriously naked. Cole's hand cupped Lynette's breast, almost casually. Ryan smiled at the realization that

Cole was a breast man, which worked, since he was an avowed legs and ass guy.

Her hand was draped along his thigh. The room was suffused with lusty smells, with a distinct undercurrent of the sweet honey-like fragrance Cole had pointed out to him and that now filled his senses whenever he was around Lynette. He shook off the emotional bullshit, or tried. Then he strode over. "Okay, then let a guy in, will ya?"

They parted, and he dropped down between them, forcing his brain to shut down when Cole's lips found his and Lynette straddled him. He was hard again, amazingly enough, but felt detached somehow, and already worried — how would this work? Where would they sleep? Why didn't he remember to give Cole a condom?

"Jesus!" he yelped when Lynette leaned down and bit his nipple.

Cole laughed and leaned back on his arms. "Okay, my turn to watch," he said, hand on his shaft. Ryan did a double take, but Cole's face was calm, happy, free of bitterness or irony. Cole leaned up and found Lynette's lips, then released her, making his way up Ryan's torso, licking and sucking then kissing him, hard, until he slid into the soft welcoming, familiar depths of Lynette's body, realizing about a beat too late he had forgotten his own condom but no longer really giving a shit.

Chapter Twenty-Four

One night, two months after they'd started their 'sex only' program, Lynette sat at the dinner table with the men, sipping a beer. The whole surreal nature of this crazy arrangement was mind-boggling. The logistics of their encounters, considering Ryan was a single dad, sometimes overwhelmed her. His place was only available if Audrey were willing to have Jamie overnight. She had been, until she'd gotten some terrifying news relative to her pregnancy and had nearly gone off the deep end. After that, Ryan felt guilty asking her. The boy's grandmother would take him sometimes but had a lot of questions about it that Lynette knew Ryan couldn't answer.

Lynette's apartment was certainly not an option, not with her mother still hanging around, asking her about her 'brewery man' all the time. So, they ended up at Cole's place a lot, although his bed was small and too crowded for her taste. They were there tonight, around his kitchen table, glaring at one another. The day been a long one for everyone, and they'd been testy, snappish and more than once she doubted her sanity for thinking two is better than one when it came to the hairier sex.

She'd thrown a heavy pepper grinder straight at Ryan when he kept complaining about the dinner she'd made, unable to find a single thing right about it. Cole had nearly fallen out of his chair laughing when Ryan had yelped, cursed and caught the thing with his skull before it fell to his lap.

'*Fuck you, you're no better,*' she'd yelled at the man still trying not to laugh too loud once he realized how upset she was. '*I'm leaving,*' she'd declared, dead serious — although she was so amped up at the thought of being between them again, she hesitated. They had only managed actual sex a few times, again, logistics and practicalities keeping their base urges at bay. But those times had been mind-blowing, deeply emotional experiences, for her at least.

Cole spoke first, leaving Ryan glowering at her, hand covering the knot rising on his head. "Wait, Lynette, I'm sorry. He's sorry. We're being shits. But we're over it now. It's out of our system. Okay?"

Ryan snorted. Lynette glared at him but let Cole draw her back to the table. "You're just saying that because you want to get laid," she said into her beer, realizing the utter absurdity of that comment. Of course, he did. That was why she was here, with them, in the first place. Something about that realization made her chest tight. Cole took her glass, set it down and put her hand to his lips. She smiled at his painfully handsome face, stuck her tongue out at Ryan and let Cole pull her into his lap.

"Yeah, I do." She felt Cole's leg move under her and heard Ryan's yelp when Cole's foot connected with his. "But more importantly, we want you to be happy."

She looked away from him, but he found her chin with his fingertips and drew her back to his lips. Dear Lord, but the man could kiss like nobody's business. She sighed and wrapped her arms around him, letting him dive into her mouth with his tongue, loving the stirring underneath her when she clenched the back of his neck and held on tight.

She studiously ignored Ryan, paying full attention to Cole, running her hands across his shoulders, then down, unbuttoning his shirt and yanking it off his arms, keeping their lip lock. She sighed, feeling another set of hands on her shoulders, easing her blouse off and unclasping her bra.

She leaned back against Ryan's torso when he reached around to cup her breasts, rasping his rough thumbs against her nipples. He teased her neck and shoulders with his lips and teeth. "Sorry," he whispered in her ear. "Truly," he claimed when she shot him a dubious look. "C'mon." He picked her all the way up off Cole's lap, having his own turn with her lips while he carried her down the hall. Ryan set her on the bed. She sensed Cole between her legs, kissing and licking up the inside of them before using that amazing mouth on her clit.

She moaned and gripped his hair while Ryan kept teasing her nipples, drawing them into stiff, needy peaks. The orgasm startled her with its quickness and ferocity. She cried out and angled her hips up, needing something, someone, inside her, but Cole just sucked at her, running his fingers along the edges of her sex.

Liz Crowe

Ryan covered her lips at the last minute, drowning out her cries. She held on to him, let the exquisite climax smother her entire universe. Ryan released her and Cole leaned back, giving her some space to recover. "Goddamn, boys, that was...hey!" Cole smiled and flipped her over in one quick movement.

She grinned, wiggled her ass and went onto all fours. She knew this drill and loved it. The men switched places and Cole got on his knees in front of her, drawing her up off her hands to meet him. His tongue-tangling kiss gave her a taste of herself, and she held on to him, suddenly needing this connection, this moment of completion so badly her chest ached. She pouted when he ended it, giving her bottom lip a nip with his teeth.

Reaching down to wrap her hand around his thick cock, she made a satisfied sound, loving the feel of him there, and of Ryan rubbing his shaft against her ass, sliding fingers inside her reaching up high, then pulling out, rubbing her still throbbing clit, then repeating the whole glorious process. She arched her back, her whole being on fire with need to be filled, taken, by them both.

"Mm-hmm," Ryan muttered, pushing her forward gently so she dropped back on her hands and knees, eye level with Cole's sex. She loved the sight of his hand around his own cock as she lapped at his head, sucked the early evidence of his desire from the tip. Ryan slid slowly into her. She slipped her lips as far down Cole's cock as she could. She was still honing her swallowing techniques, but the practice was definitely fun.

Ryan reached around to find her clit, pressing and rubbing it so her back arched more, taking all his length inside her. She sucked Cole back down, and he thrust deeper, breaching her throat a little. He threaded his fingers in her hair, tugged it, the way she liked.

"That's it," Ryan said, "Fuck her mouth, baby. She wants it, don't you, Red?" He smacked her ass, hard, making her jump and moan and her skin heat where he'd struck her.

He moved faster, going deep and hard inside her, hanging on to her hips now while she pulsed around him.

"God, Lynette, I'm gonna come. Do you want it, or should I…" His last words were drowned in a loud groan.

"Pull it out," Ryan croaked, still pounding into her. "Show me, Cole."

"Fuck," Cole muttered, and his cock stiffened as he yanked it out of her mouth. "You too," he insisted. They both pulled out of her at the last minute, coating her with cum.

"Shit," Cole grunted then flopped to his side. Lynette smiled down at him when his eyes dropped closed. She stood when she heard Ryan start the shower for her. He pulled her to her feet and wiped her back and face with a towel while the man she'd barely known as anything other than Audrey's wounded, gay brother fell into a deep sleep.

"Leave him." Ryan pulled her close for a gentle kiss, holding her face with both hands. "You're amazing."

"I know." She smacked his ass and ducked under the hot stream of water before he saw her tears. She was so weepy lately. Something about doing this, having this incredibly intense thing with these guys had turned into her an emotional wreck—a positive cry-baby. But after that first night, she hadn't let them see it. No way. She didn't need them thinking she was going soft and wanting to get married...or anything so drastic, ridiculous or utterly perfect.

Later she lay awake, listening to Ryan's soft snore, realizing that Cole was tossing and turning, tussling with a nightmare. She touched his face, saw his jaw clench and drew her hand back, remembering the story of that night when he'd woken and nearly beaten Ryan to a pulp in his sleep. But he calmed when she ran her finger down his cheek. Her skin was raw, her lips hurt and she felt like she'd just had a killer workout. But at this moment, nestled between the two men, she had never felt more complete. She propped herself on her elbow, watching Cole struggle through the dream.

She brushed her fingertip over the small globe and eagle *Semper Fi* tattoo on his biceps. He flinched from her touch, then sighed and rolled over, away from her, muttering about 'Dan' and 'fire'. Then he seemed to settle, leaving her wide awake.

She wandered out to the kitchen for some water, then lingered, leaning on the sink, pondering how she'd landed herself in this particular bizarre situation. She'd never been more physically fulfilled in her life — couldn't even fathom how it could be better on that front. She sighed, pulled her hair up in a ponytail, trying to pinpoint what was bugging her, how to quell the near constant ache she'd developed deep in her chest whenever she wasn't with them.

"Hey." Cole's voice behind her made her jump and turn, her hand to her throat.

"Jesus, you scared me."

"Sorry." He sat, Brutus at his side, snuffling around until Lynette started patting him. "Damn dog. Such an attention whore." Cole smiled before putting his head down on the table.

"What's wrong?" She rubbed his shoulders. "Cole?" He sat up, rubbed the bridge of his nose. "Headache? Need a painkiller?"

"I miss him. So much," he muttered, running a hand across his face. He'd gotten comfortable not wearing his sunglasses at home, around her and Ryan. She touched the burn marks around his eyes, trying to soothe away the stress on his face.

"Miss who, honey?" Her heart pounded. Finally, she could get his whole story — maybe.

"Dan," he said. His shoulders shook, but no tears fell. She touched his face again, and he gripped her hand, held on as if his life depended on it. "I miss him every fucking day of my life."

"Tell me about him."

"We were together for nearly two years. I was rotating home, finally. He had another year, maybe two. But we were…shit." He put his head back down on the table. Lynette stood behind him, kept massaging his neck, shoulders and arms.

"Tell me more," she whispered in his ear. Something about this moment felt exactly what she needed, to get her head around Cole.

"He was smart, scary smart. Dark hair, dark eyes, tall, even taller than Ryan. A young, innocent guy from Ohio. An only kid. Barely nineteen years old. He wanted to…" Cole's voice broke.

Lynette sensed tears pressing against her eyes. She kissed his rough cheek. "Go on," she said, threading her fingers in his hair, frightened by the depth of emotion rolling up from her gut.

"He wanted to open a bakery. His parents were chefs. They…they accepted him. Mine didn't. My father kicked my gay self out of the house and told me I wasn't welcome anymore."

"When?" she asked, her heart ripping in two at the thought of him, alone.

"Junior year of college. About the time I managed to get seduced by a married male professor who popped my cherry and made me fall in love with him, or so I thought." He took a long breath. "I'm not mad at him anymore. It was all it needed to be. But I dropped out after that and joined the Marines. Made it through basic and got assigned in Counter Intel. I'm a computer magician, remember?" He sat up and pulled her into his lap. She went, loving his words, his lips, his smell.

"Tell me more about Dan," she whispered into his neck.

"He loved books. Would read out loud to me— Hemingway, Faulkner, Salinger, King, all of it. I loved the sound of his voice. It was musical." He ran a hand down her neck then lower, cupping her breast. "He played soccer in high school. We used to play together, when we got bored. It was a great excuse to have contact. God, it was terrifying. We tried so hard not to get caught. But I loved him and we were going to be together, forever."

She stood up to get them both a glass of water. He gulped his down, his face tense. "I wasn't supposed to be there that week. On that fucking stupid convoy. But I went because Dan was going, and he said he wanted my help. We were headed into some godforsaken city that had been identified as a potential terrorist nest but abandoned. They'd left behind something like twenty computers, a giant hard drive. Shit that required our expertise. So, I went." He sighed.

Lynette stayed silent, leaning into his shoulder, the deep rumble of his voice in her ear. "We drove straight into a fucking trap. We took a dozen very smart Marines directly into it. And I was one of three who lived." He put his forehead to her shoulder. "I can't stand myself most days. That I lived. You know? Even though I'm ruined, can never have a normal life again, thanks to the attack. But honestly, I didn't care. I wanted to die with Dan."

She put her hand to his cheek then brushed his hair off his forehead. "I'm glad you didn't die, Cole," she said, pressing her lips to his, tracing their outline with her tongue. "So very glad." She shed the robe she'd been wearing and straddled him. Her need to comfort, to fix, to make him smile again nearly overpowered her.

"I'm not so sure," he said, settling his hands on her waist, his face still pensive, distracted. "I held him. Heard his last words. It was the worst thing...ever..." He hesitated. "Although this has been pretty amazing, and not something I ever thought I'd want. Now, somehow, I feel guilty. Like I shouldn't be allowed anything this wonderful, ever again."

"I know what I want," she whispered in his ear, never more sure of anything in her life.

Cole held on to her, his head still pounding with the residual nightmare and the confession session. He smelled her arousal, sweet, heavy, sexy, just like he had first identified it—like thick honey but with an undercurrent of something that made his libido roar and his heart pound with need. She kissed him, tracing his lips with her tongue while he tried very hard to dispel the images of Dan from his head.

Liz Crowe

"It's like, if you're going to be blind, it's better you start out that way. So there's no memory of sight." She held him close. "I remember Ryan. I saw him. But I never got to see you. And I hate that."

"Here." She put his hands on her breasts then moved them up her arms, tangled them in her hair. "You can see me this way. I want you, too, so much." She sighed into his skin, making him shiver.

He tightened his grip on her. "Lynette." He pressed his face to her neck, sucking in huge breaths of her.

"Shh," she said, shifting slightly against his now painfully hard cock. "It's okay."

His hands roamed all over her, his lips slid down her neck, nestled into her breasts as he gripped her ass. "Dear God, but I need to be inside you. Is it...okay?"

Lynette smiled into his hair. Ryan had been so insistent on the condom thing. He was crazed about it, but Cole had been stubborn. He liked to feel Lynette without the latex. So, they'd had physicals and tests, proven their sexual healthiness, and Lynette had gotten a diaphragm because the pill gave her migraines.

At that moment, something in him reared up with a need so powerful it terrified and compelled him all at once. It was beyond a compulsion for release. It was more elemental than that. She wrapped her arms around his neck and found his lips.

"It's fine," she said, angling her hips and allowing him to penetrate her, stretch her, forcing a moan of pleasure from her lips. "Please. Cole, I need you."

He thrust high, gripping her hips. "We can't. We shouldn't." Cole was on fire. This whole thing was insane. This woman made him mad with lust, made him want to fuck her into oblivion then hold her all night long. A woman—who would have guessed?

She rolled her hips, gripped him hard, clutching his face and kissing him. He lost himself in her, her scent, her flesh, and something gut deep and primal pulled at him. He stood, sweeping anything that might be in the way on the table to the floor and dropped her onto it. She wrapped her arms and legs around him He dove into her with his cock, into her mouth with his tongue. He wasn't just blind, he was deaf and dumb to everything but her.

"Cole!" she cried out, arching up. He caught her nipple in his mouth, sucked hard and joined her, diving over the orgasmic edge with a loud mutual cry of satisfaction. He went up on his toes with the effort of pounding into her, filling her, while she clutched at him, her body seeming to hold him even deeper than usual.

They kissed, calmed, and he pulled her up from the table. "Wow," he murmured, edging toward the blessed rest he always got post-orgasm. "Take me to bed, you minx, before I fall asleep on the kitchen floor."

He heard her then, the hitch in her breath, the distinct sob she was holding back to prove how tough she was. He put his palm against her face. "I love what you've done to me, for me, and with me."

She nodded, her tears wetting his fingers.

"Jesus, you two." Ryan's scratchy voice behind them made him jump. "Nice show. Thanks. Now, let's get some fucking sleep, okay?"

Chapter Twenty-Five

The next morning Ryan rolled over, draped his arm over Cole's hip and sighed when his brain prodded him awake at the usual ungodly hour of five a.m. He kissed the man's neck, sat up and saw Lynette curled into Cole's other side. He smiled, wondering how in the hell he'd gotten this lucky. Even when he'd caught them fucking on the kitchen table last night, all he'd gotten was a warm, tingly feeling instead of any kind of possessive jealousy that might seem more obvious.

He stretched, thinking through the day. He needed to get Jamie from Quinn and Audrey's and he had promised to take all the kids to a movie tonight — trading out for keeping his son last night. A worthwhile swap, he mused, as he stood and stared at Cole's bare torso, rising and falling in a calm sleep. Besides, now that Quinn's boys had received and accepted the presence of Audrey in their lives, they were much calmer, less demanding and more fun to be around.

He jumped in the shower and let the pounding hot water bring him more fully awake, mentally flipping through his to-do list. He needed to check in at the brewery on some of the projects they had going for judging at this year's National Beer Fest in Colorado. He felt they had a lock on a couple of categories, but his natural inclination was to baby the brews along, checking on them day and night. He toweled off, threw on some fresh clothes and wandered into the kitchen, shaking his head at the mess Lynette and Cole had made when they'd decided to screw on the table.

He cleaned up the floor and rooted through Cole's pantry for ingredients to make pancakes. After assembling everything in a big bowl, he set the griddle on high and sipped some coffee. He loved the quiet order of a morning kitchen. His mother had imposed that on him, with her insistence on a sit-down breakfast every day of his life until he left for college.

He and Quinn had never had the same one twice in a row, between fresh blueberry pancakes, omelets, homemade biscuits, muffins — the works. *'Start the day right,'* she'd say, kissing their father goodbye at the door. When the day arrived that the man did not come home from his job at the insurance company, disappearing with the secretary and about ten thousand of the company dollars, Moira had set her lips in a thin line and coped, like she always did and always with a belly full of breakfast.

"Smells good in here." Lynette leaned in the doorway, covered in a robe, her red corkscrew curls all over the place. He pointed to the coffeemaker.

"Help yourself. These will be ready soon."

She poured a cup, set it down and wrapped her arms around his waist from behind. Ryan's heart pounded a little faster. *Just sex.* That was the arrangement and he, for one, hoped to keep it that way. In the last week or so, the simple domesticity of their time together had felt more comfortable than ever. He would never admit it, but if there were a way to wake up every day like this, together, three of them, he wouldn't reject it.

Utterly impossible, Shannon. Get a grip. What the hell do you tell your son? 'Hey, uh, Jamie, here's your new mom…and Uncle Cole sleeps in dad's bed, too. Okay?'

He shook his head.

"What's wrong?" Lynette muttered into his neck.

"Nothing." He set the bowl down and turned, taking her in his arms. "You feel great," he said, lowering his lips to her neck, tasting salt and a distinct tang of need.

"Why, yes, thank you, as a matter of fact I do. Feel great." She stretched her arms up and Ryan made a grab for her exposed breast. "But…" She backed away, retying the robe. "You okay with…you know, last night? I don't want there to be weirdness. You know? Jealous bullshit?"

"If we're all together, I don't care who does what to whom." He flipped the pancakes over, let them finish then slid them onto a plate.

Lynette grabbed one and bit into it. "Together? What do you mean? We are together, right?"

"I mean, together, literally. Like last night. It doesn't feel like sneaking around and, as far as I'm concerned, it's not. But if you feel a need to have him fuck you or whatever, and I'm not around, I may have an issue with that."

"Fair. And same goes for you."

"Fair." He got out butter, syrup and honey. "And we stick with the birth control plan, right?" He stared at her. Her gaze flitted away just enough to worry him. "I am dead serious about this, Lynette. I'm glad we got the diaphragm thing sorted out for you. That takes a lot off my mind."

"I know. It's fine." She poured a cup of coffee for Cole, who'd just wandered in the room, rubbing his face. Brutus led him to a seat, then made for his food bowl after stopping to let Lynette rub his ears. She set the cup down in front of Cole and let him pull her into his lap.

"I have a great idea," Cole muttered into her neck, trailing a hand up her thigh. "You need to make a beer that tastes like this." His hand went higher, disappearing under her robe.

Ryan laughed and brought the plate of food to the table. "Dude, if I could make a beer that tasted like pussy, I would be a zillionaire by now." He put a plate in front of Cole and started eating. He was starved and watching the two of them cuddle was making him horny again.

"No, numb nuts. Like her — like, honey, and red colored, since you call her that, and maybe a little bitter, you know, to match her smart mouth."

Lynette laughed and took her own seat, grabbing several pancakes for herself. "Bitter? Me? Nice."

"Hmm...you know," Ryan mumbled around a mouthful of food. "I've never tasted a decent honey-infused common."

Lynette poured half the bottle of syrup over her stack. "But how much honey would it take to really affect that kind of a brew?"

"I'm gonna look into it," Ryan declared. "I like it."

"Sweet Bitter Honey," Cole said. "For Lynette."

Ryan laughed and grabbed Cole's hand, putting it to his lips. "No, for us. Like Lynette."

She smacked his shoulder but smiled. And Ryan got that weird, extra thump-thump in his chest when he looked at her, then at Cole.

Chapter Twenty-Six

Cole woke with a jerk, reaching up to wipe his eyes attempting to dispel the blackness that would never be dispelled. The phone was clanging Audrey's ring tone. He reached for it, then remembered he was not at his house. Lynette stirred on his left. Ryan sat up on his right, grabbed the device and handed it to him.

"We're headed to the hospital," Quinn barked in his ear. "Something's wrong. My mom's here with the other boys."

"Okay, we're on our way."

Lynette crawled out of bed, and he heard the shower start up.

"No time," Cole barked, finding his jeans where he'd left them on the floor. They'd practically ripped one another's clothes off, the six weeks between encounters too long for them all. But real life as a threesome had its challenges along with rewards and their schedules simply hadn't meshed with Ryan's need to have Jamie out of the house when they stayed over.

Audrey had seemed okay the day before when he and Ryan had dropped the boy off at his cousins' new place. She'd done her usual grumbling about being as big as two houses and cursing the Shannon twin gene for her misery. A thrill of fear shot down his spine.

"I'm not going," Lynette called out.

"The hell you aren't," Ryan yelled, jumping around trying to get his shoes on. "Let's go."

Cole sat, tried to get his bearings. Quinn's words rolled around in his head. "C'mon, man." Ryan dragged him up. "Time to go meet our nephews."

"It's too early. Her C-section isn't scheduled for another three weeks."

He felt Lynette's hand on his shoulder. He gripped it like a lifeline, panic making his chest tighten. Brutus bumped his leg. "Yeah, boy, that's right. Let's go already!" Ryan declared.

The ride to the hospital was longer than he thought possible. Thoughts of his sister rolled through his brain. She put on a huge show of being a super-strong Wonder Woman but he knew deep down she was one hundred percent terrified by this whole radical turn of events in her life. He put his face against the cool car window. Lynette touched his shoulder from the backseat. Ryan grabbed his hand.

"It will be fine. I'm sure."

Cole nodded and ignored them. He still couldn't believe his sister was having twins. Which explained the odd double heartbeat sounds he'd been getting not long after the wedding. While it was annoying beyond belief sometimes, hearing everything that no one else did, it came in handy at others. He'd touched her stomach that day, leaned in and told her to have the doctor check for a second heartbeat. She'd laughed him off for about a minute, then called her doctor's office and told them she was coming in right away.

He jumped out with his dog when he felt the car come to a halt, and made his frustrating slow way through the 'where the hell is my sister' process. Finally, he sensed Lynette by his side, talking calmly to the annoying staff. He followed her, the horrific and overwhelming smells of a busy hospital making him want to gag and run for the exit door. He gripped Lynette's hand and let her guide him.

After an interminable elevator ride, they emerged onto a quieter floor. A different set of sensations hit his nose and ears. He gulped and held on to Brutus' lead. Ryan joined them and they sat and waited. "What the hell is taking so long?" The man stood and paced, but Lynette stayed seated and quiet by his side.

"Quinn!" He heard Ryan from what sounded like the end of a tunnel. He clenched his jaw. "God, somebody throw the waiting room a bone, here."

The silence that met his ears had Cole on his feet, stumbling toward Ryan's voice. "What is it? Ryan? Somebody better start talking to me, right fucking now." He felt Ryan's hand on his shoulder.

"She's fine, Cole. C'mon, I'll take you to her." Quinn's voice sounded raw.

Cole jerked out from under Ryan's hand. "Don't hide anything from me. Damn you. What's really going on?"

He heard it. Quinn's heart — stuttering, then pounding. He lunged toward the man, using his base instincts to find him, grabbing at his throat in desperation, thinking to drag the words out of him. Ryan yanked him back. "Relax," he whispered, running a hand down Cole's arm. "It's fine."

"God damn it." Cole stood, fists clenched, in his eternal fucking darkness, needing them to stop hiding shit from him. Lynette slid under his arm.

"Quinn, Ryan, tell him."

He heard both men blow out identical breaths. He gripped Lynette into his side.

"Okay, so, Audrey's been having headaches for about a day or two, but we figured it was just stress or boredom or something," Quinn began.

"Why didn't she say anything when we —"

Lynette leaned into him. "Shh, let him finish." Her lips grazed his jaw. He nodded.

"Uh, yeah, so...she was up tonight, couldn't sleep, as usual. I sat with her a while, then fell asleep on the couch. And, uh, shit." Cole heard the man's voice break. "I woke up at three, sat up, realizing she hadn't come back into the family room." He cleared his throat and Cole realized he was either crying or on the verge of it. "I can assure you, Cole, that the sight of my wife lying on the kitchen floor in a pool of blood is not something that will exit my consciousness anytime soon. I gotta go, I need to see the boys. Fill them in on the rest, Ryan."

Cole sensed him leave and turned to Ryan. "The boys," he said, breathless. "They're okay?"

Lynette watched the drama unfold between the men. She bit her lip and tried to keep the rubbery, plastic, gross hospital smells from making her puke.

Hospitals were her least favorite place on the planet. And this whole thing with Audrey and her kids was making her antsy. She wanted to leave. She needed to stay. She stood, hands clenched together, and let the memories of the past few months wash over her.

Finally, she put a hand on Ryan's arm. "Why don't I pick Jamie up and take him home?"

Ryan glanced up at her, his green eyes snapping. He put his arm around her, which soothed her, but also made her want to run away screaming. "That would be great. Sorry. No. Don't," he said. "Stay here with us. We're gonna see the boys."

"No, no." She backed away, trying to keep from covering her mouth and running to the bathroom. Terror washed through her when the kitchen encounter she'd had with Cole weeks ago flooded her brain. Why she hadn't thought of it until now she had no idea, but there it was—she'd taken her diaphragm out already that night.

Holy fucking shit.

"I've gotta go."

Cole pulled his sunglasses off and rubbed his eyes, talking as if he hadn't heard her. His hands shook. "The boys are okay," he said. "Tyler is in the neonatal intensive care, but Lucas isn't. They think Tyler will be fine in about forty-eight hours. He was smaller, his lungs weren't ready or something."

"And Audrey?" She wanted to go into their arms, to make them hold her and face the reality of what she suspected together, but she simply couldn't. Ryan would have a cow. And he'd be right to do so. She'd promised to take the birth control thing seriously. And she hadn't, for whatever reason, that night. She clenched her eyes shut.

"Stable, resting. It's all okay. An emergency, but that's what decent hospitals are for." Ryan put his lips to her forehead. "Go home. Get some rest. Jamie's fine where he is."

"Call me?" she asked, gulping back the saliva that flooded her mouth.

Cole yanked her close. "You're sick," he said, putting his lips to her cheek. "No fever, though. What is it?" He held her arms, suddenly tense with worry.

She mentally cursed the man's ability to sense things about her. "Nothing. I'm fine. I just don't like hospitals. Congrats, guys, really. But I should go. I'll...I'll be around tomorrow."

She avoided both Cole and Ryan for a solid two weeks, needing space to process what had happened that night, on the kitchen table, with Cole without protection, their base need for each other outmatching their logic about birth control.

Dear God, what if she really was pregnant? Ryan would shit bricks. What in the hell would she do? How could she tell them?

There was a big beer and food festival in Chicago that week so she packed up and left without seeing them. She managed to avoid phone calls and texts for the most part while there. But the last night of the event, she owned up that it wasn't fair to the men who kept trying to contact her, so she texted them and informed them both that she was fine, busy, and for them to focus on Audrey and the kids.

By the time she got home, Audrey had been released with Lucas, the healthier of the baby boys. Lynette dropped her stuff at her apartment and agreed to meet Ryan at Quinn's house. She took a quick shower, then drove to the outskirts of town to the house Audrey and Quinn had bought, complete with a barn for horses and twenty acres to ride.

She sat a few minutes, gripping the steering wheel and steeling herself to see Ryan. A knock on her window made her jump. Quinn was there, smiling at her. She sighed and climbed out. "Hey, you all right?" he asked. "I was just down at the barn, watching the boys get saddled up for their riding lesson. You look like shit, no offense. Chicago that rough?"

"Uh, yeah. You know. Party, party, party." She gave him a weak smile. "So, when does Tyler get to come home?"

Quinn's face split into a huge grin. "Monday, thank all the gods. Audrey's going nuts not having him here. C'mon, Ryan's already here."

Lynette followed him in, her feet dragging like they were mired in sand. She wasn't ready to face Ryan. Not yet. But there he was, in all his tall, sexy, amazing glory. His face lit up at the sight of her. Her heart raced and her brain yammered at her to go to him. Let him hold her so she could confess what she suspected, but couldn't bring herself to admit.

He folded her into a huge hug, kissed her cheek and guided her inside. "Missed you," he whispered, cupping her ass. She stepped out of his reach. He frowned but Audrey called out then, so they walked into the huge family room where she had an impossibly tiny baby draped over her shoulder.

"I think he just threw up down my fucking back. Ryan, where the hell is Quinn?"

Lynette grabbed one of the many clean cloths lying on the table and handed it to Ryan who took the baby from Audrey and wiped her shoulder. Audrey stood and stretched, wincing a little when she limped toward the kitchen. "I swear I'm going fucking crazy. I can't stand not having both of them here, but he's such a handful…I… There you are." She stepped into Quinn's arms and he held her, whispering in her ear. Lynette bit her lip, moved by their connection and more than a little jealous of it. Ryan bumped her arm.

"Hey, want to hold him a sec? I need to wash my hands."

"Oh, no, not really, okay." She sighed when he put the tiny boy in her arms despite her protests. She'd spent a lot of years in high school and college holding other people's babies, not to mention her years in college making money working in day care centers. She was comfortable doing it but somehow, today, she felt klutzy, out of it. She sat, jiggling the baby and watching his lips purse in his sleep.

She looked up and saw Ryan move around the kitchen, assembling sandwiches for lunch. She swallowed hard, wishing like hell she could tell him her fears, but knowing it was hardly the right time or place. Audrey came back in and sat, put her feet up and sighed.

"If he's asleep, you can put him in his bed, over there." Audrey pointed to the two tiny cribs in the corner of the room. Lynette placed the sleeping boy in one of them.

"I'm going up to the hospital," Quinn stated.

Audrey's eyes flashed. "Yes, please make them tell you why they won't let him go yet. I don't like how that pediatrician keeps avoiding my eyes."

"Yes, ma'am." Quinn walked over to the crib and kissed his son's cheek. "Later, brother," he called out to Ryan, who waved from the kitchen.

"So, when are you going to tell him?" Audrey asked, keeping her voice low, after Quinn had left. Lynette frowned at her.

"Tell who what?"

Audrey pointed to her stomach. "Tell one of those men he's a dad."

Lynette's mouth dropped open. She clapped it shut, only to have it drop open again. She must look like a pure idiot. Tears stung her eyes. She swallowed hard.

"I don't know for sure. I mean, I haven't taken a test. I think I'm avoiding it. How can you tell?"

"I don't know, really, a hunch based on the fact that you look like ten miles of bad road and that you just confirmed it. Well?" Audrey's face was serious.

"I…I'm not sure. I mean, I don't know that I am, really. You know? And I don't think any of us is ready for it. I…" She slapped her hand over her lips when a wave of nausea smacked into her from nowhere.

Audrey pointed down a back hallway. Lynette got to the bathroom just in time. She gripped the edge of the sink and tried to rein in the dizziness after she threw up, then walked back out to the family room, attempting to look normal.

"Listen, Lynette, I am not judging you or Ryan or Cole for that matter. I haven't seen my brother this happy since…well, ever. So, whatever you guys are doing, more power to you. But…" Audrey took up the conversation as if Lynette had never left the room.

She sat, rubbing her lips with a tissue. "It's Cole's," she whispered. "Ryan is…" She glanced over her shoulder at him still puttering around in the kitchen. "Ryan is, was, adamant about birth control. I have a diaphragm. But I, well, I can't."

"Sister, I am not one to talk about forgotten diaphragms or condoms or any of it. Trust me. And believe it or not, I'm not going to encourage you to tell him, if your mind is made up already. Do you have…support? A ride, if you need one?"

Lynette nodded, although she didn't really. A sudden urge rolled through her to see Cole, make him help her convince Ryan it would be okay, and talk her out of the abortion she'd convinced herself to schedule while she was in Chicago. Ryan touched her shoulder, making her almost leap out of her skin.

"Sandwich?" he asked.

She shook her head. "I need to go." She stood, feeling a fraction stronger now that someone else knew her secret.

"Uh, okay." He stood, staring at her. "Call me later?"

"Yes," she said, kissing his cheek. She gave Audrey a quick hug and touched baby Lucas' still sleeping form. Resisting the urge to make the drive over to Cole's, she got home and drew a hot bath, ignored her mother and locked the bathroom door so she could think.

Chapter Twenty-Seven

Cole sat, hand on Brutus' head. The breeze coming through the window helped ease a fraction of his stress. The IT security business he'd envisioned was going gangbusters, and while he didn't regret it exactly, it was definitely more of a pain in the tail than he'd anticipated. Jake was still around, working his sales magic. The guy was smart, great with the public, getting them so many accounts Cole could hardly keep up.

But this latest assignment was giving him a serious tail-chasing vibe. A Detroit casino had hired him, promising a six-figure payoff if he could come up with a way to do what they wanted — provide one hundred percent security on all their networks, including casino floors, the entertainment venues and all six hundred of the guest rooms. But he couldn't convince them to dump the 'free wireless' concept, which was the open door invite to hackers. They kept insisting that he solve it without 'inconveniencing' their many guests.

He ran a hand through his hair and leaned back. The fact that he hadn't seen or heard from Lynette in over two weeks was making him nuts, too. He knew she'd been out of town but couldn't understand why she'd remained incommunicado since she'd gotten back. Granted, he'd been buried in work, and the awkward nature of his new business-only relationship with Jake took a lot of emotional energy. The upside was he slept better, his nights rarely haunted by dreams of fire and of Dan.

His phone rang—Ryan's ring tone. He smiled and answered.

"Hey," he started.

"I saw her today."

"Oh?" Cole's pulse pounded in his temples, but he kept his voice cool. "And how is she?"

"Looked a little ragged around the edges, but the Chicago event is long and intense."

"Sure. Okay. How's the boy?"

"He seems good. Audrey is going nuts not having them both home. You coming over later?"

"That's my plan. Ride is due here about four."

"What are you doing now?" Ryan's voice sounded strange.

"Working, trying to justify the dough the Motor City Casino just deposited in my bank account. Why?"

"Because I'm standing on your porch. Can I come in?"

Cole frowned and let Brutus lead him to the door. He put a hand on Ryan's chest, felt how hard his heart pounded then gasped when the other man yanked him close and covered his lips with an urgent kiss. He let go of the dog's lead and wrapped his arms around Ryan's neck. The hard planes of the other man's body, the rough rasp of his cheek and the distinct press of an erection against his hip made him groan when his cock rose to the occasion so fast he got dizzy from the lack of blood to his brain.

"I need you," Ryan whispered, biting his ear and lifting his shirt off before yanking his jeans down around his ankles.

"Wait, I thought we wouldn't...holy mother of..." He grunted when Ryan pushed him back on the couch, dropped to his knees and swallowed his cock all the way down. He felt a finger under his balls, another hand tugging his nipple.

His hips thrust up as he gave in to the raw, pure erotic perfection of the moment. One devoid of emotion, a need to impress or worry about pleasing anyone — the simple pleasure of getting off that he'd shared with many men.

"Stop," he croaked out. "I don't want to come this way."

Ryan took his hand and yanked him to his feet. Cole relieved him of his shirt and jeans, fumbling in his urgency. "I need you," Ryan said, pulling him close for a kiss. "So much," he whispered, pressing Cole onto the couch. Cole sighed with pleasure when Ryan coated his ass with lube, teasing him with a couple of fingers before looming over him, his cock pressing inside, making him groan and angle his hips upward so he could take Ryan all the way.

Suddenly, he smelled her, could practically taste her sweetness on his tongue. He heard her moans, her laugh, felt her hair under his hands, the bone structure of her face when he touched her 'seeing her'. A combination of amazing sensations filled all his senses. The smell of man, of Ryan, of his lust, the sensory memories of Lynette, all of it made him reach for his own aching cock.

"Deeper," Cole cried out when the climax burst across his brain. He came into his hand just as the other man let out a low moan, his left leg giving that tell-tale spasm he always had right after orgasm. "Yeah, baby. Just like that." Cole sighed, hanging on to Ryan's shoulders. The ghostly honey scent floated across his brain again. He frowned, wincing when Ryan pulled out.

"Nice." He heard her then, fury dripping off her every word. "Very fucking nice."

He grabbed his jeans and pulled them up, using his shirt to wipe the cum off his belly, nervous, embarrassed and starting to panic.

Ryan sucked in a shuddering breath and turned to face her. Lynette stood in the door, dressed in jeans and a brewery T-shirt. Her curly red hair floated around her shoulders and her eyes snapped with anger, but her face was pale, gaunt, with dark circles under her eyes he hadn't noticed earlier.

He had no idea why he'd come here and done this with Cole. If he were completely honest, it was a lot of desperate horniness mixed with worry about Lynette, his nephews, his brother and sister-in-law. Mostly he wanted to fuck something, and a simple, physical, man-to-man connection seemed logical. But now he'd allowed his selfish urges to put a look of such hurt in Lynette's eyes, he had to lower his gaze to the floor, unable to meet her stare. He'd done it again. He'd let his base, selfish needs hurt someone he loved.

"So, were you just pretending I was in the next room, Ryan? That get you past the whole having a problem with sneaking around thing?" She took a step toward him. Cole stood at his shoulder, breathing heavily. The dog whined. "Or is that rule just a guideline the rest of us have to follow to make you happy with yourself?"

"Hold on," Cole said, sitting down and pulling his sunglasses back over his eyes. "Rules? What rules? Ryan...what the fuck is she talking about?"

Ryan's chest constricted. He stared from Lynette's eyes to Cole's confused face. He had no answer. None at all. He sighed and reached for Lynette.

"Don't touch me," she snapped.

"I think you should go," Cole stated. Ryan stood between them, torn, furious and terrified that he'd ruined everything in a fit of horny selfishness.

"No, listen, guys, I'm sorry. I'm just —"

"I'm pregnant."

Ryan's vision narrowed. He locked in on Lynette's face while a slow-burning indignation lit a fire in his brain.

"Um, what?" Cole said, getting to his feet.

Ryan held out an arm to hold him back. "Really? Lynette, how could that be? I thought we had an understanding about birth control. All three of us."

Cole shoved his arm down with a strength that only hinted at what he might be capable of and pulled Lynette into his arms. She stood, not returning his embrace.

"You're a selfish shithead." She disentangled herself from Cole, glaring at Ryan. "You think you can just fuck us, both of us, one of us, whenever you want. Is that what this is about? We're a couple of Ryan's playthings whenever he wants them, just as long as we follow his rules?"

Cole yanked his sunglasses off. "I'm not a plaything, Lynette. He didn't rape me, for God's sake. We aren't cheating on you. But, of course, you guys seem to have some kind of pact you didn't let me in on so, maybe we were. Fuck."

He grabbed Brutus and tried to shoulder past them, but Ryan held on to him. "How pregnant are you, Lynette?" He kept his voice light, but he was seeing red around the edges of his vision and knew he had to keep a grip on his temper, lest he make this worse than it already was.

"Enough to know, thanks." She crossed her arms.

"Good, I'll drive you to the clinic. Get in the car."

Cole grabbed his arms and shoved him hard, making the back of his skull connect with a bookshelf. "You do not get to decide that." His voice was low, a warning Ryan chose to ignore. He pushed the man off him, making the mistake of thinking Cole wouldn't lash out.

Big mistake.

Pain exploded in his jaw, then his gut when carefully placed punches thrown by a trained killing machine landed precisely where they were aimed. He grabbed Cole's arm when the man hauled back to do it again. Ryan was no slouch and was bigger.

"You guys are pitiful," Lynette spat out. "Can't keep your stupid hands or cocks off each other, fucking or fighting. Jesus." Ryan held tight to Cole's arm, sensing the man's rage just under the surface. Brutus had Cole's other hand in his huge mouth, trying to tug him out of what must appear to be a dangerous situation for his master. "I don't need your goddamned ride, Shannon. I can drive myself to get an abortion, thanks. And you." She glared at Cole, who turned his face to her. "You should ask him about his rules sometime. About how we share but only if we're all together, in the same space. He used you today, Cole. Sorry to break that to you."

Ryan let go of Cole's hand, taking a chance the guy would not try to hit him again. He grabbed Lynette's arms, but she shook him off.

"Fuck you, Ryan Shannon. Fuck you and your 'sex only for now' bullshit. I'm done. I'll be taking a couple of days off. Got myself a medical emergency." Ryan winced and felt Cole's temper about to burst like a thundercloud over all of them. "But this whole experiment." She made a circle with her finger indicating the three of them. "Is finished."

Cole gasped and tried to pull her to him. "No, wait, Lynette, don't."

Ryan gaped at them both. "You guys have got to be kidding me." He let the anger fuel him and the words tumbled out, burying him even deeper. "This is not what we are about. We are a threesome for sex. That's all I want. That's what I thought you wanted, but obviously, I was wrong. In case you forgot, I have a family already, one I didn't expect, but it's all I need."

He let go of Lynette's arm and stepped back. They both stared at him, or at least appeared to, making his heart leap into his throat, regret making his temples pound. "I'm sorry. I...I didn't mean it that way." His voice was barely above a whisper. He meant it but knew it was too late. He hadn't meant anything more than the fact that adding another child to the mix would only complicate everyone's lives.

But, boy, did you just sound like a selfish motherfucker.

He groaned and touched his aching jaw.

Lynette ran out, slamming the door behind her. Cole stalked out of the room, turning before he went into his office. "Get out of my house. Get out of my life. I'll be at Audrey's tonight, so I don't want you to be there. I mean it, Ryan." He held up a hand. "We're done." Then he shut the office door with a firm, quiet click, which in many ways was even more final than the slamming front door.

Chapter Twenty-Eight

The hell was back. The headaches, sensory overload, throat-closing dread and the deep darkness of his reality closed in on him. Cole sat at his computer, ignoring the worried noises from his dog and the pinging of incoming emails. His phone rang—Jake's ring tone. He ignored it. He had done the dumbest possible thing. Been untrue to his nature, fallen for a woman, while being manipulated by a man to suit his own selfish pleasure.

He stood, a ball of nervous energy, needing forward motion. By the time he walked out of the office and into the kitchen, he realized he hadn't eaten all day and decided to find some food to help some of the churning in his gut.

Brutus was excellent at guiding him around to the various areas of the kitchen so he could function on his own. He could even cook some things alone. Brutus would bark when necessary and the stove had a loud timer he'd retrofitted with a Braille control panel. He put a pot of water on for noodles, grabbed a beer from the fridge and downed it while sitting at the table, brooding.

He wouldn't let Lynette do this alone. While part of him loved the thought of a baby—his baby—the practical part of him knew that was patently ridiculous. He had no business being a father, or so he kept telling himself. It was her body. She should and would do whatever she wanted about it. But he wished she'd let him help her, somehow.

He got another beer, grateful that Brutus would let him know when the water boiled. The second beer, plus all the emotion of the past hours or two made his eyes droop. The table's cool surface felt good on his hot face. He drifted off, knowing he'd meet Dan in his dreams. And he did.

The dog's frantic barking woke him. That and his lungs' urgent need for air in the smoky kitchen. He must have fallen to the floor, but could feel the heat from a fire that must be slowly engulfing the counter nearest the stove. The harsh smell of burning wood and plastic made him gag. He felt mired in lethargy, as though he was drugged, but kept coughing, unable to move.

The other fire surrounded him again. His about-to-be-ruined eyes burned, pain from his broken leg made him grunt and grab it, only to find it healed. He heard noise, yelling, gunshots. His head pounded as his lungs tried to suck in clean air only to find it full of poisonous smoke.

Something grabbed his hand, something sharp. He rolled onto his back. The world narrowed to a tiny pinprick, and he heard him—Dan—calling for him, crying out his name. He tried to roll back over and get to his hands and knees but couldn't.

"Lynette!" he yelled, but it came out a weak whisper. "Lynette, don't…" He wanted to cry, but his ruined eyes wouldn't allow it. His face was wet from something. He touched it, tasted salt on his fingertips then couldn't hear or feel anything else.

* * * *

"Hey, hold this one, will ya?" Audrey poked his shoulder and Cole held out his hands for a nephew, loving the baby smell that permeated him. "He's fed, but won't go to sleep. Work your uncle magic."

He nodded and coughed, his lungs still weak from the kitchen fire that ruined half his house. The little boy snuffled around, making mewling sounds. Cole kissed him. "Settle down, little man. Give your mom a break."

Tyler had come home finally but was still on a monitor twenty-four-hours a day and Audrey absolutely refused to leave him on his own. Especially after one scare that sent them back to the hospital for an overnight in an oxygen tent, so the household took turns being awake with him.

Cole didn't mind. He loved it. Frankly, the feel of his nephews in his arms was the single thing that grounded him in a tiny bit of sanity and kept him from doing something permanent about his misery.

He had steadfastly refused to let Ryan or Lynette near him while he'd been in the hospital a few days after the fire. Mortified for being so irresponsible as to almost burn the house down like some kind of invalid, he was grateful that at least all the computers and servers had survived.

The fire department had been able to contain the blaze to the back corner of the house. But, of course, he couldn't live there anymore. He palmed the baby's back and shifted down on the couch so the boy was nearly horizontal on his chest. He kept patting, soothing, both Tyler and himself. He stayed awake per Audrey's orders but let his thoughts drift while the infant rooted around before he fell asleep.

He wondered how Lynette was, if she'd recovered from her procedure, if Ryan had made the Sweet Bitter Honey beer and whether he'd ever retrieve that magical, connected feeling he'd gotten when he was with them both. Something was pulling at him, making him want to be up and out of here, on his own again. While that seemed right, it also terrified him at the same time. Audrey put a hand on his cheek. "Sleep, Cole. I'll sit here and feed Lucas. The bigger boys are around, so if his alarm goes off, somebody will hear it."

Cole nodded, groggy from lack of sleep. He still didn't have a handle on Quinn's other twins, but they seemed to be getting used to him now that he lived in their house. One of them, Nathan, had started reading to him the day he showed up from the hospital, burns on his hands, his lungs still weak, and alone once again. He was enjoying the *Harry Potter* books, but actually liked talking with the kid. He was a quiet, smart boy, while his brother Alex was loud, showy and, best Cole could tell, an asshole in training.

He let sleep take him. And entered the dark, quiet place where even Dan had abandoned him.

* * * *

Lynette sat on the hard plastic chair and filled out the medical forms—she had no allergies, no heart murmur, asthma, religious objections to blood transfusions. It was all very innocuous, as if she was there for a checkup. Her hands shook when she lied to the receptionist about having a friend coming later to pick her up. She mentally concocted an excuse for the phantom friend's eventual nonappearance. How hard could it be?

The waiting room felt like the inside of the cooler at the brewery. She rubbed her arms and turned in the forms, smiling weakly at the perky girl behind the desk, ignoring the rest of the women sitting around the room. She clutched her hands, pretended she was doing the right thing, making her choice as a strong, independent woman. A woman with no husband or even boyfriend to help her out, a job she wanted to keep and zero support otherwise.

"Lynette?" A nurse appeared at the door, her smile so wide Lynette winced. Jesus, these people could at least act sad. This was sad. This was bullshit. She shook her head and followed the woman down a sterile hall. She sat, got her vitals taken, had to endure a painful, boilerplate counseling session. *No, I don't feel okay about this. No, I don't really want to be here. No, I don't want to talk about it. Can we please just get the fuck on with it?* Words she didn't say but thought, loudly in her head.

"Okay, Lynette." The perky nurse was back, grinning at her like they were buddies about to get matching mani-pedis. "Get changed here, then I'll be putting the IV in to give you something to help you relax. The whole procedure only takes a few minutes. I don't see your friend yet, though. You should call and check on them before we give you any meds."

The door shut. Lynette sat. Unshed tears clogged her throat. Of all the tears she'd allowed herself while with her men — tears of joy brought on by tapping deep wells of emotion she'd forgotten she possessed — it seemed they'd dried up since catching Cole and Ryan alone, fucking, when she'd come over to tell them the truth. Memories of Cole, his beautiful green eyes, his words, his body and soul overwhelmed her, making her clench her eyes shut.

And Ryan, his brutally handsome but angry face, harsh words about their sex only arrangement, the first time they'd had sex...made love...when he'd been so gentle and loving. The men, at each other's throats, the poor dog trying to break it up.

Lynette Williams, you are a fool. Get this done. Get back to your life and leave all that shit behind.

She'd contacted the headhunter again, determined to get the fuck out of Ryan's orbit for good, hoping she could escape by leaving Ypsi Brewing altogether. She comforted herself with the memory that Ford had called her back for a second interview two weeks ago, so there was still that possibility hovering on the horizon.

She clutched the generic hospital gown and stared at her hands. Then she stood and looked out onto the busy parking lot. The memory of Cole's voice that time — when she'd conceived this kid on the kitchen table — ghosted through her brain. She knew damn good and well she'd had no diaphragm in and had taken him anyway. She clenched her jaw, gripped the curtains and let a rogue tear drip down her cheek.

She hadn't spoken to either man since rushing to the hospital the night of the house fire. He wouldn't talk to her then, anyway. Audrey claimed he was embarrassed, thinking everyone would assume he'd tried to kill himself again. But it had been an accident. She'd kissed his cheek and left the hospital room, unsaid words making her throat ache. Ryan snagged her on the way to the elevator, his eyes wild with worry. '*He's fine,*' she'd said, unwilling to engage in conversation beyond the basics.

'*I know,*' Ryan had said, tugging her close. '*How are you?*'

'*None of your business anymore.*' She'd moved out of his reach, leaving a piece of her heart in his hands before walking away.

Now, she put a hand on her still flat stomach and let what was left of her heart lead. She put her clothes back on, opened the door and handed the gown to the nurse who stood, waiting with her IV needles and drugs. "Thanks, anyway," she said, squaring her shoulders and walking out the door, already talking to the baby inside her. "It'll be okay, kid. My mom will help, and she'll only make us a little nuts."

Chapter Twenty-Nine

Ryan groaned and rolled over, reaching for his man, his woman. Then opened his eyes and picked up the heavy mantle of loneliness he'd put aside when he finally fell asleep the night before. He'd had baby duty the night before, happy to help. But he'd forgotten how much work it was.

Willing to go along with Audrey's somewhat paranoid insistence that Tyler never be left alone until the doctors let him sleep without full monitoring, he'd walked the floor holding the kid while he cried, then slept. His head ached, his heart pounded. He needed Cole. He wanted Lynette so badly he could feel it like a physical spike of pain in his gut. But the man had stayed sequestered in the guest room, and Ryan hadn't the energy to try and lure him out.

He had no one to thank for the present state of affairs but himself. He knew that. Plus, he'd nearly lost Cole again. Despite what Audrey had said, he knew that whole fucking fire thing was his fault.

He sat, tried to rally the energy to get on with the day. Lynette had been completely distant, not communicating with him beyond the necessary words of work. He kept wanting to ask her questions, to make sure she was okay with everything. She'd been gone for three days, during which time he assumed she'd taken care of it. And of course, that was his fault, too.

He rose, took a shower, got dressed, drank coffee, played his father role and went to work on autopilot. Lynette was there already, doing her thing and ignoring the shit out of him. As usual.

Quinn called about halfway through the day. "Cole went home today."

"Oh?" He tried to remain casual. "The new place?"

They'd decided to buy a new house, a handicapped accessible one, for him, about a mile from Audrey and Quinn's place. A fresh start, sans memories and bullshit. Ryan thought it was a good idea. And only wished he could help. But he'd done enough already, hadn't he?

"Yeah. Audrey's not happy about it. She's having some kind of serious let-down moment right now. But on the up-side, Tyler's off the monitor."

"Great." He felt lame but had no words while he watched Lynette through the maze of stainless-steel fermentation vessels. She was leaning back, talking with one of his younger brewers. They guy smiled at her, touched her arm. They both laughed and the look on the guy's face made the hair on the back of Ryan's neck stand up.

He gritted his teeth and looked away. He'd slammed that door shut but good with his reaction to her news and his selfish sharing rules bullshit. She wasn't his to possess or be jealous of or even care about anymore.

But he did. So much so that it kept him awake every night.

"You okay?" Quinn's voice sounded a million miles away.

Ryan sighed. "I've made my bed, brother, and now I'm wallowing around in it. Nobody's fault but mine."

"Well, that is just about the lamest shit I have ever heard come out of your mouth. And I've heard my fair share of it."

Ryan winced at his brother's angry tone, mainly because the man was right. He'd never shied away from what he wanted. Why he couldn't manage to reach out to either of the people he loved right now, to at least make some sort of amends, was beyond him. He felt encased in cotton, numb, marking time and avoiding what mattered. And he couldn't seem to change that. "Yeah, well…"

"I hear Lynette is leaving us."

Ryan sat up, his face burning. "What?"

"Yeah, she put in her resignation yesterday. I thought you knew." Quinn's voice trailed off. "Well, anyway…"

"Exactly. I gotta go." He tossed the phone down on the table and waited a half second before bellowing out that asshole kid's name who was eyeballing his woman.

Hold up, Shannon. Not your woman. Not anymore.
Fuck it.

"Hey, Roberts! Get your ass back here and show me how you jacked up my fermentation log with your bullshit entries."

The kid scurried back to him. Lynette met Ryan's gaze for a few seconds then turned away. The rest of the day was a blur of work, avoidance, checking on the

Sweet Bitter Honey, which was in secondary fermentation and smelled heavenly.

He suddenly wished Cole were here, sticking his nose in the beaker of rich red, honey-infused brew. Fury washed over him. He dropped a beaker of the brew into the sink, watched in shatter into a zillion pieces before he stomped out of the brewery, out to his truck and pointed it toward home. He touched the quick dial on his steering wheel and smiled when Jamie's voice filled the cab. "Hi, Daddy. Can we go swimming? Tracey said we could."

"How about this, buddy—how about I pick you up early, like now, and we not only go swimming, we get ice cream for dinner?"

"Yay, Daddy! Ice cream for dinner!" The kid dropped the phone with a clatter that echoed around in Ryan's ears a second until he realized Jamie had forgotten to hang up. He set his jaw. Time with his son had been rare lately. He'd been so focused on his own selfish needs.

This was good—getting him back on track, thinking about what was really important, like his family or what was left of it. Without fully acknowledging that he considered both Cole and Lynette as family, he cranked the radio and ignored the throbbing empty space in his soul—where he'd had true happiness once and managed to toss it away.

Chapter Thirty

Lynette watched Ryan stomp out of the brewery after letting a beaker of her namesake brew shatter in the large sink. She gulped and had to grip the leg of a tall fermentation vessel to keep from running after him. She missed him so much. They'd developed such a great working camaraderie both before and after climbing into each other's pants. She cursed herself for letting it get too personal. Plus, bonus, she was on fire with lack of attention, that much was certain.

Her hormones were like a roiling stew, making her hot, cold, ecstatic and irrationally furious in turns. The doctor said that she should be able to hear a heartbeat at her visit in about two weeks and the crippling nausea had ended, leaving a void of horny energy she had a tough time dispelling alone.

She sighed and leaned her head against the cool metal. She had to leave, even though she was worried about her new insurance plan covering what would be a fairly obvious pre-existing condition. Now that all the doctor visits, hospitals and shit were mapped out in front of her, it made her a more than a little breathless. It was an expensive thing, this pregnancy, and at the end of it she'd have a child to support.

She pulled her phone out of her pocket and tried not to call Ryan, but she wanted to hear his voice so badly, to relay this mess, get his advice. Anything. But he'd made it clear that her getting pregnant was the end of his interest in her, period. And Cole still wouldn't respond, no matter what she did.

She had talked to Audrey and Quinn, but even they had no explanation for the full shutdown that Cole had embraced. Maybe if she told him the truth, that she was still pregnant, it might help. She shook her head. No, this was her issue now, not anyone else's.

A tiny voice of reason reminded her that she could tell him, should probably let him know and that would likely break down his new emotional stronghold, the one that resisted both her and Ryan. But her stubborn streak clicked in, prohibiting it.

While she stood pondering her dilemma, her phone buzzed with a call from Audrey. "Hi, how's the baby farm?" she asked. Audrey had been a good friend through all of this, but even she couldn't convince her brother to let Lynette back in his life.

"Oh, fine, smells like puke and shit, and I don't think I've had a shower in about a week. But, you know, great. Listen, I just dropped Cole off at his new place. I left him there because he wanted to be alone, but..."

"I'm not going to his house, Audrey. He doesn't want to see me any more than Ryan does."

"Sweetie, you aren't trying hard enough. Those boys may think they are stubborn alpha males, but I think you need to take over, show them you know what's best. I swear you guys could make it work."

"No." Lynette leaned back against the fermenter.

Audrey's silence filled the space in her head. Lynette cleared her throat. "What about...you know, the dog thing?"

Audrey sighed. Lynette heard a small cry. "The trainer was there with the new dog and Cole actually seemed glad, willing to listen and learn this time. Because of his history, the Purple Heart and all that, he got pulled ahead for a new program, one that actually supports vets and their service dogs. It's a girl dog this time. Daisy."

"Oh, well, that's..."

"Yeah, I gotta go handle some kind of baby disaster, but I wanted you to know that he's there, and I think he misses you, a lot. The trainer is also a veteran, so Cole's probably getting whipped into shape on many levels right about now."

Lynette ran a hand over her eyes. "I'm glad for him. He needs this. I miss him, so much." Her heart ached with remorse. If asked right then, she wouldn't even be able to enunciate which 'him' she meant. She'd give anything to see them both, hold them, let them hold her and soothe some of the near constant anxiety out of her.

But it was too late. Between the three of them, there was just too much stubborn bullshit. It wasn't worth the effort. It would never work. Their own personalities and issues and society's inability to accept a true polyamorous relationship precluded any sort of serious domestic arrangement. It would likely be more of what they'd had already—intermittent blazing hot sex, interspersed with long periods of time apart pretending that they were just fuck buddies.

"Oh, honey," Audrey said. "I know you do, but this is up to you now. Take control and don't let the men ruin everything. Okay?"

"Okay. Maybe. Probably not." She rubbed her side, which had been aching in yet another weird way, like everything about her lately.

* * * *

The next few weeks flew by and before she knew it Lynette could sense her body change, adjust. Every time she brushed the small hard bump under her shirt, she couldn't help but smile. She'd ended up turning down the Ford marketing job and had told Quinn and Audrey the truth about the baby, but had threatened them within an inch of their lives if they told either of their brothers anything more than the bare facts.

Besides, Ryan had gone out of his way to avoid her for weeks. They barely communicated, leaving their assistants to handle the sales meetings for them.

According to Audrey, Cole had been whipped into shape by his new dog trainer who practically lived at his new house. Audrey claimed it was the best possible thing for him.

"I wish you would just go see him and tell about the baby," Audrey said during their weekly catch-up phone call.

"Well, I might. I don't know. Something is holding me back." Lynette had looked down when her phone dinged with a new incoming call. Cole's number flashed, making her breathless. "Uh, he's calling me now."

"Good, go, make up to him and Ryan. You have to fix it, Lynette. Otherwise, it will never happen. You know that."

Her heart stuttered at the sight of his name on her phone's screen. She would never in a million years admit it to anyone, but she missed her men, both of them, so much she cried herself to sleep almost every night, like the lame, weepy, knocked-up woman she was. The thought of life without them, even as complicated as it was together, made her miserable. But she was damned if she could figure out how to fix it now, with so much water under the bridge and time spent not communicating.

She clicked over to Cole's call without another word. "Hi," she said.

"Oh, uh, hey."

"Did you butt dial me or what?" She tried to keep it casual, but the sound of his deep voice made her break out in a chill.

"No." The silence spun out. Lynette let it. "I got a package. And, um, was wondering if you'd help me with it."

"A package? What are you talking about?" She pushed herself away from her desk.

"A box came in the mail, about a foot square. I had the postman read me the return address. I think…" His voice broke. Lynette was instantly on the alert. "I think it's from Dan's mother."

"I'll be right over." She tossed her stuff in the car then called Audrey.

"What's Cole's new address?"

"Thank God!" Audrey said and gave it to her before hanging up.

She pulled up in the driveway of a tidy-looking brick ranch house, complete with a ramp, rails and all sorts of things indicating accessibility. It was nestled in a tree-lined neighborhood of similar-sized homes, the streets and sidewalks full of little kids riding bikes, skateboarding or playing in sprinklers. She got out, took a breath and walked to the door. It opened before she could knock. Cole was there, holding his sunglasses. The new dog stood next to him, tongue lolling out, but he wasn't holding on to her. "Aw, look at this one." She crouched down and let the dog lick her face. "She's pretty, Cole. What's her name?"

"Daisy," he said, his jaw clenched. "And trust me, we are bonded, thanks to the hard-ass ex-Marine who trained us."

"Relax, honey, it's okay." She put a hand on his shoulder. He flinched, so she took it off. "Where's the package?"

Chapter Thirty-One

Ryan laughed when Jamie ran for the pool, arms and legs pumping. He jumped, scattering a few families that were already there. "Sorry." Ryan slipped in and grabbed the kid before he drowned. They splashed around, threw a Frisbee, played Marco Polo and variations on that annoying theme for a couple of hours.

Ryan had made a point to do this weekly now, after their first impromptu swim a few weeks ago. He was determined to at least get this part of his life right — the part where he was a half-decent father to his son.

A harsh conversation with none other than his own mother, the usually supportive Moira, ghosted through his brain. He'd been sitting late at night, sucking back bourbon and wondering if he'd ever feel good about anything again, when she'd called. He'd grabbed the phone at the sight of her name, thinking some one of their many aunts, uncles or cousins were dead, given the usual nature of her late-night calls. She'd been staying with Quinn and Audrey a few days, taking her turn at holding one twin infant while the other one got fed.

"Ryan James Shannon," she'd began right away, making him wince and wish he'd ignored her call. "I did not raise you to be this person."

"Ma," he said, biting down on a bourbon-infused ice cube and staring back out into the night sky. "I'm not in the mood."

"Don't you talk back to me, young man." Something in her voice made him sit up straight, put the booze glass down and pay attention. "I just had a very distressing conversation with your brother and I want you to tell me just one thing."

He let the silence expand and fill the space where he should be answering her, like he'd been raised, as she liked to remind him. But his throat hurt, his head pounded and he was suddenly propelled straight back to that moment when the doctor had handed him his son. His heart pounded and his skin got clammy. He stood up and paced.

"Did you break up with that lovely girl because she was pregnant?"

"Um, huh?" This was not what he was expecting.

"And that young man, Audrey's brother, why aren't you talking to him? He is a wounded soul, Ryan, and if what I am hearing about you is correct, you not only walked out on Lynette, you left Cole behind, too, for reasons I refuse to accept."

Ryan made a mental note to kick Quinn's ass for spilling his secrets. One thing he'd always wondered was how he could possibly explain the nature of an honest to God three-way relationship to the woman whose opinion he valued above all others. And now, apparently, his do-no-wrong brother had done it for him.

"Ryan, love." His mother's voice softened, making him tense because he knew that meant harsh words were imminent. "I realize you've had a hard go of it. You put so much of yourself into being an athlete, and I let all those coaches convince me to let you do it, to focus on nothing but that for so many years. Then, when it was taken from you, you did exactly like I feared you would. You collapsed and became a shell of the man you could be. Then, God brought you a son, our sweet boy Jamie, and you returned home, and..." She paused for a breath and Ryan resisted the urge to be a cynic about 'God bringing him a son,' knowing that would be the wrong move at this point.

"Oh, Ryan." He could tell she was near tears, which she had used so much in his life to exacerbate the guilt she could lay thicker than mortar. "I don't pretend to understand you and the choices you make with...men. I love you more than life, and I want you to be happy. But you are being a right arsehole now, and I will be damned if I'll let you."

"But, Mom, you don't understand."

"I do understand one thing. You must make this right. At least agree to talk with these people. Don't pull away, turn in on yourself like you do, not now. They need you."

"No, Ma, they're just fine without me. Besides I'm got Jamie to focus on and the brewery and—"

"Ryan." Her voice was sharp and angry and strange to his ears. "I know you're trying to be a good father, and I love you for that, but there are more people in this equation now, partially thanks to you. Quinn tells me you were the catalyst for the...um...relationship and the one who ended it, for reasons no one understands other than to say 'oh, you know Ryan can't take the responsibility or the pressure.' And that, young man, I will not accept about you. Not anymore."

Ryan rubbed his eyes, sat and stared around the pool, letting his mother's words poke holes in his psyche. She was right, but he had no idea what do to about it. Shit just happened to him, he justified. Cole had been in his path one day and so he'd acted on it. Lynette had appeared in his life and so he'd done the same with her. She'd suggested making it three, so he'd facilitated it.

And now?

Now, it was up to him. He had to fix it. But terror coated his brain. Fear that they would reject him and that it could be too late paralyzed him. *And that, ladies and gents, is Ryan Shannon in a nutshell it seemed – the reactor, the non-actor, the passive grown man with a son and an empty bed and heart.*

He tried not to groan aloud when he flopped back onto the lounge chair, listening to Jamie's delighted squeals while he raced around the sandpit with some buddies.

Ryan brooded and glared at the happy family groups. He was such a shithead. Such a loser. He'd clutched happiness in both hands and had tossed away – why exactly? Because life hadn't gone like he'd planned? Because Lynette had forgotten birth control once? He'd used the people he loved, made them feel like…what had she called them? Right, playthings. Making up rules he got to break to keep the equilibrium of their triangle to his liking.

He sat back up, watching his son scamper around the other, larger boys. Poor kid – stuck with a single dad who barely knew the first thing about raising children, other than making sure he had a good breakfast. He dreaded the coming years — the adolescent angst, girlfriends, underage drinking or pot smoking or whatever the fuck it was teenagers did.

He sank back, putting an arm over his eyes. Visions shot across his brain — Lynette, their first time together, the amazing feel of her body against and around his. Her soft lips, sweet smell, crazy laugh and bizarre sense of humor.

Jesus, he missed her. And not just the sex, either, although lack of that had turned him into an adolescent with a boner anytime he saw her. He loved how great she was with Jamie. How she fit in pretty much any place or situation she found herself. Jamie kept asking for her, too, which was annoying, since Ryan had no decent answer or excuse about her absence.

And Cole — Ryan winced, thinking of his handsome face, deep voice, tough-shit demeanor and his hard, rough, masculine physique, hotter than anyone had a right to be. The few times they'd fought had been epic, but they had matching temperaments and when the three of them were together, it was indescribable and sublime — and he fucking wanted it back. Permanently. He didn't care who knew or disapproved.

He was nearly forty years old, a single parent, and he was lonely. He'd been proactive about the sex part. It was time to get his shit together and work for the emotional connection he knew he wanted. He jerked up, realizing he must have dozed, unnerved by a shout to his left, his dad radar homing in on the noise.

He shielded his eyes from the late-afternoon sun. The group of boys that had just been in the sandpit was gone. The swimming area was fenced in, so it wasn't like they could get out anywhere or anything. He heard the shout again, this time around back, at the snackbar. He jumped to his feet, his vision tunnelling. Something was seriously wrong and he sensed it. Rounding the corner, he saw a group of kids in a circle, and several moms with phones to their ears, looking frantic. He sought out Jamie's bright blue trunks in the group, his brain absolutely refusing to take in what his eyes showed him. His boy was the one on the concrete encircled by other kids, his face ashen grey, his small body completely still.

"Hey, there he is! Mr. Shannon, something's wrong with Jam—"

Ryan pushed past the pimply teenaged lifeguard and jerked the boy into his lap. "Somebody call..." His voice faded when he realized his son wasn't breathing.

An older lifeguard grabbed Jamie, laid him on the grass nearby and started administering CPR. Ryan sat, incredulous, unable to process it. The mothers were fluttering around. "Did he choke? What did he eat? Is he allergic to anything?"

Ryan heard it but didn't at the same time. Allergic? He had no idea. Nothing had indicated that before, although he did get a rash when he ate too much peanut butter—which was pretty much all he would eat for a period of time about a year ago.

He must be choking, Ryan reached out, needing to touch the boy's still hand when the EMTs appeared with a gurney and took over. Ryan stood and watched, frozen with helplessness while they worked to get his son to breathe again and experienced his entire universe collapsing inward on itself. He wanted his family, but he'd ruined that, and now?

"Lynette," he whispered as he watched them try to revive his son. "Cole, somebody call..." He slumped back to the grass, realizing that he neither deserved their support nor did they owe it to him. But he needed it now more than anything. He couldn't do this alone anymore.

Chapter Thirty-Two

Cole sat, trying to ignore Lynette's cloying scent. Her honeyed essence was somehow magnified, multiplied times a thousand, probably because he hadn't seen her for so long. He had to clench his hands into fists to keep from yanking her to him, kissing her, holding her, shaking her silly for being so obstinate. He gritted his teeth. Ignoring the wet nose of the dog that was not Brutus, he found the package on the table and pushed it toward her. "Can you open it? Tell me what it is?"

He heard paper ripping, tape being removed. Then his ears picked up on something else, something strange and yet familiar. He tilted his head, then decided it was just the dog. He reached out and felt Daisy's soft head. It was okay. Not Brutus, but fine. He scratched her ears, nervous, waiting. The dog put her head on his leg, whining. "It's okay," he whispered.

He truly did feel centered with this dog in his new house. The new pain-med cocktail kept the headaches at bay much better. For the first time in over a year, he was beginning to feel a bit like the old Cole, thanks in no small part to Frank, the guy who'd literally lived with him the last two weeks, reminding him that no real Marine would wallow and allow the lame funk he operated under. Frank and Daisy were a package deal, the man claimed. Cole didn't get to keep her without the come-to-Jesus portion Frank provided.

'*You are alive, Marine,*' the man had barked after Cole had cursed him to high heaven for the second or third time, while he sat sullen and brooding, sunk in his now comfortable morass of pain and self-pity. '*Get on your feet and listen to me.*' Frank had been a drill sergeant, no surprise there, and the familiar cadence had snapped something into place inside Cole's brain. He'd jumped to his feet, fast, and stood, listening carefully while Frank commanded him.

'*You are not allowed to be this way, not anymore. You're fit, a survivor, a Marine-forged bag of muscle and bones, and I will be damned if I let you sit there and sulk your way through the rest of this life.*'

Cole's body had tensed, and his heart had pounded but he'd felt it then. The small beating pulse of purpose, starting somewhere in his gut and working its way up to the base of his skull. Flashes of sensory memory — sights, sounds, smells and touches from Dan, Ryan, Lynette, Audrey, his baby nephews — made him flinch but he had stood tall and firm and kept listening.

'*I will not allow you to toss this chance away. This dog was trained at great expense to be your eyes, your companion, and you sit there and ignore her like so much shit on your shoe? Hell, no.*' Frank had been in his face then, breathing heavy and speaking straight into Cole's by now eager ear. '*The enable-Cole-to-be-a-lame-ass time is fucking over. Do you hear me? This.*' He'd grabbed Cole's hand and put it on the dog's harness.

He'd shivered all over, guilt and anger running rampant through him.

'*This is your new reality, and you are too smart, too strong and too worthwhile to let it slip away because you are a whiny-ass child. You are not a child. You are a man. Fucking act like one. Now.*'

Frank had kept talking. And Cole had kept listening. And by the time the man had left, he felt good. Not great—that would likely never happen again now that his time with Ryan and Lynette seemed over—but good and independent enough to allow a small bit of satisfaction to creep in under all the usual 'my life sucks' bullshit that he'd been living with for the last year and half. He even entertained the concept of reaching out to Ryan and Lynette, once his emotional boot camp was over, hoping he could relay some of his own remorse at how he'd acted to them both.

Then, this package showed up the day after Frank left, and he'd called the first person he thought might help. Ryan had ignored him. So, his next call had been to Lynette, and he'd never been happier to sense another human being in his space.

"Um, let's see, there is a picture. You and…oh, this must be Dan."

He sucked in a breath. His hands shook. "What else?"

"A handwritten letter—looks like it's from Dan's mom. And what looks like a flash drive taped to a piece of paper that says "To Cole, from Dan.""

She rustled around some more, and he heard them. The distinctive clink of metal on metal. He put his head on the table. She took his hand and put the clinking metal in it. He closed his fingers around Dan's dog tags, felt their edges cut into his skin.

"And one more thing," she whispered. He sat up, held out his other hand and clutched the fabric of what must be a folded American flag to his chest. His chest constricted. "Cole," Lynette said. "Honey." She put her hand on his face. "Take a breath."

He did, but it made a noise, and he realized it was a sob. He sat, gripping his dead lover's dog tags and the flag they'd draped over his coffin, crying like a fucking girl. Lynette came around behind him and put her arms around his neck. They stayed like this a while, until he got control. "Read it to me, please?"

She sat. Cole heard the rustling of paper, and that same strange, almost sub-radar blipping noise, but the sound of Lynette's voice drowned it out.

Dear Cole,

My name is Janice Anderson. Daniel was my son. My only child. I hope you can understand and forgive me for taking so long to do this, but I was only able this past month to go into his room and open up the box of his stuff that the Marines sent me. I feel terrible about keeping this from you, but please know it wasn't intentional. I knew my son well. He was smart, talented in the kitchen, athletic, loving and gay. And I was proud of him.

Lynette sucked in a breath and continued. Cole's eyes burned, but his heart was starting to release a small fraction of the agony he'd lugged around since coming home, blind and alone.

He had a package of stuff with your name on it, including this photo of him with a handsome, blond man sitting on a beach who I assume is you and this computer drive. I didn't access it, because it had your name on it. He left one for me, too. He recited his favorite recipes to me, told me how much he loved me and his father, who died not long after Dan's accident. He read us some passages from a few of my favorite books – The Great Gatsby, Of Mice and Men, Pride and Prejudice. *And sang me a song – my favorite Rolling Stones tune, actually. I've listened to it so many times I get angry at myself for waiting this long to find it.*

It's obvious to me that he loved you. He said so on his recording. Told me about how you met, how smart you were, although you tended toward being an overbearing asshole, pardon my French. And how right you were for him. I don't know if you realize this, Cole, but you were Dan's first boyfriend. His first real sexual experience. I didn't know that until he told me on the recording, and part of me wishes I still didn't. Some things are better left private even between parents and children. But there it is. He somehow knew he wouldn't be coming home from that horrible place and he wanted me to know everything.

So, I'm giving you as much of him as I can and ask that you forgive a lonely woman's tardiness, her inability to face reality and go through her dead son's things in hopes of finding something special – which I did. I found you.

Yours sincerely,
Janice

Cole shook all over. His head pounded. He stood, bumping his legs against the table then sat, still clutching the dog tags and flag like a little kid with his blankie. His mind was blank, dark, on fire and frozen all at once.

Lynette touched his hand. "Do you want me to plug in the drive? I can leave you with it. So you can have some privacy."

"No!" he croaked out. "Please d-d-d-don't leave. If you don't mind listening with me, I mean. Use my laptop. Should be on the coffee table."

"Sure thing," she said. "Come, sit by me."

The dog led him to the couch. He dropped onto it, still hanging onto the tags for dear life. He let her put her arm around him but sat frozen and stiff against her.

Lynette held his hand and they listened to the sound of Dan's voice, the words rolling through him like waves, making his head pound at first, then somehow, relaxing him. When he began to sing in between reading from their favorite books, the second the first lyrics of a sappy Alan Jackson song rolled out into the room, Cole couldn't breathe. "Turn it off..." he croaked out, grabbing Lynette's hand hard. "God."

But Dan's voice kept coming. He read more passages from his favorite books. *Catcher in the Rye, The Old Man and the Sea, The Stand*, even some non-fiction stuff Cole liked like *The Tipping Point* and *The Blind Side*. Long stretches of nothing but reading, bringing the man back to him as though he'd never left. Cole kept a death grip on Lynette's arm, mesmerized.

Then a new sound, a second voice. Cole's. Laughing while he taught the hapless kid to play poker. Or tried to anyway. He gulped, remembering how that session ended. Dan stopped recording before their arguments about the statistical unlikelihood of having two royal flushes in one game ended in loud, energetic sex in a hotel room.

"Oh, Cole." Lynette held him close, rocked with him back and forth. Dan spoke after reading a few more snippets from books, recited the sports stats of his favorite baseball team—the Reds, which Cole had almost forgiven him for—and his favorite football team — Ohio State, which Cole would never forgive him for. He said simply, "Cole Traynor, I love you. Now go and live your life. Because I know you're not — you're holding back something, probably from someone who loves you as much as I did. I release you. I want you to be happy."

Cole identified it then — the unmistakable sound of a small fluttery heartbeat. He dropped the dog tags and the flag, turned to Lynette and gripped her arms. "You didn't do it, did you?"

She stayed quiet, sniffling.

"Answer me, damn you." He heard her sharp intake of breath. "Oh, please, Lynette, please tell me I'm not hearing things." His voice sounded strong to his own ears, reflecting a strength he'd retrieved, thanks to Dan's recording.

Finally, he knew what he wanted. She stood, drawing his ear to her stomach. He held on to her, listening, gripping her so she'd never leave him again, then spoke. "I knew he was a virgin. He was a lot younger than me, and so amazing."

Lynette ran her hands through his hair, soothing, calming. He let her and then he sensed it again — the sound of his baby's heartbeat.

"I love you." He stood, holding her close and kissing her so hard he didn't know where his lips ended and hers began.

She broke away. "I'm so scared, Cole. Ryan is… Wait, did you say you loved me?"

"Shh…" He put his fingers to her lips, ran them across her cheeks, nose and eyes, brushed away her tears. "We'll get him back. It will be fine. And yes, I did."

Both of their phones rang within seconds of each other. He pulled his out of his pocket. It was Audrey's tone.

"Quinn's calling me," Lynette said. Cole felt a lick of dread in his gut when he answered.

He listened to his sister's voice a few seconds before he dropped his phone. He heard Lynette's gasp, felt the dog dancing around his ankles. The dog that wasn't Brutus...

Cole gritted his teeth and let Daisy's softer, less aggressive presence soothe him. She was a licker, which was something Frank had tried to break her of, but Cole didn't mind. She got nervous, or thought he was, and she licked his hand until he told her to stop, but usually not until he actually did feel better for it.

"It's Jamie," he said. He grabbed her arm. "Get your keys. Let's go."

Chapter Thirty-Three

Lynette raced into town from Cole's new neighborhood, cursing and running red lights while Daisy barked enthusiastically. Cole white-knuckled the armrest. "Jesus, Lynette."

She ignored him. Her heart was pounding so fast it hurt. Her eyes burned. She had gotten one of her men back and was ready to work on the other one. But Jamie, he was… "Oh shit." She hit her brakes and screeched to a halt at the red light before the hospital.

Cole put a cool hand on her arm. She started to shake him off but something about his touch calmed her. He peeled her fingers from the steering wheel and kissed them. "It's okay. It will be fine. It has to be." He let go of her and faced ahead again. "I mean, if you don't fucking kill us and my new dog getting there."

"Don't be a backseat driver. It's unbecoming." She scratched away from the signal, jerked the wheel to the left and was jumping out of the car at the emergency room nearly before she had the thing in park.

Cole and Daisy followed on her heels. They skidded to a stop at the security check. Lynette tried to relay that it wasn't her or the blind man with her who needed help. They were there to find a boy. "My nephew," Cole piped up, gripping the dog. "James Shannon."

"Cole!" She heard Audrey's voice, saw the woman's tired eyes when she rounded the corner. "I just came down to find you. They moved him upstairs to the pediatric intensive care unit."

"Fucking-A, Audrey, what happened to him?"

"Anaphylactic shock. Turns out he's allergic to cashews."

They got in the elevator. Lynette held on to Cole's hand as Audrey gave them the details. Jamie had been having a reaction for the better part of an hour they believed, having been given a trail mix fruit and nut bar by one of his friends' moms. He'd been itchy, the boys claimed, his eyes kept watering but he'd been playing in the pool and the sand so they figured he was just overheated, with eyes full of pool water. By the time the kid's mom had figured out something was wrong, he'd had a grand mal seizure and stopped breathing. That was when Ryan had found him.

"Oh God." Lynette put a hand over her mouth. Cole tightened his grip on her other hand. "Is he...I mean..."

"He's still out. The problem is, even after they got him breathing again, he wouldn't, he won't, wake up. They aren't a hundred percent sure how long he was without oxygen." Audrey sucked in a breath, rested her hands on the elevator rails. "Ryan is catatonic. He won't talk to anyone, not even Quinn. Well, except when he's roaring and tearing the medical staff new assholes because they won't let him hold Jamie."

Lynette's heart clenched. Ryan and Jamie's bond was special, she knew. She'd observed it first-hand. This was the worst possible thing that could happen to him. She leaned back, waiting for the elevator doors to open. Audrey turned to them both. "Listen to me," she said, her green eyes snapping. "Get your fucking shit together. He needs you."

"Our shit is fine, sister dear," Cole said, putting Lynette's hand to his lips then touching her stomach. "All of it."

"Good."

The doors opened and Lynette rushed out, her need to see Jamie for herself so great she nearly tripped over Quinn, crouched down on his ankles outside a closed door. He stood and pointed to the glass window. Lynette peered in, saw the boy's small form dwarfed by the bed, all sorts of bleeping monitors surrounding him.

"Jamie," she whispered, touching the glass. As if he heard her, Ryan looked up, still clutching his son's hand. His face was hard, set, angry. She bit her lip. The self-loathing and fury hovered around him like a dark cloud. "Can I go in?"

"No," some bossy nurse said, without even looking up to see who spoke.

"But, I'm..."

"This is the boy's mother," Cole said, shoving her in the door. "Thank you very much." Lynette looked over her shoulder. "Go. It's okay," he whispered to her.

She made her way over to the bed, terrified, horrified and sick to her stomach. Jamie's face was gaunt, his chest rose and fell on its own, but his eyelids weren't moving. She touched Ryan's shoulder. He didn't look up, kept his gaze trained on the boy, a small hand clutched in his large ones. They stood together, watching Jamie breathe for nearly an hour in complete silence.

"You didn't do it, did you?" Ryan's voice was raw, rough, when he finally spoke.

"No. I didn't." She knew what he meant. "I love you, Ryan. I love what we had. And I want it back."

He glared up at her then resumed his visual vigil. "Well, I'm sorry to hear that."

"Why?" She put her hand on his neck, hoping to dispel some of his tension. "You love me, too. I know you do."

"You don't know anything about me." His voice broke. He rested his forehead on the bed.

"I know enough," she said, leaning down to kiss his cheek. "Can he come in? If you tell them, and I go..."

"Good luck with that."

She backed out of the room, motioned for Daisy to bring Cole forward. He put a hand on her face. "You okay?"

"I'm fine. And if you spend the next seven months asking me that every minute, we are going to have an issue. You go in." She opened the door. "Hurry before Nurse Ratchet gets back."

Ryan's eyes ached but he refused to take them off Jamie, as if by watching him he could force the kid back, make him wake up with the sheer force of his will. He heard the door open and close again but ignored it. He clutched his son's hand and tried like hell not to yell and throw anything.

How in the fuck had he not known? This was his only son and he'd failed him. Let him eat something that almost killed him.

"Hey." Cole's low voice made him shiver.

"How did you get in here?"

"Told them that dog therapy was the best thing for situations like this."

Ryan glanced down and saw the yellow lab with the pink bow on her service harness. It all crashed in him then. He stood, stumbled away from the bed. He'd lost his son. He'd been given one simple thing to nurture and he had fucking blown it. Cole stepped forward and let the dog sniff around the bed. Ryan put his hands on his head, willed his heart to stop pounding and watched while the dog made concerned noises down in her throat.

Cole whispered something Ryan couldn't hear. His brain was starting to shut down. Jamie would never open his eyes again, he just knew it. He'd never hear his delighted giggle or hear the 'yay, Daddy' words from his lips. He slid down the wall, his head on his arms. He felt tears form but could not let them fall.

A sudden noise made him look up. He gaped at the sight of the huge yellow dog, now up on the bed, whining and nosing at Jamie's hand. Then amazingly, she stood over him and licked his cheek. "Cole, get her down." He started to rise.

Cole held out a hand, his face still trained toward the bed. Ryan took a step closer, threaded his fingers through Cole's and watched Jamie's eyes flicker and move under his eyelids. When they opened, their deep green was the most beautiful thing Ryan had ever seen. The crazy nights of colic, the anger at the kid's druggie mom, his early resentment at the whole mess dispelled in his brain. All he saw, all he heard, all he felt was the pure unconditional love that the little boy threw his way every single day. "Jamie," he whispered, still holding on to Cole's hand.

The dog looked up, wagging her tail like mad, still perched on the bed. She licked the boy's face again, softly, slowly until he looked right at her and smiled. "Yay, Daddy! You got me a dog!" The boy sat and threw his arms around the animal's neck. She sat, panting and grinning at the men.

"Yeah, buddy, we got you a dog." Cole sat, put his arm around him while Jamie kept a death grip on the lab.

"What in the name of heaven is going on in here?" The nurse burst in, trailing a couple of doctors. "Shoo, shoo, get down." She glared at the men. Cole started to let go of Ryan's hand, but he held tight, watching the doctors check out his son. The dog resumed her spot on the floor next to Cole.

"Good girl," Cole muttered.

"Amazing girl," Ryan said, looking up and catching Lynette's eye. "I love you," he said, looking at Lynette and speaking to Cole. And he knew he'd never spoken truer words in his life.

Chapter Thirty-Four

"Ow!" Lynette lurched up from the couch, hand to her back. Daisy ran over and tried to put her slobbery dog mouth around Lynette's palm. "No, no, I'm fine, sweetie. Just getting too awkward for my own good." The dog whined and licked her knee then went back over to Cole who sat nearby, plugged into his headphones, working.

In the last few weeks, Ryan and Quinn's mother, Moira, had jumped in with both feet and had convinced Lynette to have her mother evaluated by a doctor. They'd discovered that she was suffering from early onset dementia, which would be tough to handle, but at least she'd agreed to hire a live-in helper — paid for by Quinn and Audrey. "Go," she'd whispered to Lynette. "Be with your men. And don't you ever tell me two isn't better than one." Lynette had blushed to the roots of her hair before holding her tiny, bird-like mother close.

Ryan came in, holding a tray of cheese, bread and a six-pack of beer. She narrowed her eyes. "No fair. I can't drink."

"You'll drink this. It won't hurt the kid much, I promise." He showed her the carrier. It was emblazoned with the Ypsi Brewing logo and woman's head with curly red hair who wore a set of dog tags around her neck. "Sweet Bitter Honey has just won a gold medal at the National Beer Fest, I'm told by my assistant brewer. Congrats." He handed them each a glass, and they lifted them together.

"Holy shit, dude, you can really do this, can't you?" Lynette smacked her lips, staring into the rich, amber-colored liquid. She frowned, stuck her finger in it to grab something that seemed to be clanking around the bottom of the glass, then sucked in a breath. "What the hell?"

She grabbed Cole's from him, under his loud protests, and made him put his finger in it, guiding him to a small object at the bottom. She sat with Cole who had an adorable, puzzled look on his face, staring at Ryan and palming a small platinum ring. Ryan plucked the glass from her, still half-full.

"What is this, Ryan?" Her voice was soft. Cole put his hand on her leg.

Ryan leaned over, took the ring from her and slipped it onto her left ring finger, then did the same with Cole's, who was still speechless. "This is just us, making a commitment, in front of each other for now."

"But..." Cole spluttered. "We are, we can't, Ann Arbor is liberal and all, but even this might be a stretch for the kids' school forms."

"I want this, I want you and I don't want there to be any ifs, ands or buts." Ryan gripped their hands and put them to his heart. Lynette bit her lip and leaned in to touch her forehead to his, while putting her other arm around Cole's neck, drawing him into their circle. "You and Cole should get married, legally, so the baby has...you know..."

"Fuck that," Cole said, standing and pulling them with him. "Lynette knows I'll take care of my child, financially and otherwise. We don't need a legal document for that."

"We have to be realistic, Cole." Lynette knew Ryan was right. "Let's do that, take the legal step so there aren't any questions, ever." She pulled Ryan close. "I want an attorney to spell it out clearly — Cole and I are the baby's biological parents, but you're a legal guardian. We can do this. I've been checking. And we can be together, all of us." Her new resolve about this was steadfast. She didn't care who knew or what they thought, not anymore. Not at the risk of sacrificing her ultimate happiness.

"You're okay with that?" Cole pulled Ryan close, and the two men stood, making Lynette's breath catch in her throat at the sight of them.

Ryan nodded. "It's my idea, so, yeah. But after the baby is born, I want to have a commitment ceremony, for all three of us." He grabbed their glasses and handed them back out. They clinked them softly, then sipped. Ryan took hers away after she'd just had a taste of the amazing, rich, sweet red brew.

"Enough for you, little mama," he said softly.

"Ugh, this sucks." She flopped back on the couch, putting her feet up on the coffee table, staring at the ring on her finger that matched the ones both of her men wore. Ryan and Cole drained their glasses. Then Ryan winked and pulled her to her feet, folding her into his arms. He nuzzled her neck and cupped one of her newly lush breasts. "How about you show off some of that epic sex drive tonight?"

She sighed and leaned back, letting her overheated libido take over. "Baby, I don't know if even the two of you are enough for me lately." She groaned when Ryan brushed his hand along the curve of her stomach, reaching down to press his finger against her sex.

Cole came up behind her, turned her chin around and captured her lips. "We'll take that challenge."

She let herself fall into their arms, completely confident they would catch her. They each took a hand and lead her back to the bedroom that Cole had outfitted with a California King bed, a cushy chaise lounge and a spa-worthy bathroom including a tub that would easily hold three people. Ryan eased her down, propping a huge pillow under her head, kissing her lips then lower, sucking her newly sensitized nipples. Cole took up the kiss, and she sighed, stretching and letting relaxation and happiness course through her. The men's hands met over the mound of her stomach, fingers entwined. She put her palm on theirs, still kissing Cole, her back arching up when Ryan increased his attention to her breasts.

"How do you want it tonight, Lynette?" Cole whispered, running his hands down her face, in her hair. "Your wish is our command."

She opened her eyes and cupped Cole's face with one hand, pulling Ryan back up with the other. "I want you." She kissed Cole's lips. "Inside me." She turned her head to give Ryan a kiss." And I want you inside him."

Both men raised their eyebrows. She laughed, then gasped, putting her hand to her stomach. Cole sat up, alarm on his face. "What is it? What's wrong?"

Ryan just smiled and slid down to his elbow. "Feel it?" he asked, passing his hand over her belly. She nodded, pulling Cole close and placing his hand on her stomach, near Ryan's. The baby did it again. A little flutter, then still.

"Holy shit," Cole whispered, his face a mask of amazement. "Why did it stop? Is he okay?"

Lynette laughed at the innocent worry on his face. She kissed him. "First off, you don't know if it's 'he'. Secondly, the interior beating I will take has just begun. You'll get plenty of opportunity to feel it. I've been feeling it for a week or two already. And now...can we please resume our prior activity?"

Ryan kissed her. "Okay. I'm gonna orchestrate this one. You, up," he said to Cole who stood and tugged his jeans off, making her lick her lips in anticipation.

"Wait," she said, putting a hand on Ryan's arm. "Show me..."

Ryan gave her a wicked grin, then turned, gripped Cole's thick cock and licked and sucked the man to a near orgasm. Her body twitched and pulsed in response to the amazing show in front of her. She moaned when Cole fisted Ryan's hair and pumped his hips. "Stop," she demanded. Ryan lifted his mouth off Cole's dick.

The other man panted, put his hands on his hips. "Count backwards from fifty," Ryan muttered, making her smile. "Roll over, Red, up on your hands and knees." He patted the bed. She grinned and obeyed him. She wasn't heavy enough in the front for it to be uncomfortable in this position. If anything, it relieved some of the pressure on her spine. She wiggled her hips.

"C'mon, boys. Show me what ya got."

Cole sighed when Ryan placed his hands on Lynette's hips, showing him how she was positioned. He'd nearly blown down Ryan's throat and was still hanging on by a thin thread, but he leaned over her, cradled her stomach, his baby, their baby, in his hands. Then reached higher, cupping her full breasts, sucking in deep breaths of her incredible, intensified scent. "You sure?" he sighed into her ear, already positioning himself, needing to be inside her so badly it took all he had to hold back. But he did.

"Yes, Cole. I'm sure." Her voice poured over his psyche like her namesake beer, calming and enervating him at the same time. "Please, now." She arched her back and he slid into her, loving the new sensations, the heat and pull of her changing body. "Oh, baby," she sighed when he stroked deep.

Cole nodded, still thrusting in and out of Lynette's depths. "Ah, shit," he cried out when Ryan's cock breached him.

They synchronized their rhythm, each stroke from Ryan sending him deeper inside Lynette. He had never in his life felt so complete. His eyes hurt, but the rest of him roared with need. Ryan's cock reached his gland, then retreated, making him grunt and press harder into Lynette.

"Coming," she cried out, but he smelled her a half second before she declared it, her rich odor swirling around his head. She groaned when her pussy clutched him, drew him deep.

Cole waited, wanting to make it last, letting his woman and his man have their release before he let his own cloud his brain, sending flashes of phantom light behind his eyes. "Oh my God," he groaned, draping his torso over Lynette's back.

Ryan pulled out, and he withdrew from Lynette's body, smiling when he sensed her collapsing over on her side. He dropped down and held her, loving the lush smell and fullness of her. "I love you," he whispered, shivering with post-orgasmic pleasure. "Sleepy now," he muttered into her neck. And he fell between them, Lynette and Ryan, and slept, dreamless, for hours.

Epilogue

Five months later they stood together, hands clasped in front of nearly two hundred people, the combined forces of both Ypsi Brewing and Traynor Distribution Company plus several of Cole's Marine friends and plenty more beer royalty. Daisy sat, panting at Cole's side. Ryan looked at them both, the crazed events of the past year rolling around in his head, passing behind his eyes in a montage of lust, love, drama and most recently messy, loud and terrifying childbirth.

He smiled at Lynette, put his hands to both of their faces. Daisy pushed her nose into his leg. The baby made a funny mewling sound. Jamie rushed over to her seat, put his hand on her face. "Daddy, I think Danielle needs something."

"It's okay, Jamie," Lynette said, her natural unflappable nature having taken to motherhood like a duck to water. "She's fine. Come on up here and stand by your dad, okay? Grandma will hold Danielle."

Moira smiled and pulled the pink-swaddled newborn from her seat and handed her to Lynette's mom, who had tears streaming down her face.

The boy nodded, giving the baby one last concerned look, then jumped up to stand between Cole and Ryan. Cole put a hand on his head. The boy gripped both men around the thighs, his eager gaze directed at Lynette.

Ryan had never felt better or more nervous. He smiled at the justice of the peace who'd agreed to preside at their commitment ceremony. He watched while Cole took Dan's dog tags, kissed them both then knelt down to fasten them to Daisy's collar. The dog shook, sending the tags tinkling in a somehow appropriate way. A slight, but attractive older woman stood by Cole, her huge dark eyes full of tears. Cole put an arm around her.

"Thank you," Janice Anderson said. "I wish all of you the very best." She kissed each of their cheeks then took her seat.

Cole took a deep breath. Ryan put his arms around them both while they repeated traditional words, exchanged kisses then turned to face friends and family, his heart bursting with happiness. He stood between them, held them close and whispered, "I love you. Thank you."

They each kissed his cheek. Jamie jumped up into his arms. "Yay, Daddy! Family!"

The crowd laughed.

Ryan smiled. "Okay, people," he said, holding his son. "Let's party."

Lynette sat, exhausted in mind and body, holding her daughter's sleeping form to her breast. Daisy led Cole over and he dropped into a chair. "I love that dog," she said, plopping Danielle into her father's arms. Cole smiled, and her heart swelled with happiness. The man kissed his daughter, cradled the infant to his chest and pulled the blanket away from her face se he could run his fingers down her face. The girl made a satisfied sound and settled herself, her lips pursing as she fell into sleep in her favorite spot nestled into her father's neck.

Jamie clamored into Lynette's lap. "What are you doing up this late, mister?" She kissed his hair. She felt Ryan's hands on her shoulders. He crouched down on her other side.

"Over here, buddy," he said, pulling Jamie off her lap. "Lynette's too tired."

"But…" He held out his hands, flexing his fingers.

She laughed. "Selfish, like his dad," she said. She sat between her men and watched the celebrations continue. The next thing she knew Ryan was picking her up, carrying her somewhere. She muttered into his neck but let the blessed sleep consume her.

"Relax," Cole murmured in her ear.

"Sleep," Ryan said. The two voices combined like a lullaby as they laid her down someplace soft and covered her with something warm.

The warm wet dog nose shoved into her neck, then retreated, satisfied that she was settled. "Daddy!" she heard Jamie just before she dropped off, napping at her own wedding but no longer really caring. "Mommy's sleepy. Where's my sister?"

She smiled and held out a hand. Cole took it and pressed it to his lips, then rose and kissed Ryan before they retreated, leaving her to a few moments of well-earned rest.

Want to see more from this author? Here's a taster for you to enjoy!

Brewing Passions: Tapped
Liz Crowe

Excerpt

The man must be out of his ever-loving mind.

Evelyn tried hard not to yell, or otherwise overreact, ever aware of her reputation as one of the sole females in this testosterone-soaked world of beer sales. But she simply could not stand for this sort of manipulation.

She rose to her feet. "I won't do it."

From his position behind the desk, her boss, Grant Taylor, president of Tri-City Distribution, tipped back in his chair and appraised her from head to toe. "He asked for you specifically. And I am certain I don't have to remind a professional such as yourself that Fitzgerald is our best craft beer brand—one of our *only* craft beer brands and the one I hope to use to build a better beer portfolio." He feigned a pitiful look.

"You look like a constipated crocodile when you do that." Even as she accepted that her day had just grown that much worse, if it were cosmically possible, she slumped back into the chair on the other side of his desk.

"Evelyn, honey, it's not that bad. He's a good guy, really."

The foul liquid that passed for coffee at the Tri-City offices polluted her throat, giving her a few seconds to think. After only two years in the beer and wine sales business, she'd found her niche, and she even had an incentive trip to Barbados from the Corona guys nearly within her grasp. A day spent—more like wasted—trying to shove hipster beer down the throats of savvy buyers at her best stores would not get her any closer to that goal. Evelyn stared out of the window at the annoyingly perfect blue sky.

"Grant, you know I need a heads-up longer than an hour. Seriously, I have to shuffle the whole sales day. Jesus. I don't even know where—"

Grant held up a hand. "Spare me, please. I know you've already committed where Fitzgerald products are placed to that gorgeous, top-selling brain of yours. You sold more of their amber, IPA and Winter Spice bullshit than anybody. Don't kid a kidder." He grinned at her.

Stress bloomed in her chest and spread, bringing a familiar anxious mantra to the forefront of her mind.

This stupid job is the only thing between me and the homeless shelter.

Nothing would make her jeopardize what she'd built out of, essentially, nothing. A two-year associate's degree was all she'd been able to afford before she'd started working in a trendy downtown craft beer and cocktail bar. When a Tri-City sales rep had mentioned they were hiring and how much she could make in commission, she'd jumped at it.

Who knew she'd be a sales star?

"Fine. But if you think I'm gonna suck up to the Chosen Son of the Fitzgerald fortune, you are sadly mistaken. He can ride in my car and go on calls with me, but he'd better understand that I have a full day already set and I won't be giving him any special attention." She drained the last of the caffeine then set the mug down on Grant's desk with what she hoped sounded like a decisive bang. A sudden puff of air blew past her, ruffling the papers on Grant's desk.

Her boss's eyes widened. He pointed to something behind her and started to open his mouth.

"No," she cut him off. "Don't say another word. You know I'm right. Everybody knows he's just a trust-fund baby, opening a brewery with his daddy's money, then gallivanting around the world, getting his degree" — she hooked her fingers in the air around the word — "in brewing science. Jesus. Who needs a degree in that? He should just stick to improving his golf handicap and deflowering debutantes."

The petulant sound of her own voice annoyed her, but stories like Austin Fitzgerald's made her the maddest. She'd been raised by a single mother who'd waitressed by day and, she'd later learned, turned tricks at night while the young Evelyn had done homework and watched TV at her aunt's house. Her mother had died during Evelyn's second year of college, forcing her to quit after she'd figured out that the modest funeral would eat up every cent her mother had managed to save.

Grant cleared his throat and stood, buttoning his suit coat. She watched him, her brain still on fire with helpless frustration. Even if she'd agreed to haul Fitzgerald around, she had no plans to sell craft beer that day.

"I *need* to schmooze my wine buyers today, Grant. I can't be babysitting this guy." The back of her neck tingled when the ends of her hair fluttered in another sudden breeze. She frowned, observing her boss stick his hand out as if about to shake hers, a big smile pasted on his face.

"Well, if I weren't deathly allergic to both golf and debutantes, that might have been a career choice," came a low, raspy voice from right behind her.

Evelyn's entire body broke out in goosebumps.

"Grant, good to see you again," the voice continued.

She gritted her teeth and rose, giving Grant what she hoped was a sufficiently withering look before turning around. Deep green eyes met hers. She was struck dumb by their depth and humorous sparkle. Dark jeans and a simple navy blue crew-neck—undoubtedly cashmere—sweater, brown box-toe loafers and a camel-colored dress jacket completed the look. He would have been at home on a *GQ* model as easily as he navigated a brewery floor. Close-cut dark-brown hair topped a clean-shaven, angular face.

A face that seemed pretty amused by her at that moment.

"And you must be Evelyn Benedict, saleswoman extraordinaire." His smile lit up the room, rendering Evelyn speechless. Grant nudged her arm until she stuck out her hand. Austin's warm, firm grip lingered long enough to make her uncomfortable.

"I see she's mesmerized by the size of my...trust fund already." He glanced over her shoulder at Grant then at her, pinning her in place again with that intense, still amused gaze. "Austin Fitzgerald, the albatross around your neck for the day." He gave her palm a friendly squeeze before letting go. "At your service."

Austin's gaze remained squarely on hers. She had on her best thrift store designer suit over a silk blouse open at the neck. Used to men eyeballing her from tip to toe, she found it refreshing for one not to automatically zero in on her cleavage.

"Never had such a lovely babysitter before, Grant. Thanks."

She swallowed when his eyes narrowed, then frowned as he gazed quickly up and down her front, lighting an unwanted and unexpected fire in her belly. Since when did she like it when some guy checked her out in such an obvious way?

He shrugged, sidestepping as if to get out of her way, the moment between them over. "Ready to go when you are. Rumor has it you have a big day ahead," he said, the expression on his handsome face suddenly neutral.

"Yes. I do." She strode past him, needing to regain her composure. Loud, masculine laughter echoed in her ears all the way to the ladies' room. She splashed water on her face and stared in the mirror while her heart took up a loud drumbeat in her ears.

He is nothing but a spoiled-rotten trust-fund brat. No matter if he wears it like a stockbroker-slash-daytime drama hero. I do not need this distraction right now.

* * * *

Austin tried to focus on the guy behind the desk as they stood in the claustrophobic office. But his brain spun with a combination of fresh perfume and sudden, kneejerk lust for the woman who'd just stalked out of the room.

The day suddenly looked a lot better — less 'annoying ride-along crap' and more 'honest to God, get to know a beautiful woman.' He had countless headaches back at his brewery to deal with. Didn't need the time away any more than she seemed to want him around, but he grinned at the sight of her rich golden-blonde hair and deep blue eyes when she emerged from around the corner. Her expression was flat. He sensed her determination to resist whatever had occurred between them earlier.

Yeah. Not if I have anything to do with it.

"After you." He held out a hand and followed her down the narrow hall toward the parking lot door, adjusting himself behind the zipper of the stupid jeans he'd grabbed off the rack yesterday, desperate for something to wear that was suitable for selling and not brewing.

Good Lord, but she's hot.

Alarmed at his instant, adolescent response to her, he held the door open. She breezed past him. He had to shut his eyes against the quick breath of light, clean scent that invaded his nose again.

He helped put his sample bottles in the trunk of her one-step-from-the-graveyard car, then climbed into the immaculate interior, watching as Evelyn pulled out her itinerary for the day and studied it, a frown marring her perfect face.

"Okay, so I'm trashing this, I guess." She tossed the papers into her briefcase with a sigh. "Let's hit it, shall we? By the seat of our pants? Not the way I usually like to approach a work day."

"Yeah, good plan." Without even realizing he was doing it, he touched the hand she had resting on the gear shift between them. It was meant as a 'we're in this together' sort of gesture. Nothing more. She stared at it, then up at him. Utterly unprepared for the spark that leapt from her skin to his, he swallowed hard and jerked his arm back.

"Sorry," he muttered, grabbing his own thigh while she backed out of the parking space. Trying to quell the alarm rising in his chest, he risked a glance at her while they waited at a light. Her angry stare made him smile and hold up both hands. "Don't nail me for harassment, okay? My mommy and daddy won't bail me out anymore, or so they claim."

Her quick laughter was music to his ears.

"I'm sorry. I was just…" Her jaw clenched and he had to force away the urge to run his finger over it if only to get her to relax. Such a beautiful woman should not be so uptight. A surge of protectiveness nearly suffocated him.

Wow, Fitzgerald. Get a hold of yourself.

For a guy who'd never worried about where his next meal — or his next pair of designer sunglasses — would come from, Austin remained fairly introspective. He was well aware of his reputation, but hearing it tumble from Evelyn's mouth earlier had pissed him off, making him want to prove something to her.

The fact that he'd finally given in to his mother's harping on about marrying the Masterson girl had honestly slipped his mind since laying eyes on the gorgeous creature behind the wheel. He suppressed an inward groan at his dilemma. But couldn't resist encouraging the connection between them. He somehow sensed she'd love to play along. Some light flirting, nothing more or less. Harmless, really.

"It's okay. Really. Just an awkward moment we'll laugh about with our kids someday."

She snorted. "Sure we will. Just before you dump me and the brats for the trophy wife your mommy always wanted for you."

He narrowed his eyes, hoping she didn't realize how close to the truth she'd gotten about the mother-approved arrangements. When she grinned at him, two amazing dimples appeared on her cheeks, making him grateful he was sitting, since his knees had officially turned to jelly.

He looked away from her. Staring straight ahead, making a mental count to ten, he calmed his breathing, reminded himself he was there to work. Evelyn cleared her throat at that moment, effectively ending the internal break-up monologue he'd begun with his almost-fiancée.

Valerie, a girl who would have been a debutante — had such things existed in Grand Rapids, Michigan — as heir to the Masterson restaurant empire. She was an interior designer of some repute, pretty, bossy, and desperate for the Mrs. Fitzgerald designation. He liked her well enough and was so sick of the nagging about his continual reluctance to put a ring on her finger that he'd been ready to close the deal.

He put a hand over his eyes and muffled a groan at the mess he was about to make. All over this one, single, first impression.

But what *an impression.*

"All right, we'll swing north and hit the big chain stores first." She spoke as she drove, and Austin used every ounce of his willpower not to stare at the leg exposed by her short skirt, at the way her thigh muscle flexed when she worked the clutch, gunning the engine too high every time. "I'm close to getting the winter lager placement alongside your amber. Then I know the boys at Beer Baron and Hop Town would love to see your rock-star face, so we'll stop in there."

He glanced over to gauge her level of seriousness. The tingling sensation in his scalp at her ironic smile alarmed him all over again. Every single memory and thought of the woman he'd been half-heartedly screwing for years had gone in the blink of Evelyn's amazing blue eyes. He swallowed hard and listened to her talk business.

"Also, I'd like to drop in on a couple of new boutique beer and wine stores that opened last month. Your esteemed presence gives me the excuse I need."

"Uh, okay. You're in charge. Just give me the high sign when I'm supposed to speak."

"Oh, don't worry, you'll figure it out. I'll have to do some inventory stuff at most of these places, so there will be time for you to bond with whatever management is on hand. A few of them are ladies — you'll make their day, I'm sure."

Unable to stop himself, he touched her again, this time letting himself own the heat that passed between them. "Don't be jealous, honey. I'd never cheat on you."

"Ha! I'll farm you out in a heartbeat, *sweetie*. You'll do whatever it takes to increase our bottom line. Hope you took your vitamins." She yanked her hand out from under his.

Smiling at her once more, he shifted in his seat to relieve the pressure building under his zipper.

He'd been damn close to asking Valerie to marry him, willing to leave her and her bitch of a mother to the wedding arrangements, ready to nod in agreement at what he hoped were the proper intervals. His mother had finally stopped haranguing him, left him to run his brewery in peace and he'd made a similar peace within himself, realizing the Faustian bargain he'd struck.

But now, as he sat in the passenger's seat of Evelyn's car staring out the windshield without seeing anything, a long-buried urge almost blinded him. And he knew Valerie was history.

PUBLISHING

Sign up for our newsletter and find out about all our romance book releases, eBook sales and promotions, sneak peeks and FREE romance books!

About the Author

Amazon best-selling author, mom of three, Realtor, beer blogger, brewery marketing expert, and soccer fan, Liz Crowe is a Kentucky native and graduate of the University of Louisville currently living in Ann Arbor. She has decades of experience in sales and fund raising, plus an eight-year stint as a three-continent, ex-pat trailing spouse.

With stories set in the not-so-common worlds of breweries, on the soccer pitch, in successful real estate offices and at times in exotic locales like Istanbul, Turkey, her books are unique and told with a fresh voice. The Liz Crowe backlist has something for any reader seeking complex storylines with humor and complete casts of characters that will delight, frustrate and linger in the imagination long after the book is finished.

Don't ever ask her for anything "like a Budweiser" or risk bodily injury.

Liz loves to hear from readers. You can find her contact information, website details and author profile page at http://www.pride-publishing.com